T0345304

SWARNALATA

SWARNALATA

TILOTTOMA MISRA

Translated from the Asomiya by
UDAYON MISRA

ZUBAAN
128 B Shahpur Jat, 1st floor
NEW DELHI 110 049
EMAIL: contact@zubaanbooks.com
WEBSITE: www.zubaanbooks.com

Orginally published in Assamese 1991
First published in English by Zubaan 2011
This edition published by Zubaan Publishers Pvt. Ltd 2018

10 9 8 7 6 5 4 3 2 1

ISBN 978 93 85932 45 8

Zubaan is an independent feminist publishing house based in New Delhi with a strong academic and general list. It was set up as an imprint of India's first feminist publishing house, Kali for Women, and carries forward Kali's tradition of publishing world quality books to high editorial and production standards. *Zubaan* means tongue, voice, language, speech in Hindustani. Zubaan publishes in the areas of the humanities, social sciences, as well as in fiction, general non-fiction, and books for children and young adults under its Young Zubaan imprint.

Typeset by Jojy Philip, New Delhi 100 015
Printed at PrintShoot, Manesar, Gurgaon

Swarnalata
An Introduction

Set in the middle part of the nineteenth century and straddling the provinces of Assam and Bengal, *Swarnalata* deals with that exciting period in the country's history when colonial modernity was beginning to make its presence felt and issues relating to widow re-marriage and women's education were catching the imagination of the educated sections of society. The novel is woven around the life of Swarnalata, daughter of Gunabhiram Barua, the leading social reformer of nineteenth century Assam. It takes the reader on a journey with Swarnalata as she grows up in the sleepy little town of Nagaon in Assam, where her father is a senior government official, and then moves to Calcutta to study at the Bethune School where she meets many of the leaders of the Brahmo movement of that time. Through a deft interface of history and imagination, the novelist gives the reader a glimpse into the Assamese society of the period and how the complacence and obscurantism of ages summed up as tradition was beginning to be questioned by new ideas based on reason and tolerance. It is through Swarnalata's two most intimate friends, Lakhipriya and Tora, that issues relating to the position of widows and that of the subaltern converts to Christianity are foregrounded in a very forceful manner. The child-widow Lakhipriya's poignant life, her struggle to educate herself, the rather unexpected support that she receives from a conservative and tradition-bound father, the humiliations that she faces and her eventual triumph in securing a job as a teacher and marrying the man of her choice makes for absorbing reading and effectively throws light on one of the major social issues of the nineteenth century. By contrast, the independent-minded Tora represents the comparatively liberated girl who because of her Christian faith is free to chart her own course in life, untrammeled by customs and tradition which tend to suffocate her many Hindu friends. Yet, even though they are devout Christians wedded to the idea of unquestioning duty and sacrifice, both Tora and her husband, Henry, are not without their doubts and are quite skeptical about the stated intentions of their missionary mentors.

The different strands of the novel, which is divided into three parts, are held together by the symbolic Bilwa-Kutir where Gunabhiram and his wife Bishnupriya live along with their children. It is from Bilwa-Kutir that the new ideas of change and progress start percolating into the medieval society of Nagaon, thereby setting off social tremors. That the traditional Hindu society of his time tolerates Gunabhiram because of his power and privileges but refuses to accept him, reveals the challenges that reformers like him had to face even to bring about the smallest of changes in people's outlook. As the scene gradually shifts to Calcutta , the canvas opens up to include debates centred around the two major schools of the Brahmo faith, issues relating to indentured labour in the newly set up tea estates of Assam, questions of self-rule and independence and, of course, the entire issue of women's education. Amidst all this intellectual ferment which marked the closing decades of the nineteenth century, the novelist does not fail to present an intensely sensitive portrait of the human relationships and the moments of tragedy and triumph which marked them. To sum up, *Swarnalata* is a moving portrait of social flux and transformation that marked the closing decades of nineteenth century Assam and Bengal and which set the stage for the birth of the succeeding age.

Udayan Misra
Guwahati 2010

Part I

1

The wide road which skirted the river Kolong was lined on both sides by sonaru and simolu trees. It was the month of April. From the swaying branches of the trees heavy with red and yellow blossoms, could be heard the halting notes of an oriole. Occasionally, one's gaze was caught by the glistening wings of the keteki as it made its way across the azure morning sky, calling for its mate. A few yards along the lane which broke off from the main road, stood a newly built chapel. By its side were two bungalows belonging to the American Baptist Mission. A portion of the chapel also served as the school house and it was here that every morning from seven to nine Miss Orell Keeler, the young missionary woman, would teach the girls to read, write and sew. Some elementary lessons on Asamiya and arithmatic followed by Bible Studies took up the first hour. Then the girls learnt to sew and darn. The younger girls were taught to make button-holes and to darn while the older ones learnt how to stitch cotton jackets and blouses.

As the daily routine of this somewhat unconventional school drew to a close, the older girls sang Christian hymns in Asamiya, Miss Keeler accompanying them on the organ. The seniors would sing, "*Jagate Madhye Joto Lok*"[1] and the younger ones would join

---

[1] "*All the people of the world.*"

in the refrain, "*Jesu Christat Paritraan*."[2] Once school was over, the girls would rush out of the mission compound, bidding good-bye to their two-hour confinement. And, even as they walked back home, merrily laughing and chattering away, the little girls seemed to become one with the vibrant landscape all around them. Miss Keeler's school had just twenty girls and most of them were Christian converts from poor families belonging to Nagaon and its surrounding villages.

On that April morning of the year 1876, two small girls, some nine or ten years old, were walking back home from school. One of them was wearing a green cotton mekhala with floral motifs and an embroidered calico jacket. The other girl too was wearing a similar jacket along with a yellow cotton mekhala. By the look of it one could easily guess that the cotton jackets had been stitched at the school, the calico cloth having come as Christmas gifts from the foreign ladies. One of the girls was the daughter of a teacher of the mission boys' school; the other was Golapi's daughter. Golapi was the Baptist Mission's Bible reader. Her job was to go from house to house and read from the Bible.

As the two girls approached a beautiful well-kept bungalow by the side of the road, their steps slowed down. The bungalow was just like the ones in which the British lived. It had a wide front verandah with windows much larger than those of Assamese houses. The doors and windows had glass panes fitted on them. There was a nicely tended flower garden in front of the house and right in the centre of this garden there was a large Bilwa tree. It was from this tree that the house had taken its name, "Bilwa Kutir". Under this tree, at a spot properly swept and cleaned, a girl some five or six years old was playing kitchen with a maid-servant somewhat older than her. The younger girl was dressed like European girls of her age. She was wearing a long frock

---

[2] "*Jesus Christ our Saviour.*"

with frills at the wrists and neck, and her hair was tied with a red ribbon. Her fair complexion, large eyes, sharp delicate nose and a pair of dark, arched eyebrows seemed to hold all the promise of future grace and beauty.

The two schoolmates kept on staring at this small girl through the bamboo stile-gate in front of Bilwa Kutir. To the people of Nagaon, the family living in this beautiful house had for long been the object of great curiosity for a variety of reasons. The owner of the house, Gunabhiram Barua, had come to Nagaon some years back as the Extra-Assistant. There were very few Assamese holding such high government posts in those days. But the people of Nagaon were also fortunate to have had, some twenty years before Gunabhiram's arrival, Anandaram Dhekiyal Phukan as a Sub-Assistant. Anadaram had initiated several measures for the good of the people. Yet, much to their sorrow and chagrin, Phukan had died at an early age. Many still remembered that poignant scene when Anandaram's child, Radhikaram, had lit his father's pyre virtually from Gunabhiram's lap. That was why Gunabhiram was no stranger to the older residents of Nagaon. But his views and actions did not seem to conform to common practice and this added an aura of distinction to Gunabhiram's personality. Before coming to Nagaon on transfer, Gunabhiram Barua had publicly accepted the Brahmo faith. To the conservative Hindus of the time there was little difference between acceptance of Brahmoism and conversion to Christianity. The liberal approach of the Brahmo religion and its rejection of rituals compared favourably with the religious beliefs and practices of the Protestants. That was exactly why, on hearing that Jajnuram Kharghoria Phukan had embraced Brahmoism, Anandaram Dhekial Phukan's father, Holiram Dhekiyal Phukan, had rushed to Calcutta to save his brother from becoming a Christian! Ever since then, the influence of the Brahmo faith had been quite strong in that family. During his student days in

Calcutta, Gunabhiram too had come into contact with many Brahmo friends and well-wishers of his family.

Apart from accepting the Brahmo faith, Gunabhiram had done something so daring and sensational that anyone else in his position would have been socially ostracized by the Brahmin community to which he initially belonged. Not content with writing a play called *Ramnavami* advocating widow-marriage, Gunabhiram had married a Brahmin widow named Bishnupriya Devi, just a year before he moved to Nagaon on his new assignment. But no one had openly dared to boycott him socially because everyone was overawed by his strong personality, his wide learning and, above everything else, the high government post which he held. All this, however, did not prevent "Barua Hakim" from becoming the subject of curiosity and common gossip. That was why, even when Gunabhiram's little daughter played kitchen like countless other girls of her age, it attracted a lot of attention.

Swarnalata looked up from her play when she became aware that the two girls from the mission school had been staring at her for some time. She had often seen them passing by her house on their way to school. Though curious, she hesitated to take the first step and speak to them. The two girls kept on staring at Swarnalata for some more time and then slowly walked away. As soon as the girls vanished from sight, Swarnalata seemed to suddenly remember something and rushed indoors.

2

The name Bilwa Kutir evoked memories of the ashrams of ancient days. But, there seemed to be something very British in the architectural design of the house. When the British first came to Assam and discovered that heavy rains and floods kept the low-lying areas submerged for the greater part of the year, they decided that houses on stilts like the ones built by the neighbouring Burmese, would be best suited for the climate. They were surprised to see the Assamese villagers facing untold hardship during the monsoons, living virtually submerged in waist-deep water during those wet months and wondered why they too did not build their houses on stilts like their Mishing neighbours. Commenting on this, an American missionary had written in the *Orunodoi:* "The people of Burma and other nearby countries live in elevated houses built on bamboo stilts. If the people of Assam too build such houses, then it would help them in many ways and it would greatly reduce the occurrence of fever and other ailments. If, however, they were unwilling to live in such houses because of tradition and caste practices, then a small kitchen could be built on the ground where meals could be cooked and eaten. But, the stilt-house is best suited for bedrooms, living rooms and store-rooms." Gunabhiram knew the utility of such houses right from his childhood days. Anandaram Dhekiyal Phukan who was initially his guardian and later on his brother-in-law, used to live in such a bungalow during his tenure in Nagaon. At that time, Gunabhiram had stayed with him for several years. The Phukan family had always maintained close links with Commissioner Jenkins Sahib and the missionaries and it was but natural for its members to be influenced by the ideas and living style of the foreigners. That was why Bilwa Kutir was a beautiful synthesis of the stilt or chang-house and the typical Assamese houses. It had the living rooms and the study in front, built high above the ground in the chang style. Behind it, encircling the back courtyard, there was the kitchen, the prayer-room, the servants' quarters and the cowshed. These were of mud and thatch and built on level ground. During the rainy season it was quite inconvenient for the family to go to the kitchen from the chang-house. But, for the sake of tradition and custom, the Barua family didn't mind this. Later on, however, a covered passage was built connecting the kitchen with the main house.

Swarnalata, who had just left her play under the Bilwa tree, had reached the wide verandah at the back of the chang-house in search of her mother. Though she had come in running, the moment she stepped into the house, she checked herself. She suddenly became conscious of her footsteps on the wooden floor of the bungalow. She knew that her mother had always cautioned her against running about noisily inside the house when her father was in his study. Disturbing him at his work was considered almost a crime in Bilwa Kutir and everyone seemed to be aware of this.

When little Swarnalata crossed the sitting-room and reached the rear verandah, her father was not inside the house. It was time for him to go to the Court and he was in the kitchen having his food. The kitchen consisted of three rooms: the main hearth-room, the room where tea and snacks were made and then the dining room. Although every now and then Bishnupriya cooked a special dish for the family, it was the Brahmin cook who prepared all the meals in this large household which never seemed to be short of guests. Bishnupriya, however, made it a point to personally serve the food to each member of the family. On this particular morning too, she had just served food to her husband and was sitting by his side on the floor when Swarnalata came rushing in and hugging her from behind, said: "Ai, I want to go to school too! It is so nice to see the Christian girls going to school. Can't we too become Christians?" An amazed Bishnupriya looked up at Swarnalata and said in a tone of mild reproach, "Don't say such things, Maisena." But, Gunabhiram, who had stopped eating and was looking at his daughter intently for sometime, said softly, "Aijani, one can get educated even without becoming a Christian, my little one. Well, let tomorrow be the day for your Bidyarambha. You'll start your lessons from tomorrow."

That evening after his return from Court, Gunabhiram was relaxing over a cup of tea, when Bishnupriya asked him hesitantly: "Are you really thinking of sending Maisena to the Mission School? Ever since you told her about starting her lessons from tomorrow, she has been pestering me about it." Barua thought for a while and said, "I have no apprehensions about sending anyone to the Christians for education. One should be liberal in such matters. The missionaries teach in the Western style and there is much to learn from that teaching too. All these years we have never had women's education in Assam. It's only the Christians who are giving some attention to this matter and we should be happy about it."

Bishnupriya could not agree fully with her husband on this. Engrossed as he was in his government job and his studies, certain problems did not seem to touch him much. It was Bishnupriya who had to face them at every step of her life. On most occasions she tackled these issues on her own because she did not want to create any situation which could adversely affect her husband's work. But, even as she had in her own quietly

determined manner borne the onslaughts of society, Bishnupriya
hoped that she would be able to protect her children from all
the unpleasant consequences of certain decisions taken by her
husband which seemed to violate the accepted customs. Often
she would gaze at Swarna's innocent face with concern and pray
silently: "O Lord! May she never be unhappy in life." Behind this
silent prayer lay the centuries-old fear of all the hardened social
customs and practices which have shaken the purpose even of
the great social reformers. There were reasons for this too. When
all the wheels of society move in the same narrow groove, then
for those few who wander out in search of a wider road, life
becomes even more difficult. And unless accompanied by a group
of determined fellow-travellers, these pioneers too eventually fall
back into the earlier groove. In the case of Gunabhiram Barua,
however, his strength of mind continued to remain unshaken
because in his intellectual circle there seemed to be no dearth
of such fellow-travellers and well-wishers. Even in a place like
Nagaon, he had come across a number of courageous persons
who had, in several spheres, succeeded in overcoming insular
social attitudes.

But Bishnupriya's problems were of a different nature. The
society which she had known intimately before she married
Gunabhiram, could no longer accept her with ease. Yet, she had
not been able to break free from it. She still seemed to hold on to
some of the practices and superstitions of the traditional Assamese
Brahmin society. At heart she was very lonely. There was none
amongst her acquaintances, except her husband, who could help
her get back her lost confidence. This was why sometimes she
felt rather helpless and a sense of guilt seemed to overwhelm
her. It was during such moments that she fervently prayed to
God to protect her husband and children. She had four living
children now. The two daughters by her first marriage, Kalipriya
and Damayanti, had both been married off at an early age.

Swarnalata, Satyabhiram and Karunabhiram were the children from her second marriage. Satyabhiram had died in infancy.

Bishnupriya pondered over her husband's comments on women's education and said: "It seems, quite a few educated Hindus are doing hard work for the cause of women's education in Calcutta these days. Instead of sending our daughter to the Mission school, can't we send her to a school run by our own countrymen?"

There were very few Assamese gentlemen in those days who were better acquainted than Gunabhiram with the efforts made by Ishwar Chandra Vidyasagar and other learned people in Calcutta to promote women's education. Even in his student days in Calcutta, Gunabhiram had acknowledged Vidyasagar as his guru and had been much influenced by his actions. Inspired by Vidyasagar's views on women's emancipation, he had, in those days, written a letter to the editor of the missionary journal *Orunodoi* in which he had advocated equal opportunities for boys and girls in the field of education. Gunabhiram had cautioned the readers of *Orunodoi* that if Assam as a nation was to make progress it must discontinue the evil practice of denying education to girls. But, much to his disappointment, Gunabhiram noted with dismay that even twenty years after the publication of that letter little had been done to promote the cause of women's education in the region. This was exactly why both he and Bishnupriya were in a quandary about their daughter's education. Except for the school run by the missionaries, there wasn't a single other for girls in Nagaon. Yet, from his conversations with the missionaries, Gunabhiram knew only too well that the main thrust of their education policy was proselytisation. Behind their efforts at spreading western education lay their unflinching faith in Christianity and their aim of bringing all the "unfaithful" within the only "true fold". It was this faith in their mission that had inspired all these men and women to travel all the

way from faraway America and spend their time in some of the
most difficult terrains in Assam. Though Gunabhiram was quite
liberal in his attitude to religion, yet he hesitated somewhat to
hand over his young girl to the care of a set of people who
were directly involved in the spread of Christianity. He deeply
believed in shedding one's petty prejudices and in learning to
view the world in the light of modern liberal ideas brought in
by western education. But, for that, he did not see any need to
give up his Hindu faith. To him, the Brahmo faith was a higher
stage of Hinduism and represented a unique synthesis of ancient
Vedic beliefs and modern rationalist views. Exactly because of
this, Gunabhiram had tried to inculcate in his children the values
of western thought and education as well as those of the Vedic
tradition. The problem, however, for Gunabhiram right then was
whether he could give his daughter such an education in Nagaon.
Having thought over all this, Gunabhiram finally decided that
Swarnalata would receive her primary education from a private
tutor at home. Once that was done, there would be enough time
to leisurely think about the future.

3

⚜

In those days the Nagaon Bar had several Assamese and Bengali gentlemen practicing as lawyers without possessing any formal degree in law. In deference to old procedures, the government had permitted them to continue with their practice. However, these persons were not considered as "pucca" lawyers. One such lawyer was an Assamese gentleman named Panchanan Sarma. Although not very articulate in English, he was quite proficient in Asamiya, Bengali and Sanskrit. Sarma had helped Gunabhiram to get his book *Assam Buranji* ready for the press. Because of this, he was seen at Barua's study almost every evening. Despite having great respect for Barua's scholarship, Sarma would not accept anything from the kitchen of Bilwa Kutir except an occasional areca nut and betel leaves. Neither Bishnupriya nor her husband showed the slightest trace of displeasure over this. Their own relatives had not kept any social links with them. So, they were not surprised that new acquaintances avoided eating at their place for fear of losing caste.

Gunabhiram decided to request Panchanan Sarma to be Swarnalata's private tutor. On the very evening of that day when he had talked with Bishnupriya about Swarnalata's education, Gunabhiram broached the topic when the two of them were in the sitting-room after evening prayers. At first, Sarma appeared dumb-struck and stared wide-eyed at the person making the suggestion. A private tutor for a girl! Does he really wish to make his daughter a teacher in the Christian school? Sarma found the whole idea preposterous. Whatever little education is needed to read the *Ramayana* and the *Mahabharata* could easily be given to a girl by her own parents. After all a girl who would very soon be given away in marriage and sent off to another home needed to be taught domestic skills like cooking and weaving instead of wasting time in teaching her Mathematics and Grammar. His own daughter Lakhipriya was some two or three years older than Swarnalata. But, Sarma had never thought of giving her a school education. The girl had however, on her own, learnt the Assamese alphabets. In the mornings and evenings she would sing Ai-naam, Bia-naam and devotional songs with her mother and grandmother. She had also learnt by heart some of the verses from the Lakshmi-panchali. Always busy in doing odd-jobs from helping in the kitchen to setting up the loom, Lakhipriya spent whatever spare time she had in looking after her younger brothers and sisters. How would the household run if his daughter were to take to studies, Sarma reflected.

Panchanan Sarma, however, did not share his thoughts with Gunabiram. He was well aware of Gunabhiram's views on women's education. Even then, unable to conceal his astonishment at Barua's decision, Sarma made a general statement: "Sir, in our part of the country, one never hears of girls from respectable families being educated. You are daring to do something unusual because you possess a very liberal mind." What Gunabhiram said in reply to this was something he had said on countless earlier occasions. He had also expressed these views through his writings published in different journals: "I am not out to do anything spectacular or new, Sarma. Even the Shastras say that girls be given the same education as boys. In ancient days, girls too were given the sacred thread and sent to the guru's place for receiving education. This practice was given up only after the coming of child-marriage.

Had the Almighty not wished that women have equal access to knowledge and wisdom as men, then perhaps He would have created them just like the animals. In the advanced nations of the world educated women have written good books. If our womenfolk also acquire such knowledge, it would be beneficial to both the husband and the wife."

Panchanan Sarma had heard such comments from Barua Hakim on earlier occasions too. But he did not believe that good intentions and honest arguments alone could change the world. Everything that Barua said appeared out of the ordinary to him. Barua's views did not at all conform to the accepted practices of Assamese society. Yet, realising full well that he would not be able to counter Gunabhiram's arguments, Panchanan Sarma avoided contradicting him. For politeness's sake, however, Sarma declared: "Wise persons like you should show the way. Others will soon follow. As for me, I will start teaching Swarnalata from tomorrow."

4

The happiest hours of the day for Swarnalata were those spent walking with her father in the morning. Gunabhiram was very regular and on every rain-free morning he would take a walk along the bank of the Kolong, talking about many things to Swarnalata. How the leaves breathed, how to distinguish the different calls of the birds, how the river Kolong emerged from the mighty Luit and then re-entered it at a later stage—he would tell his daughter all this and many other things. Swarna understood only some of the things he said. But, even if she did not understand everything, she felt happy that her father was talking to her like a grown-up. Swarna had great regard for her father. Having observed her father discuss matters with all the wise and accomplished people who visited Bilwa Kutir, little Swarnalata was convinced that her father was the wisest person on earth. She seemed to believe that it was her father alone who would be able to give the answers to the countless questions which filled her mind. One morning as father and daughter were passing by the beautiful bungalows of the sahibs, Swarna suddenly asked, "Deuta, the sahibs go to church, don't they?" Gunabhiram nodded rather absentmindedly. He had been thinking about something else and had been quiet for some time. But Swarna's second question alerted him, "Does one lose one's caste on going to church, Deuta?"

Gunabhiram gave a puzzled look and asked: "Who's been teaching you all this, Maisena?" Swarna replied hesitantly with some apprehension, "Panchanan uncle was saying it yesterday."

They walked silently for a while, but unable to suppress her child's curiosity, Swarna asked once again, "Deuta, how does one lose caste?"

Gunabhiram kept quiet for some time. He was really angry with Panchanan Sarma. In just two days he had put such wrong ideas into the child's head! But, it didn't take long for Gunabhiram to realize that people with obscurantist views like Panchanan Sarma seemed to see matters of caste as part of one's tradition. So, what was the point in being angry with him? Though he himself would not like his children to imbibe such ideas, yet could he keep them in the dark about the existence of such beliefs? Deciding that it would be best to give a rational answer, Gunabhiram said in a sombre tone: "Caste divisions are one of the evil practices of our country. A person's nature is his real caste. One who possesses a good nature, naturally belongs to a higher caste. He who indulges in evil practices actually belongs to a lower caste. How will one lose caste by going to church? It is God who is worshipped in a church. Can worship be seen as an evil action? There is nothing more holy than the worship of God, be it in whatever religion." As he finished speaking, Gunabhiram turned to look at his daughter. He saw a look of helplessness etched on her beautiful face. All of a sudden Gunabhiram realized that Swarna was still a child. How could she ever understand such intricacies? With great tenderness he told her: "Next Sunday I will take you to the church to see the service". A smile broke out on Swarnalata's face. That means, father isn't angry with me after all, she thought.

On Sunday mornings there was always a festive though sober atmosphere in front of the newly-built church. All the Christian families from in and around Nagaon would gather here, dressed in their best. Most of them were ordinary folk and from their appearance they seemed to be from the Mikir tribe. There were also one or two Assamese and Bengali families. What marked out this group was that, unlike the other common folk in their neighbourhood, each one of them wore some kind of footwear. But, it was evident from their self-conscious gait that they were not used to wearing shoes or sandals, except on Sundays. The men were mostly in shorts or pantaloons and shirts. The women were dressed in cotton sarees or riha-mekhala and they had their heads partially covered with their sadors or saree ends.

When Gunabhiram and Swarnalata reached the church, the service was just about to begin. Nodding to a few acquaintances, they proceeded to a pew in the front of the hall. Swarna was wearing a beautiful frock with a silk scarf over her head. Dressed in choga-chapkan, Gunabhiram was sporting a fine cap of black velvet. Soon after they sat down, the service commenced. The parson who was conducting the service was earlier called Sonaram, but now he was addressed by the more dignified name of Charles Sonaram. Swarnalata had seen him before. But, she didn't understand why, with all the sahibs and mem-sahibs being present in the church, it was left to Sonaram to conduct the service. How could the Christian religion be the religion only of the sahibs, thought Swarnalata, even as she listened to Sonaram reading out from the Bible in Asamiya. Although she wasn't listening attentively to what Sonaram was saying, yet she was quite intrigued to see a simple, ordinary person like him speak so fluently and confidently to a gathering of so many important and well-placed people.

As soon as Sonaram finished his sermon, Miss Keeler began playing a quiet sweet tune on the large organ which stood at a corner of the church. Swarna recognized Miss Keeler as she had come to Bilwa kutir on a few occasions to meet Bishnupriya. Keeping tune with the notes of the organ, a group of boys and girls started singing a hymn. As Swarna stood looking at the group, it suddenly struck her that she had seen one of the girls before. She was the girl who always used to pass by Bilwa Kutir on her way to school. Swarna knew her as "Golapi's daughter". She didn't know her name. As long as this girl kept singing along with her companions, Swarna kept looking at her, virtually entranced. The simple girl in the green cotton mekhala–sador suddenly seemed to rise quite high in Swarna's estimation.

As people started trooping out after the service, Swarna's eager eyes were busy searching for Golapi's daughter amongst the groups of men and women. Meanwhile, Miss Keeler and a few other missionaries were walking ahead with Gunabhiram Barua. As Swarnalata walked past a small group of people, the girl she was looking for came forward and asked her with a shy smile:

"What's your name?"

"Swarnalata. And yours?"

"Tora."

"You sing so well," Swarna said with great admiration.

A smile of deep contentment lit up Tora's face and eyes. Although Swarna was younger than her, yet it pleased her beyond measure to receive such appreciation from the Hakim's daughter. Moved to say something as complimentary to Swarna, Tora blurted out spontaneously: "You are indeed very beautiful." At this, Swarna blushed in embarrassment. She looked around for a few moments and then started running to catch up with her father who had by now walked much ahead of her.

In the meantime, Tora was surrounded by her companions. Everyone was eager to know what had passed between her and the Hakim's daughter. They had seen the girl who lived in the Anglicized surroundings of Bilwa Kutir only from a distance. No one had dared to speak to her. But, Tora was different. It was not in her nature to shrink from any situation. If she wanted to do something, she would do it without any hesitation. This was why the missionaries liked her so much. It seemed that they just couldn't do without Tora.

5

Tora had lost her father, Sendura, when she was just an infant. Sendura was the *sais* of the Commissioner Sahib. He used to stay with his wife in a small hut within the compound of the sahib's bungalow. Actually, he had come to Nagaon and started serving in the Commissioner's household after being socially ostracized by his village for having married Golapi. He was of the Kalita caste while Golapi belonged to the fisherman community. Sendura had a cheerful happy disposition. He could continue to smile even after running for over a mile behind the sahib's coach. Because of his cheerful nature, the sahib also had a lot of affection for Sendura. So, when Sendura was stricken with the deadly cholera, his master visited him in his hut and even volunteered to teach his wife Golapi how to make barley-water for her sick husband. He had called over the government doctor to examine Sendura, but all efforts had proved in vain. The epidemic carried off thousands of people in Nagaon that year. When all indigenous medicines failed to control the pestilence, people tried to appease the Burha Dangoria, the spirit which they thought was responsible for their misery. Day and night they sang Nam-Kirtan and offered pujas to all the spirits and deities. The Sahib had warned Golapi that if she too joined in the community prayers, then the government physician wouldn't treat Sendura. So, Golapi had kept herself away from all this. But when she saw that the doctor's medicines were not proving effective, she decided to take the path of faith like all the other folk. One evening, she quietly slipped out of the hut with her little three-month old infant clutched in her arms and a one-rupee coin in her hand, to join the mass prayer to Burha Dangoria held in a neighbouring village. Quite late at night the mass-prayer ended and the people built a raft of plaintain trees on which they placed an offering of rice, pulses and jaggery. Then they set it afloat on the river Kolong. Golapi prostrated herself on the bank of the river and offered a fervent prayer to her Istadevta to carry off the God of Death on the raft so that Sendura could become well again.

The commotion made by the people at the bor-sabah disturbed the reverend padre Miles Bronson who lived in a cottage nearby. He came out of his house and started walking towards the Commissioner's bungalow. Sometime back, he had visited some of the families afflicted by the cholera epidemic and had even given some of the patients the medicine that that had arrived recently from America. This drug had proved to be effective in the case of several of the mission school students who had been afflicted by the dreaded disease. As Bronson approached the Commissioner's bungalow, he noticed someone hurriedly open the gate and run towards him. Bronson recognized the man and asked in concern.

"Why, what's the matter, Bapuram?"

Bapuram was the Commissioner's servant. He was somewhat taken aback when he saw the white man and answered hesitantly: "Nothing has happened, huzoor. Sendura's condition is critical. I am going to call Golapi."

"But where has Golapi gone so late at night?" asked the surprised padre.

"The people have organized a bor-sabah to propitiate the Burha-dangoria. She has gone to pray there," replied Bapuram haltingly. He was in mortal fear of offending the padre because he knew that the sahibs got angry when they heard of such practices.

"God save these people," murmured Bronson to himself and walked in haste towards Sendura's house.

Sendura's body was beginning to turn limp and cold. Bronson lifted the man's eyelids with his fingers and peered into his eyes. He realized at once that the final moment had arrived. But in a last effort to revive the patient, he quickly got some mustard oil heated and started massaging Sendura's limbs. After a while, Sendura opened his eyes with a great deal of effort and called for Golapi in a voice that was barely audible. Bronson's eyes were moist. He laid his hands on Sendura's head and in a voice filled with great compassion, tried to assure him: "Golapi has gone to pray for you. You too must pray to God now. He alone can save you".

As Sendura kept staring at Bronson sahib's serene and dignified face, it seemed as if he had recognized him. Clutching Bronson's warm hands with his own cold ones, Sendura entreated feebly, "Sahib, save me please". Bronson placed his hands on Sendura's head and started praying to Jesus Christ. At that moment it appeared as if this saint of a man was the very embodiment of love and mercy. Slowly but finally, life ebbed out of Sendura.

Meanwhile, Golapi had quietly entered her house. She felt greatly relieved after the community prayer because her faith reassured her that after the Nam-Kirtan Sendura would finally recover. But, as she stepped into the house and saw Bronson Sahib praying by Sendura's bedside and Bapuram sobbing away in a corner, she knew that it was all over. Seeing Golapi, Bronson rose and went outside. He had faced plenty of similar situations in life and had always tried to give a little bit of peace to the many helpless and unfortunate ones at the time of their death. Disease, death, helplessness and frustration in his own life had turned this great soul into gold purified by fire. Even then, he could not help being deeply moved by the sorrows and misfortunes of others. Life's cruel realities had not succeeded in turning him into a total Stoic. As Golapi began to wail over her husband's body, Bronson re-entered the room with slow steps. With his hand on Golapi's head, he started to console her. Unaccustomed to receiving such warmth and affection from respectable people, Golapi was moved to believe, even in her moment of utter misfortune, that this man was in fact an incarnation of God. From that day onwards, she started looking upon Bronson as the saviour of both herself and her child and resolved to follow his guidance for the rest of her life.

After Sendura's death Bronson sahib and his wife started taking an added interest in Golapi's well-being. As for herself, Golapi didn't have any close relatives. Even if there were some, they avoided her for fear of having to take responsibility for the widowed mother and daughter. It was Bronson who got her a job as chowkidarni of the mission school and had a small house built for her at Christianpatty. Bronson's wife, who used to give lessons to a few elderly persons at her residence, also started teaching Golapi who proved to be a sharp pupil. But more than her eagerness to learn, it was her desire to please her missionary teacher that made her master her lessons very quickly. Once she could read small books like *Bare-Motora* and *Phulmoni Aru Koruna*, the missionary couple encouraged Golapi to read the Assamese journal *Orunodoi* which the missionaries were publishing from their printing house in Sivasagar.

Golapi didn't suffer from any self-doubts in accepting the Christian faith. Even before becoming a Christian, she had come to view her neighbours at Christianpatty as her own people because it was they who looked after her during her difficult days. Moreover, it was only after coming into contact with the Bronson couple that Golapi had come to know something about religion and what it stood for. Earlier, when she had taken part in pujas and other rituals, she could not understand what they signified. She did everything mechanically with the hope that by doing so, she and her family would be saved from the anger of so many known and unknown gods. But now she could read about religion in her own tongue. She could even ask questions to the priest regarding her doubts. Golapi was a fast learner and as soon as she accepted her new faith, the missionary ladies started taking her along with them for their proselytizing work amongst the village women. Meanwhile, her daughter Tora had also reached school-going age and when she was put in the mission school, Golapi's religious activities began to widen.

6

❧

Every evening the atmosphere at Bilwa Kutir was pervaded by the sweet sound of music. However, the songs that were sung here did not spring from the usual earthly pangs of unrequited love. Rather, they were all in praise of the eternal Brahma. It was an everyday practice for Gunabhiram and his family to sit on a bamboo mat spread on the earthen floor of the prayer-room adjoining the kitchen and take part in these musical offerings to God. This routine was seldom violated. The prayer room contained no idols or pictures of gods and goddesses. An earthen lamp on a brass-stand stood on one end of the bare room and near it on a low table were kept copies of the *Gita*, the Bible, Upanishads, Kirtan, Bhagabad, Maharshi Devendranath's *Brahma-Dharma* and other religious books. The prayers were usually led by Gunabhiram himself. After reciting the Gayatri-sloka quietly to himself, Gunabhiram would, in his deep bass voice, read out slokas from the Vedas and the Upanishads. Among others, the verse. "*Asato ma sat gamayo, tamaso ma jyotirgamayo*" was a special favourite and it was always sung. Both Bishnupriya and Swarna would join in the singing of the slokas. Sometimes, after reciting the Sanskrit slokas, Gunabhiram would recite the Lord's Prayer of the Christians and then explain its meaning in Assamese. The prayer session would usually end with Gunabhiram and Bishnupriya jointly singing a Borgeet either of Sri Sankardeva or Sri Madhavdeva. Whenever she sang the Bargeet, *Pawe pari Hari*, tears would invariably stream down Bishnupriya's cheeks. Swarnalata did not understand why her mother always wept when singing that particular Bargeet. It was only many years later that she came to realize that her mother's tears actually sprang from the deep hurt and social insult she had suffered which was still etched deep in the innermost corners of her heart. Those tears, Swarna came to know, weren't tears of weakness. Rather, they signified the strength of mind and confidence of someone who could surrender herself totally and unhesitatingly to the Almighty. An entranced Swarnalata would listen to the songs sung by her parents and the spell of experiencing something other worldly would continue to hold her even after her father concluded the day's prayer session with the words, *Brahma Kripahi Kevalam.*

Bilwa Kutir would be suffused in an atmosphere of peace and calm following the evening prayers. After attending to her two-year old son Karuna, Bishnupriya would sit reading either a book or a journal in a corner of the wide rear verandah. Gunabhiram would be in his study. And for Swarnalata too this would be the time to take her lessons from Panchanan Sarma. Having finished with the first alphabet book *Barna-Mala* in a very short time, Swarnalata had now started with the *Bare-Motora* and the arithmetic book which her father had got from the Orunodoi Press of Sibsagar. Swarna had completed her initial lessons at half the time other pupils would take at school. This little girl's zeal for learning left Panchanan Sarma amazed. For someone who had believed all these years that girls possessed less intelligence than boys, this was quite a revelation. Ever since he started giving lessons to Swarnalata, Panchanan Sarma had also started thinking of something else. He had so far not taught a single alphabet to his own daughter, Lakhipriya. Yet, in the case of his two sons, he never let them skip their morning and evening lessons, and missing school was just out of question for them. His sole aim seemed to have been to get them through the Entrance examination so that they became eligible for government jobs. But, for his daughter his only concern was to find a suitable groom and get her married at the earliest. It was not that Sarma did not love his daughter or was not concerned about her future. It had simply never occurred to him that he was being unjust to her by denying her education. Now, however, his ideas seemed to be undergoing a change. He began to think that if, alongwith Swarnalata, he could also give a few lessons to Lakhipriya, his filial duties towards her would be adequately taken care of before finally giving her off in marriage. It was with this thought in mind that Panchanan Sarma, after finishing Swarna's lessons for the evening, addressed Bishnupriya:

"Nobow, from tomorrow I think I'll bring Lakhipriya along to join Swarnalata in her lessons. After all, being a girl, how long will she be staying at home? If she's taught to read and write, it may be of some use in her future life."

A smile of happiness lit up Bishnupriya's face. She had always wanted Swarna to make friends with a girl of her age belonging to a good Assamese family. All these years, Swarna had come to know a few children from the Brahmo families and most of them were Bengalis. The Baruas did not have much social contact with the Assamese families in town. The upper-caste Assamese looked upon them as some sort of mlechhas because of their acceptance of the Brahmo faith. Over and above this, Bishnupriya, a Brahmin widow, had married a second time. How could orthodox society accept such a marriage? Thus, even though the upper caste families of Nagaon treated the Barua couple with respect in public, yet in their heart of hearts they didn't like their children to come into contact with the family living at Bilwa Kutir. Bishnupriya was only too aware of this. More than her own sense of loneliness, it was her daughter's lack of friends which saddened Bishnupriya. That was why she seemed so happy with Panchanan Sarma's suggestion and gladly approved the new arrangement.

7

Before taking Bishnupriya into confidence about his plans for Lakhi's education, Panchanan Sarma had not broached the topic in front of his family members. That evening, on returning home from Bilwa Kutir, he called his daughter and informed her in a sombre tone:

"From tomorrow morning be ready to go out with me to Bilwa Kutir. Swarna and you will do your lessons together."

Even as Lakhi ran excitedly to give the news to the other members of the family, a storm of sorts seemed to break over the house. There was none in the family to support Panchanan's decision. Lakhi's grandmother, her widowed aunt and her mother all joined in to condemn this strange and unheard-of move. They firmly declared that a Brahmin girl should never read or write. Besides, if people came to know that the girl was being allowed to visit the unclean house of the Hakim-saheb it would become virtually impossible to get her married into a respectable family. Panchanan's two brothers were marginally educated. Yet, on this question of women's education there seemed to be no divergence of views between them and the womenfolk of the family. Bholanath, the elder brother, started quoting from the scriptures to convince Panchanan that the true meaning of women's education lay in their doing their household duties well and in providing succour and satisfaction to the husband at all times. Educated women were by and large thought to be women of ill repute. They spent their leisure time reading bad books. These and many other arguments confronted Panchanan Sarma. But, even as the opposition to his move mounted from all sides, his resolve to educate his daughter seemed to grow. Eventually, after a lot of altercation, exchange of harsh words and emotional collapses of the women accompanied by tears, Panchanan had his way. He asked Lakhi to accompany him every morning to the Hakim's place. But, Sarma insisted that during her lessons, Lakhi would have to sit only on the mat she would carry from home and she should not touch any eatables at Bilwa Kutir. On her return from Bilwa Kutir, she would enter her house only after having a bath. Sarma laid down these terms not just to ensure peace in his household but also because he believed that social stability depended a lot on the womenfolk observing these customs strictly. Those same rules which in his own case he had never considered to be rigidly applicable, he now thought to be absolutely essential for his daughter. The very nature of a man's outdoor duties made it impossible for him to follow all the social norms.

A natural friendship sprang up between Swarna and Lakhi from the very first day. Swarna was of a shy nature and couldn't mix easily with strangers and new acquaintances. But Lakhi was the opposite. Being the elder daughter of the family, she had from a tender age conducted herself in the world of her elders like a perfect miniature housewife. There seemed to be a motherly glow about her when she sang lullabyes to put her little brothers and sisters to sleep, or when she mashed the rice and curry and coaxed them to eat. She seemed every inch the perfect housewife when she helped her mother in the kitchen or her father in the prayer room. It seemed that Lakhi was born to be a mother or a housewife, play and prattle didn't seem to be part of her little world. So, it was natural for her to assume the role of an elder sister as soon as she set eyes on Swarna. Being the Hakim's daughter and also somewhat advanced in studies, it was Swarna who should have exuded some sense of authority. But instead, Lakhi established herself as senior both in age and experience and Swarna accepted the position without any hesitation. After their lessons, when the two girls would play under the Bilwa tree, Lakhi's almost ceaseless chatter would often leave Swarna amazed. On the first day itself, Lakhi's sharp and experienced eyes detected the flaws in Swarna's play-kitchen and she giggled like an experienced housewife. "My Lord! When will the rice be cooked and ready on such a hearth? Move aside, let me make a real fire-place." Saying this, Lakhi's supple little fingers set to work to create a nice mud-chula. Then she neatly arranged the cooking utensils on the hearth. "One shouldn't mix up the hearth on which one cooks rice with the one in which the tea is made," she said. "On this side will be the rice-hearth and on that side the tea-hearth." Thus, talking continuously, she quickly arranged the toy-kitchen to resemble the kitchen in her own house. As Swarnalata watched her, she felt that Lakhi was a born housewife working busily in a real kitchen. What was play for Swarna, seemed to be part of the day-to-day chores for Lakhi.

Tired of playing kitchen, Lakhi proposed one day that they should play at "puja". Swarna was quite excited on hearing about the new game and began running around at Lakhi's directions to collect material for the game of worship. In a few moments Lakhi stuck some flowers and leaves on a lump of clay and turned it into a goddess. Then she prepared an altar decorated with sewali flowers. "The priest will sit here," she said, "and the sacrifice will take place at this spot." While Swarna watched in consternation, Lakhi set up the sacrificial post.

"How are sacrifices made?" asked Swarna in fear.

"It's so simple! The goat will have to be slaughtered at one stroke, like this—," Lakhi raised her right hand and in one sweep carried out the action of bringing down the machette on the goat's neck. A sudden feeling of fear and revulsion swept over Swarna's face. In a tone of disbelief, she said, "But if you do that, the goat will die!"

Lakhi burst out laughing, "But, it is supposed to die when it is sacrificed! What a simpleton you are!"

In an instant, Swarna became grave. "In that case, I won't play the puja game any more. I don't like sacrifices."

"O Lord! Sri Bishnu! One should never speak against sacrifices. The Goddess will be offended," Lakhi said in a serious tone. Swarna's features were distorted with fear. Without further protest, she followed Lakhi's directions mechanically and played the whole game. But, her heart was not in it. It seemed that all of a sudden the spot underneath the Bilwa tree had transformed into a place of some unknown primitive fear for Swarnalata. In the meantime, Panchanan Sarma had taken leave of the Baruas and the game had to come to an end. But, Swarna didn't dare venture to that spot below the tree the next morning, till it had been swept clean by the servants.

8

Miles Bronson, after failing to get much of a response to his proselytizing efforts in upper Assam, decided to shift his workplace to Nagaon. The Baptist missionaries too started converging on this small town and their work began to bear fruit. In Nagaon, Bronson himself started co-ordinating the two-fold task of spreading the words of the gospel along with education. These missionaries from far-away America had selflessly given themselves to fulfilling these tasks, believing firmly that once people became exposed to western education, they would naturally be attracted to the noble precepts of the Christian faith. With this belief as their guiding force, they had overcome all possible obstacles and engaged themselves totally in their chosen task. When in summer the wives of British officials sought refuge in the colder climes of Shillong, Darjeeling or Shimla, Mrs Bronson, Miss Keeler and the other missionary women would brave the scorching afternoon sun and go from house to house in order to preach the Gospel among the women. This they called their "jenana work". The missionary ladies knew from their past experience that direct talk about religion evoked little response from the womenfolk. So, they would approach the women first by teaching them knitting, sewing and other handicrafts. Only after gaining their confidence would they carefully broach matters of religion. But despite their cautious efforts, they met with little success in most of the Hindu households. In some of the houses they had to leave from the outer courtyard itself after being told that the menfolk didn't approve of the visits by the ladies from the mission. Sometimes, after being asked into the sitting-room, the lady of the house would tell them politely: "Your religion is good for you. Our religion is good for us. We do not understand what you say about your religion. So, there is no point in wasting your time here". But, the missionary women would not give up hope even after such harsh reactions. They seemed to hold on unwaveringly to the belief that even the most impregnable of barriers could be pierced one day with the words of truth and love.

The doors of Bilwa Kutir, however, were always open for the missionaries. Both Gunabhiram and Bishnupriya never failed to receive Bronson and the other Baptists with warmth and courtesy. They seemed overwhelmed by the sense of commitment of the missionaries to the cause of the Assamese language. Towards Christianity, they didn't have any ill feeling, primarily because the founder of the Brahmo faith, Raja Rammohan Roy, believed in one God and in the unity of all religions. He had also said that the teachings of Christ had great relevance for modern times. So, it was but natural that to the liberal Brahmos any form of religious intolerance was not the acceptable norm of social behaviour. So, whenever in the afternoons the missionary women visited Bishnupriya, she would listen to their discourse without the least hesitation and would also read the Assamese books on religion and ethics which they often left behind.

Golapi too would come to Bilwa Kutir, sometimes alone and sometimes with the missionary women. Bishnupriya would learn sewing and knitting from her and then teach Swarnalata. Ever since Swarna and Tora got acquainted in the church, Golapi would also bring along her daughter to make friends with Swarna. Swarna looked upon Tora with great admiration.

She felt that none could equal Tora—whether it was singing, sewing, knitting or studies Tora was unparalleled. The two girls would talk a lot whenever they were together. Swarna was very curious to know about Tora's school life. Listening to all the stories about the memsahib's school, she started yearning to go to such a school. She felt that instead of sitting in a corner at home with Lakhi and memorizing the mathematical tables, it would be so much more fun to be in a class with many other girls of her own age. Finding Swarna an avid listener, Tora would open up her own dream-world. She would often get carried away by her fancies and create an illusory world which she tried to portray as the real one. One of her favourite dreams was centred round the hope that Miss Keeler would take her to America some day and she would visit distant lands in ships that sail on the seas.

"How far is America from here?"

Swarna would ask in awe and bewilderment.

Tapping the floor with her feet, Tora would declare confidently: "America is on the other side of the earth. When it is night here, it is daytime over there. Everything there is the reverse of what we see here. When we sleep here, the people in America are awake. And can you believe it, all the people there are white like our mems and sahibs? There isn't anybody there like you and me."

Swarna would, with her beautiful eyes wide open, try to visualize those strange people and their strange land. She found it hard to believe the stories about that land which lay below the earth. She would ask Tora in a tone of disbelief: "Who told you about all this?"

"Why, our neighbour Bogi baideo's father Dhaniram. He had accompanied Bronson Sahib to America some years ago. Bogi baideo has told us all everything about America. In her house there are many precious things brought from America."

"Can you go to America all alone? Won't you be afraid?" Swarna asked with disbelief.

"What is there to be afraid of?" Tora replied defiantly. "I will go with the missionaries. Even the waves of the ocean respect them. The moment they call upon Lord Jesu, no harm can befall anyone."

"Can't the sea waves drown the Christians?"

"No, they cannot, because Jesu used to walk on water. That is why whenever Christians fall into the sea, they are picked up by Jesu."

Tora's words were full of an unshakeable faith. She always enjoyed adding her own details to all that she had heard from her mother and the missionaries. She was eager to kindle a spark of faith in Swarna's mind about her own beliefs. That was why she added something of her own while recounting the miracles of Christ to Swarnalata. And, as if in a trance, Swarna would keep listening to Tora. Whenever she raised any doubts, Tora would, like an experienced preacher, give a quick reply.

Hakim Gunabhiram Barua used to go quite often to tour moffussil areas. In those days the railway was yet to come to Assam. Apart from the boat in the monsoon months and the bullock-cart or horse-drawn carriage in winter, there weren't any other means of travel or communication. However, horses and elephants were also used by government officials during their visits to the interior areas. A trip from Nagaon to Guwahati, a distance of some seventy-five miles, would mean taking the road for some thirteen miles upto Raha and then crossing the Kolong river. In those days there was no bridge over the Kolong. One had to cross the river by boat and then cover some ten miles by road, after which the Dimul river had to be crossed. After the Dimul, one had to cross the Kapili, Kiling and several smaller rivers. And, when the monsoon rains flooded the river

banks, the roads would simply disappear. As a result, if one had
to tour during the summer months, one invariably had to take
the boat. Though travelling by boat was time consuming, yet
it had its own advantages. The rough bumps, the mud and the
slush where the carriage wheels could get stuck or the horses
slip and fall, could be avoided. Above all these, there were fewer
chances of not reaching the dak bungalow in time and of being
stranded in some far-off unknown place and having to spend
the night there. Compared to all these advantages the only likely
hazards in a river journey were the swarms of mosquitoes in
summer and the possibility of boats getting stuck in the sand
bars in winter. Nevertheless, the fear of a mishap was always
there and every traveller had to be mentally prepared for it. But,
usually the boatmen were so skilled that one could easily leave
the question of safety to them. Moreover, in a boat journey, all
the physical hardship was borne by the boatmen. Those who had
the privilege of travelling in the sheltered tents of a pair of big
mar-naos or under the thatched roof of the khel-nao, did not
have to face much discomfort on the journey.

Having considered all these options, Gunabhiram decided to
take Bishnupriya, Swarna and Karuna along with him on his
official tours that year. Bishnupriya hadn't been anywhere after
they came to Nagaon following their wedding. Thinking that a
trip outside would brighten her spirits, Gunabhiram decided to
visit his Bengali friend Kailash Nath Ray who was the manager
of a tea-garden near Bheleuguri. His wife belonged to a Brahmo
family of Calcutta, and he too had accepted the Brahmo faith.
Mrs Ray was very fond of Bishnupriya and the latter too looked
upon her as a dear relative. Whenever the Rays visited Nagaon,
they used to stay at Bilwa Kutir and they had often invited the
Barua family to come and be their guest at the tea garden. So,
Gunabhiram decided to spend a few days at Bheleuguri with his

family after finishing his official work at Raha, Jamunamukh and nearby places.

Swarnalata was extremely excited about the river journey ever since she heard about the plans. She didn't remember having ever gone on a long journey outside Nagaon. However, she had heard many a strange tale about such journeys from the visitors who came to Bilwa Kutir from different parts of the province. In those days one could hear many a spine-thrilling account of a journey from Jorhat to Nagaon. As one crossed the dense Nambar forests, it appeared as if the dhan-gulois, the jakhinis and the Burha-dangorias all lay in wait to frighten the wits out of the weary traveller! Swarna had also heard many stories about boat journeys. Her father had given her detailed descriptions of all that one could encounter during river journeys from Calcutta to Guwahati. Therefore, Swarna could break through the confines of Bilwa Kutir as her imaginative journeys took her around the country.

As the day of the journey approached, Swarna was eagerly waiting for a chance to share her excitement with her two new friends. But, Lakhi didn't show much of an interest in it. Like someone who was very experienced in such matters, she said that she knew all about such river journeys for she had travelled with her family upstream of the Kolong upto Arikati for the holy dip in the Brahmaputra on Ashokastami day, and she hadn't liked the journey at all. It was always better, she felt, to travel by bullock-cart. Seated under the thatch one could view so many enchanting scenes, whereas in a boat one had to guard oneself from the sun during the day and the mosquitoes at night. Listening to Lakhi's disheartening account, Swarna was worried for a moment, but her enthusiasm could not be dampened. She waited eagerly to tell Tora about their planned trip. She seemed to derive some secret pleasure over the fact that she would be able to score a

point over Tora by taking, if not a sea-journey, at least a river
journey before her. But, to her disappointment, before she left
on her trip, Swarna didn't even meet Tora. A school girl from the
mission told her that Tora had gone to "camp". The girl couldn't
say what the camp was and Swarna concluded that it must be the
name of some nearby village.

When the Barua family finally proceeded to their boats with
all their luggage, it appeared as if they were starting on a journey
to some far-flung lands. Bed-rolls, utensils and a good supply
of provisions formed the major part of their luggage. They had
also brought with them a servant, a cook and the young girl
who always stayed with Swarna. A room of bamboo and thatch
had been built on the large mar-nao and every effort had been
made to provide as much comfort as was possible to the Hakim's
family. A clerk and a court-writer followed the mar-nao of the
Baruas in a khel-nao. A part of the khel-nao too was covered
with a thatched roof and underneath it, beds had been made on
straw. The two boats would be brought together during meal
times and everyone would eat on the mar-nao.

As soon as the boats set sail, Swarna sat near her father and
sought the answers to the countless questions which arose in
her mind. Gunabhiram with a lot of patience, answered all her
queries. As the boat crossed the jail building on the bank and
moved near the opening of Khanajan, Gunabhiram explained
to his daughter how Anandaram Dhekiyal Phukan had used the
convicts to deepen the bend of the Mori-Kollong and thereby
shorten the river route by some two miles. Remembering
Anandaram with reverence, he told Swarna:

"See Maisena, nothing is impossible for man. With a little bit
of will and intelligence even a river can be tamed."

Swarna paused for a moment and then asked: "Can the waves
of the ocean be tamed too?"

Gunabhiram was a bit puzzled. But, in support of his own

argument, he said, "Till now no one has been able to achieve that. But, in future as man's knowledge expands, this too could be possible."

"Deuta, isn't it true that Jesu could walk on waves?"

This time Gunabhiram understood where Swarna's question was leading. With a smile he affectionately laid his hand on his daughter's head and answered: "There are such stories in all religions. Whether these are true or false one must use one's reason to find out. That's why one should study and increase one's wisdom."

Swarna didn't quite follow what her father said, but, her experience with elders had taught her that grown-ups always avoided direct answers. So, she decided to stop there. Meanwhile, attracted by other sights, she forgot what she'd been saying.

The heavy mar-nao was proceeding at a sluggish pace. The boatmen were pushing long bamboo poles deep into the water and manouevering the boat forward. It took almost the entire day to reach Raha. It had grown dark as they crossed Phuloguri. All of a sudden, a lot of flickering lights appeared on the river. At first everyone thought they were fishing boats. But, as the boat moved closer they turned out to be plantain-rafts. They had been put into the river with some prasad and a small lighted earthen lamp. The moment Gunabhiram saw these rafts, he cautioned everyone not to drink the river water without heating it. Seeing the rafts, he knew that cholera had broken out in the nearby villages. This was how the village folk sent their offerings to the deities whenever epidemics struck the region. Swarna was very scared on hearing all this. Meanwhile, a swarm of mosquitoes which had been hovering over the passengers, started troubling them. To avoid being bitten by the mosquitoes, they quickly finished their food and took shelter under the mosquito-nets.

On the first night the boat anchored at Raha ghat. There were several other boats at the ghat. Most of these belonged to

Marwari traders. These boats used to carry cotton, lac and other goods from the Naga Hills, North Cachar and other interior areas to Guwahati. Some of the trading boats which came from Guwahati went upstream of the Kopili after halting at Raha. This made Raha an important junction for such boats and added to its commercial importance. Every week there used to be a large village market at Raha and it was here market that Christian missionaries from Nagaon would often distribute free, small booklets or pictures of Jesus among the people.

Gunabhiram had some official work at Raha. So, after anchoring the boats, they all went to the dak-bungalow. The next morning, the boats started moving upstream. The river Kopili being full of swift currents, the two boats inched their way forward. As they left Raha, the paddy fields which had lined both banks, gradually began to disappear. It was then the month of Aswin. Although the flood waters had started receding, yet there were long stretches of shallow on both sides of the river. Here and there one could still see a paddy field. But, almost the entire area seemed to be covered by swamps and undergrowth. After moving upstream for some time, the boats passed through a stretch which was covered with tall river reeds. Most of the region appeared deserted. The banks would open up a bit whenever the boats approached human habitation. Then the boats would be anchored and the passengers would come ashore and straighten their limbs. The servants would go into the nearby villages to bring vegetables and poultry and meals would be cooked on the shore. But sometimes coming to know that the hakim's boat had anchored, people would of their own accord bring milk, curd and vegetables from their kitchen-gardens. Gunabhiram, however, never accepted anything without payment. Even if the people entreated that their goods be treated as gifts, Gunabhiram would insist that they accept payment. Sometimes he even sounded harsh.

Swarna would be thrilled with the village scenes. Young Mikir women coming to bathe in the river would keep staring at the boats and then suddenly burst out laughing. Swarna would look away in embarrassment. But she would be filled with affection for these girls when they waved at her and her little brother. Groups of naked children would hover near the boats as long as they were achored and keep staring at the passengers. To Swarna they appeared to belong to some other world. She would be filled with curiosity to know what they ate and how they lived. Her father would tell her: "They are Mikirs. They have a culture of their own. But since our people know so little about them, they are looked upon as uncivilized races. Even the British had at first thought our people to be uncivilized barbarians. But those British who have read and heard about the culture of our country, they realize how ancient and rich it is. That's why people should be properly educated. Education alone instils in us respect for all races."

"But such things aren't there in the books I have read," commented Swarna.

"You'll understand everything when you grow older. There's plenty about our neighbouring tribes in the *Orunodoi* volumes at our house."

Slowly the two boats advanced through a huge forest area. Large, tall trees lined both sides of the river. Some of the branches drooped and almost touched the water. Watching the monkeys frolic on the tree branches was great fun for Swarna and her brother. The colourful kingfishers would dive into the water and then swiftly return to the trees. As the sun played on their wings, rainbow colours would flash. Egrets sitting on the branches of a dried tree would suddenly spring to the sky as the boat approached. Watching them fly till they disappeared from view, Swarna would be transported to her own dreamland. Sometimes a group of teals would wing their way above their heads like a string of beads across the sky. Swarna felt that their unknown

cries carried a message for her. Gunabhiram would point to
the sal trees and say sadly: "One day these valuable trees will
disappear from our forests. Timber merchants from Darrang have
been felling these trees for the past few years. The ones you see
now are new ones. With the traders' eyes on them, these too are
bound to disappear soon."

Gunabhiram had some official work at Kampur. So the party
stayed the night at the dak bungalow and began their journey the
next morning. In the afternoon the boats approached a village
called Baliram. They hadn't thought of anchoring the boats there.
Seven days of boat-journey had exhausted the passengers and
everyone wished to reach Jamunamukh as quickly as possible.
But having seen two other boats anchored at the Baliram ghat,
the passengers could not rein in their curiosity. Even their
boatmen, who had come to recognize their comrades manning
the other boats, wished to draw close. As the boat which carried
Gunabhiram and his family approached the shore, they heard
lilting music. Swarna looked at the shore in amazement. The tune
appeared very familiar to her. And as their boat drew closer, she
seemed to recognize the singer's voice. It was Tora's. And, as their
boat touched the shore, Swarna saw a strange sight. On a mar-
nao Miss Keeler was playing the organ and, standing by her side,
a few girls were singing hymns. Meanwhile, quite a number of
people had gathered on the shore. As soon as the singing of hymns
was over, another missionary woman started distributing some
pamphlets among the people. Most of them flipped through the
pamphlets and then returned them. Although these were written
in Assamese, yet there wasn't a single person among the group
of villagers who could read. Understanding the problem, the
two white women left their boat and came ashore and started
speaking about Jesus in broken Assamese. At first everyone seemed
to listen with attention to what they were saying. But when the
missionary ladies explained to the people that the purpose of

their coming to the village was to set up a girls' school there, the crowd slowly began to leave. Only a small group of children stayed on to listen. In the meantime, Gunabhiram, Bishnupriya and Swarna had come ashore. A surprised and happy Tora ran to meet them. "The name of this village is 'camp', isn't it." Swarna eagerly asked Tora.

"What are you saying! This village is called Baliram. There are a few Christian families here. That's why we have come here. Such a trip is called coming for camp. We have been moving around like this by boat for fifteen days. We'll be returning home after about a fortnight."

"So many days!" Swarna exclaimed. She was already tired with just a week's river journey. Meanwhile, Gunabhiram was about to take leave of the missionary group when he saw some villagers coming towards them. They were accompanied by a man who seemed to be a gaonbura or headman. With hesitant steps the villagers approached Gunabhiram and the missionaries. Thinking perhaps that Gunabhiram also belonged to the group of missionaries, they told him that though they didn't have anything against the Christians because they always said the right things, yet they did not approve of the setting up of schools for girls. The few young men of the village who had gone to school had lost interest in their fields. Now if the girls too started going to school, who would manage the housework? The men appeared quite excited while presenting their case.

Like a leader of the missionary group, Gunabhiram explained to the villagers that with whatever the girls learnt at school they would be able to do their household chores better. Moreover, only if the girls were educated could one expect the children of the villages to improve. He told them about the harm that could befall the young ones if the mothers were uneducated and ignorant. Miss Keeler too narrated a story in broken Assamese. The gist of her story was that a wise and educated mother can bring back a straggler to the right path. Slowly, the attitude of some of the village elders seemed to soften. Someone whispered to one of the villagers as to who Gunabhiram actually was. In a flash the news spread and the village folk assured Gunabhiram that all arrangements would be made to make the stay of the missionaries comfortable in their village. They also agreed to the setting up of the school. But they wanted to be assured that the girls who would attend the school would not be asked to give up their faith. Gunabhiram told them that in Calcutta and other big cities many girls had gone in for higher education. But they had never given up their own religion.

After explaining all this, Gunabhiram returned to his boat. He saw before him the image of another great man who, facing almost unsurmountable odds, was waging a single-handed struggle for the cause of women's education. The example set by Vidyasagar had always inspired Gunabhiram in his life's struggle. He would consider himself lucky, if he could do for the Assamese people only a fraction of what Vidyasagar had done for the Bengalis! But watching the dark dense forests on both sides of the river, Gunabhiram was filled with a feeling of despair. Calcutta was lit up by so many glittering lamps. Would he alone be able to bring some light into all this darkness in Assam?

10

The week in the tea-garden passed amidst fun and gaiety. Kailash Nath Rai and his wife overwhelmed the Barua family with their love and affection. Right from the first day, when the vehicle came to pick them up from the river-ghat, till the last there seemed to be no end to their hospitality. Guests were indeed rare in the tea estate and Raibabu and his wife wished to delay the departure of the Baruas as far as possible. But, because of the pressure of official work, Gunabhiram couldn't stay for more than four days. Both Bishnupriya and Mrs Roy were moved to tears as they said good-bye. Since she got married to Gunabhiram, Bishnupriya had never received so much affection from anyone.

By the time the Baruas returned home, some twenty days had passed. During this period a major change had taken place in Lakhipriya's life. Her marriage had been fixed with the younger son of Ramprasad Goswami of Kaliabor, Govindaprasad. Even before she had completed nine years of age, Panchanan Sarma had been on the look-out for an eligible groom. But his search became more determined after his wife and mother started prodding him after Lakhi started taking lessons at the Hakim's house. Contacts had been made with several families. Eventually, Lakhi's marriage was fixed with the son of the Goswami family of Kaliabor because the horoscopes matched. The young man was said to be suitable in all ways. He had read upto class four

in the Nagaon High School. But finding it difficult to continue
his studies staying at someone else's place, he had come back
home and was now teaching in a near-by primary school. People
from the groom's family had already come and seen the girl. The
wedding was fixed for the month of Magh. After the marriage,
the girl would continue to stay at her mother's till puberty.

At first Lakhi didn't know anything about her marriage. It
was only after everything had been finalized and her mother
and grandmother had started washing her hair regularly with
monisal and enlarging her earlobe holes so that the *keru* would
go in, that it gradually dawn on her that some major change was
about to take place in her life. The weaving of silken mekhalas
started in the household loom. Two women weavers from the
nearby village were employed to weave rihas and mekhalas with
intricate designs and also clothes which would be offered as gifts
to the elders. After all, everything that was being done in the
Sarma household now seemed to have only one purpose—that
of Lakhi's wedding. Lakhi had been feeling quite lonely without
Swarna so, she liked the new situation at home. Especially as
everyone seemed so concerned about her food, dress and overall
appearance, Lakhi's childlike mind bubbled with happiness.
She waited eagerly for Swarna's return so that she could relate
everything to her. She went to Bilwa Kutir with her father
the very next day after Swarna and her parents returned. But,
the eagerness with which she had waited for all these days
seemed to have ebbed away and Lakhi looked quite dejected.
Panchanan Sarma went and sat near Gunabhiram and started
enquiring about his muffasil trip. Lakhi clutched Swarna's hand
and moved towards their place of play beneath the bilwa tree.
On other days Lakhi would chatter away without a break. But
today it was Swarna who was doing all the talking. The boat-trip,
the meeting with Tora, incidents in the tea-garden, as Swarna
hurriedly related all this, she didn't even notice that all the while

Lakhi was silent. When she became aware of Lakhi's silence, she asked: "What's happened to you Lakhi? Why are you so sad?" Lakhi just kept mum. As Swarna continued looking at Lakhi's face in amazement, she saw her friend's beautiful eyes fill with tears. Swarna had never seen her cry before. A bit perplexed, she again asked Lakhi, "Please tell me what's happened."

"I'll no longer be able to come and read with you. I will be married in the month of Magh." With this, Lakhi burst into tears. She had never thought that she would have to break the news of her wedding in such a manner to Swarna. But, that morning when she was about to come to Swarna's place, her mother had said, "Say good-bye to Swarna. You needn't go again to her house before the wedding. There'll be lot of problems if someone tells the groom's household that we are on visiting terms with the Hakim's family."

It was only then that Lakhi suddenly realized that the wedding didn't just mean nice new clothes and golden ornaments. Whatever little freedom she had, was now about to be bartered. Lakhi leaned her head on the bilwa-tree and cried her heart out. Swarna's face turned pale with fear and sadness. She thought marriage was a terrible thing. Would she too be given off in marriage by her parents? Her tiny heart seemed to flutter with some unknown fear. When Lakhi, tired of crying, turned around to look at Swarna, she saw that Swarna too was sobbing away. Forgetting her own plight, Lakhi started consoling Swarna: "Don't cry, Swarna. I will try to come over sometimes to your place. Please pay attention to your studies. And, of course, you must come to my wedding." Lakhi tried a brave smile as she uttered the last few words. She didn't really understand why Swarna was crying. She was still too young to know that at a certain stage in one's life, tears just well up on seeing others cry. Taking Swarna's tears to be a sign of her affection for her, Lakhi was filled with a sense of gratitude.

11

⁂

After Lakhi's wedding was finalised, Gunabhiram and Lakhipriya thought things over and decided to arrange a new tutor for Swarna. They felt that Swarna would not be able to receive a true education from a person who, despite being educated, had decided to give off his little child in marriage. At that time a lot of people were writing for and against child-marriage in newspapers and journals in the different provinces of the country. While still a student in Calcutta, Gunabhiram Barua had written in the *Orunodoi* that both the boy and the girl should attain a mature age at the time of marriage. If the age difference between the two was a big one, then the relationship between the husband and wife became more like that of a father and daughter. They wouldn't be able to develop the friendship and affection of equals and this would result in complications in their family life. Gunabhiram had acquired these ideas from the Brahmo society of Calcutta. One of the main objectives of the social revolution initiated by the Brahmos was to bring about a radical change in the marriage practices of the Hindus. Brahmo leaders like Keshav Chandra Sen and Rajnarain Basu had been waging a relentless campaign against child-marriage and polygamy and in favour of widow re-marriage. Devendranath Tagore, Keshav Chandra Sen, Sivnath Shastri—each one of these Brahmo leaders tried to outdo the other when it came to matters relating to women's liberation. Each tried to show that he was more liberal than the other. Devendranath was the first to get his daughter married in the Brahmo fashion. Keshav Chandra took the initiative for women's education and Sivnath Shastri fought hard to ensure that women and men sat together during the prayer-sessions. The Brahmos of Nagaon were duly informed of these developments through the newspapers and journals which they received. As a result, something of the intellectual storm which had hit Calcutta, also touched Nagaon. Even in this distant corner of Assam, the Brahmos could hear, though faintly, the impassioned pleas of Brahmananda Keshav Chandra. The fierce differences of view between *Tatwabodhini Patrika* of the old or "Adi" Brahma Samaj and the *Indian Mirror* of the new generation of radical Brahmos created a sensation even among the Brahmos of Nagaon. However, it was mainly Keshav Chandra Sen's revolutionary ideals which had influenced Gunabhiram and several other leading Brahmo samajists. Every Sunday, after evening prayers in the new Brahmo temple built at the initiative of Gunabhiram, different issues relating to their faith would be actively discussed and debated. The discussion would be lead by the Headmaster of the Bengali school, Gurunath Dutta and by Gunabhiram Barua himself. It was Gurunath Dutta who led the prayers as the Acharya. But in Devendranath's Adi Brahmo Samaj only Brahmins were allowed to hold such office. However, in matters relating to caste, the Brahmo Samaj of Nagaon was guided by the principles of Keshav Chandra Sen.

Gunabhiram's heart turned heavy at Panchanan Sarma's decision to get his minor daughter married. He started having many apprehensions about Swarna's future. That's why after Sunday prayers, he raised the matter of child-marriage while sitting in discussion with Dutta and others. The Calcutta Brahmos were fighting tooth and nail to get a ban introduced on girls below fourteen being married. But were the other sections of society touched by such issues?

"Haven't they been affected?" asked Duttababu. "We are all aware of the writings on this issue in the journals these days. The other day the *Abala Bandhav* of Dwarkanath Ganguly carried a good write-up on child-marriage. The point is that the educated sections are bound to be influenced by such writings. But with the uneducated it is a separate matter. It will take a lot of time for their condition to be changed."

"Generally, when we refer to someone as educated, we mean the Brahmins, Kayasthas and other high castes. Whereas by uneducated we mean the lower castes. This is where we have been making a big mistake. Among the lower castes of Assam, Orissa and other provinces, evil practices like sati and child-marriage are virtually absent. Only among the upper castes are these practices growing roots. So, it is actually the upper castes who need to be rid of these evil customs."

Gunabhiram didn't say these words just for the sake of debating matters. Everyone present realized that they were the expression of his deepest feelings and bore the mark of his own experience. After a brief lull, a young lawyer named Durganath Ray spoke out excitedly: "The really educated among the Brahmins and the Kayasthas have already accepted the Brahmo faith. As for those who are still stubbornly holding on to their superstitions and evil customs, there is no saving them. They will always make fun of the Brahmo samajists as *Brahma-Jnani* or the supremely wise. We needn't worry our heads over such narrow-minded people".

Durganath Ray belonged to the new generation of Brahmos. He had heard the fiery speeches of Keshav Chandra Sen at Calcutta. He also knew Sivnath Shastri. As such, unlike the members of the Adi Brahmo Samaj, Durganath was in no mood to compromise with the Brahmins. The elder Brahmos like Gurunath Dutta and Gunabhiram Barua were not in the least lacking in brotherly affection towards this young lawyer. But, they felt that Durganath's over-enthusiasm needed to be kept in check.

"You haven't come out with very wise words, Durganath. If we Brahmos show so much self-pride, then the very purpose with which the Brahmo Samaj was set up would be eventually lost. We wish to build a new Bharat which will be free of evil practices like caste and untouchability. We have to surpass the other civilized nations. Therefore, it would be our duty to pull those who are making fun of us, from darkness to light."

It was Gurunath Dutta's habit to change the course of a discussion in such a manner whenever the possibility of bitterness arose. Because of this quality of his, everyone looked upon him with a lot of respect.

After the discussion concluded that day, Gunabhiram took Gurunath Dutta aside and told him about the problem of getting a private tutor for Swarna. Gurunath suggested that the responsibility be given to a teacher of his school, Rajaninath Das. Swarna should also learn a bit of English so that she could go to some good school for higher studies.

"I am very worried on this score. Till today our Nagaon does not have a good school for girls," said Gunabhiram in a tone of sadness.

"Don't you worry," assured Gurunath Dutta. "If the Almighty desires, then one day Swarna will study in Bethune College. And we have heard that an English woman, Annete Akroyd, has joined hands with Dwarkanath Ganguly to set up another girls' college in Calcutta. It's called Hindu Mahila Vidyalaya. It is being said that the method of teaching in this school will be quite different. Certain differences are reported to have sprung up regarding this between Keshav Chandra Sen and Dwarkanath Ganguly. Be that as it may, we'll consider all the aspects before fixing up a good school for Swarna. What do you say?"

Gurunath Dutta's words seemed to remove a heavy burden from Gunabhiram's mind. But he felt unhappy at the very thought of sending Swarna to Calcutta. How would he send his little darling daughter so far? And even if he decided to send her, would her mother agree? Yet, both Bishnupriya and he had so many dreams for their Swarnalata. They wished to shape her as an ideal of the new age. Maybe for that they would have to steel their hearts. As Gunabhiram was returning home clasping his daughter's hand in his, such were the thoughts which kept him engrossed.

12

Ever since she returned from camp, Tora's days had been hectic. She would be taking her annual examinations just before Christmas. Those days there were only two primary schools for girls in Nagaon. One was the newly set up Bengali school, and the other the school run by the missionaries. The total number of pupils of both the schools didn't exceed fifty in number. The annual examinations were held at the house of Nakulbabu, a teacher in the Bengali boys' school. His home took on a festive air during the exam days. The examination would be held in a large room. The examinees from both the schools would number some twenty or so. Apart from the teachers of the Bengali girls' school, some missionary ladies would also be present during these examinations. For Tora, this examination was of great importance. If she did well, the mission would send her to the "Normal" school run by the government where she could train as a teacher. It was Miss Keeler's wish that after finishing her Normal training, Tora should start teaching at the newly established girls' school at Baliram. While returning from camp, she had talked about it with Golapi and Tora. At first, Golapi did not like the idea at all. For Golapi, who had brought up her daughter with so much care after her husband's death, the very idea of sending Tora so far away to work was difficult to accept. Miss Keeler had listened patiently to all her protestations and then, looking into the distance while the boat moved on, she had said:

"My mother had similar apprehensions, Golapi. I was also her only child. But her unwavering faith in God helped her overcome all her misgivings. She happily accepted my becoming a missionary. Yet I know that when I was about to leave, she was heartbroken. Even then, she did not dissuade me. Just see, here I am in Assam having come all the way from America's Boston city, and yet I don't feel lonely at all. For me now, all of you are like my parents, my own brothers and sisters. If I have done it, why can't Tora?"

Golapi fell silent, listening to Miss Keeler. She immediately changed her view. Tora, however, was thinking of something else.

"So, I will not be able to go to America with you?" Tora asked in a sad tone.

Smilingly, Miss Keeler patted Tora on the back and said:

"Why are you worrying? I have promised, one day I will take you along to America. But before that you will have to learn to work amongst your own people. Only then will you be able to proudly tell the Americans that you are a little Assamese missionary."

From then onwards Tora started dreaming of becoming a missionary. She couldn't imagine anyone else who could outdo Miss Keeler in knowledge and wisdom. She decided that like Miss Keeler, she too would spread Christ's gospel, would teach in a school, give music lessons—what could be more glorious? This explained Tora's new-found enthusiasm since she returned from camp. One day she went with her mother to meet Swarna. It was there that she learnt of Lakhi's marriage. She had once seen Lakhi when she, along with some missionary women, had gone to her house to do "jenana" work. She now recalled how Lakhi's grandmother had summarily sent them off from the front courtyard itself. Such experiences were not new to them and Tora didn't take it otherwise. But she was quite moved when Lakhi had hesitatingly come out to meet them at the gate. She remembered presenting her with a small book of morals. Having now heard of Lakhi's wedding, Tora was not at all surprised. She had little time to think of it or even feel sorry for the small girl. For, with Christmas being just a week away, she had so much to do. She would have to help the missionary ladies decorate the Christmas tree. Then, the hankies had to be embroidered, the table cloths stitched and small gifts packed for all the loved ones. Also, gifts would have to be sent to those children from the Mikir Hills whom they had recently met. Tora seemed to be in a hurry and left Bilwa Kutir after insisting that Swarna should come for the Christmas celebrations.

13

Miles Bronson had specially invited Gunabhiram Barua for Christmas Day celebrations in the Nagaon Mission. Although on several earlier occasions, Gunabhiram had joined these celebrations, he had never brought Swarna with him. But, this time, noticing his daughter's eagerness, he decided to take her with him. Christians from Nagaon and nearby areas—Assamese, Bengalis, Mikirs and others—thronged the Mission compound, celebrating the birth of Christ in full gaiety. Gunabhiram exchanged greetings with all those whom he knew and then sat on the chair specially kept for him. Though Swarna sat next to her father, yet her eyes kept roving trying to spot Tora among the boys and girls seated on a bamboo mat on the floor. But she didn't see her anywhere. Meanwhile, the children were getting excited with the beautifully decorated Christmas tree placed in front of them. In the absence of a real Christmas tree, some other sapling had been decorated with coloured streamers and flowers, with stars and small toys. As Swarna kept looking at the tree in amazement, suddenly the tunes of a Christmas carol being played on an organ could be heard. A fascinating scene then opened up before Swarna. Dressed in sparkling white from head to toe, there was Tora as the Virgin Mother. She was carrying on her lap a Christ-like doll. A group of children all dressed in white led Tora towards the audience and, singing all the while, made her sit on a decorated altar. They then acted out the story of the birth of Christ through songs and music. Finally, when the angels from heaven, the poor shepherds and the wise men from the East knelt before Mary and the infant Jesus, Swarna felt that Tora was really some goddess. Swarna had seen plays before. Sometimes when theatre groups came to Nagaon, her father would bring them over to their house and all of them would enjoy the acting. Swarna loved seeing the yatra plays. But this function was sober and solemn in quite a different way. The deep notes of the organ, the lilting tunes of the carols sung in chorus, and the snow-white dresses of the participants seemed to fill her with some sacred sort of happiness.

As soon as the acting was over, one could hear shouts of joy among the children. Father Christmas was advancing with faltering steps, a big bag slung over his shoulder. Seeing his white flowing beard, red cap and white and crimson clothes, young and old started clapping excitedly. Santa placed his bag underneath the Christmas tree and then started pulling out gifts for the children. As he called out the names, the excitement among the young ones rose. A surprised Swarna was looking on with a fixed gaze when she heard her name being called out. At first she couldn't believe it. But the old man repeated her name a second time and called out clearly, "Swarnalata Barua". Meanwhile, Tora had joined the group of children and was now gesturing to Swarna to go and collect her gift. A puzzled Swarna stood by her father's side and stared helplessly at him. When Gunabhiram smiled and asked her to go, Swarna somehow managed to walk up to the tree and collect her gift. She was blushing all through. But she felt good at the thought that she was being given equal importance with the others. After a while, as she walked back home with her father, clutching with both hands her little gift, Swarna felt that she was drifting away into some dream world.

Returning home from the Christmas celebrations, Swarna

just couldn't wait to show her mother the gift she had received.
She rushed indoors. But seeing visitors inside, she hesitated for
a while. Lakhi's parents were there. Swarna didn't remember
having seen Lakhi's mother in Bilwa kutir before. Yet, the
presence of visitors could not dampen her excitement. Handing
the colourfully-wrapped gift to her mother, she almost cried out:
"Look, what they have given me! But how did they know my
name?" Bishnupriya smiled affectionately at her daughter and
said: "Knowing that you would come, Tora must have kept the
gift ready for you. Such a sweet girl. May god bless her." In the
meantime Swarna opened the packet and found an embroidered
handkerchief and a small needle-case. Happily she kissed the
handkerchief. Observing mother and daughter all this while,
Lakhi's mother was dying to say something. In a soft tone she
now said: "Swarna, haven't you come from a Christian's place?
Go and have a good bath and cleanse yourself."

Swarna opened her eyes wide in surprise and looked at her
mother. An embarrassed Bishnupriya hinted at Swarna to go
inside. When Swarna left, Mrs Sarma smiled and said: "After all,
she is a little girl. If she is not taught these things from now
onwards, she'll face problems in the future."

Bishnupriya didn't say anything. Perhaps she did not wish to
offend her guest. Nevertheless, a feeling of disgust seemed to
cover her face. Mrs Sarma, however, didn't even notice it. She
took the brass sarai from the small boy who accompanied her
and placing it before Bishnupriya, said: "You must have heard
about Lakhi's marriage. The wedding has been fixed for the 15th
of Magha. We have come to invite you." Mrs Sarma's face was
gleaming with pride and happiness. Her words seemed to convey
a new sense of self-confidence. But on hearing what Bishnupriya
had to say, her enthusiasm was somewhat dampened:

"You seem to have decided too early on marriage. And Lakhi
was ever so interested in studies. Nowadays people insist that

girls should be given a proper education. In our days things were different."

"How can we say that Lakhi is too young for marriage? A girl is considered grown-up the moment she enters her tenth year. She'll be attaining puberty in a year or two. If one keeps on waiting for girls to be educated, then the marriage age will pass. Won't you too have to get your Swarna married within a year or two? Society will scorn us if we can't get our daughters married in time."

"We are not thinking of getting Swarna married. Her father wishes that she be properly educated. Marriage, of course, depends on fate," Bishnupriya let her words fall slowly. Mrs Sarma just kept on nodding with fixed eyes. That she did not at all approve of what the Hakim''s wife was saying became evident from her gestures. She, however, could not muster courage to protest openly. She had heard about the strange views of the Hakim's household. In women's circles, she had even heard of Bishnupriya being referred to as a woman of disrepute. But such slander could not stand in the face of Bishnurpiya's elegant personality which expressed itself through her grace and beauty, her taste in dress, her sobriety of manner and her sophistication in speech. For a moment Mrs Sarma stood confused. She really couldn't decide as to what was right and what wrong. But she was not used to thinking deeply about such matters. Whatever the greater section of society believed, she too accepted without dissent. She hastily accepted the tamul-pan offered to her by Bishnupriya and then left. Bishnupriya saw from a distance that after glancing around, Mrs Sarma flung something towards the patch of vrindaban grass which grew in a corner of the garden. Perhaps it was the tamul-pan which she had given her. Bishnupriya hung on to the verandah railing for a long time. Somehow her past seemed to come back to her whenever she met people like Mrs Sarma. But she would so much like to forget that past. The present was too invaluable for her. Hand in hand with Gunabhiram, she had already moved out into a wider world and she still had so far to go. Her first husband, Parashuram Sarma had given her a lot of love and affection. But at that time her mind had been as warped as Mrs Sarma's. She was not even aware of her own limitations. Yet she had been quite happy to live in that darkness of ignorance. Thinking of all this made her smile. She thought of all the mental agony she had to go through in order to reach this little light of knowledge. Yet, she reflected, it was so strange that the real pleasure of living seemed to lie in such a struggle.

14

The Maghotsav of the Brahmos closely followed Christmas. On the eleventh day of the month of Magha every year the Brahmos celebrated the founding of the Samaj by Raja Rammohan Roy. Most of the Brahmos of Nagaon were Bengalis. But their continued stay in Assam had added a local Assamese flavour to their tongue. However, in matters of marriage and higher learning, they had kept up strong links with Calcutta. During the Mahotsavs, they naturally took the lead and this resulted in the songs and speeches being made mostly in Bengali. But it had always been Gunabhiram Barua's wish that the Brahmo Samaj be brought nearer to the Assamese heart. That's why on this year's Mahotsav programme he was thinking of including some Assamese devotional songs. Gurunath Dutta and several other Bengali gentlemen had happily agreed to this. Gunabhiram requested Chandrakanta Mahanta of the Garmurh satra to sing some borgeets on the day of the Mahotsav. Mahanta readily agreed and even offered to teach a borgeet to Swarna and another Bengali girl. This was why Swarna had been very busy ever since Christmas ended. On the one hand she had to learn to sing the borgeet, and on the other there were the lessons in English and Mathematics from her new tutor, Rajaninath Das. Rajaninath was a strict person. With Panchanan Sarma, Swarna would sometimes doze off during lessons. But, now if she became absent-minded even for a second, Rajaninath would snap shut the book and say angrily:

"If you are not interested in studies, you may leave. Go and ask your father to find a groom so that you can go off crying to your in-laws."

For Swarna no punishment could be greater than this. Within seconds her eyes would be filled with tears and her face flush with shame. Rajanibabu would feel sorry at this. But he didn't believe in indulging his students' whims. So, the lessons would start once again. Rajanibabu had already assessed Swarna's intelligence. He knew that given the proper opportunity, Swarna could well be the first girl in Assam to get through the Entrance examination.

Meanwhile, Swarna found herself another occupation. The sewing kit which she got as a Christmas gift gave her hours of happiness. Whenever she got any time, she sat down to embroider her handkerchiefs. Bishnupriya who had been patiently trying to instruct her daughter on the intricacies of sewing, would watch her little daughter struggle with the needle and thread, with motherly pride and affection.

On the Maghotsav day, the precints of the Brahmo temple were filled with people from early morning. A temporary shed was erected to accommodate the invitees. The guests included not only the leading Brahmos of the district but quite a few Hindus, Muslims and Christians as well. All of them were provided with chairs to sit on. One could also enter the temple with one's shoes on. Nonetheless, some of the Indian guests opted on leaving their shoes outside.

The function began with recitations from the religious texts. After portions from the Vedas, the Upanishads, the Bible and the Koran were read out, the singing of Brahmo-sangeet began. The Bengali songs composed by Bishnuchandra Chakravorty were rendered beautifully in chorus by an accomplished group.

This was followed by the singing of two psalms of David by some little boys of the Baptist Mission. In the end, the audience was enraptured by the singing of borgeets and the ghosa by Chandrakanta Mahanta and his two little pupils, Swarna and Ranu. When Mahanta rendered those reverberating lines "suna suna re sura, boiri promana" from one of the favourite borgeets of Sri Sankardeva, accompanied by the khol which he played himself, the entire audience began applauding enthusiastically. Most of the Bengali Brahmos present there had not heard a borgeet before and so they were pleasantly surprised that there were such melodious devotional songs in the Assamese language as well. When finally, Swarna and Ranu, dressed in traditional Assamese attire, sang a borgeet to the rhythmic beat of the khol, both Bishnupriya and Gunabhiram were filled with pride and happiness. They were happy not just on hearing Swarna being praised, but that their daughter had been able to present before such an audience a glimpse of the rich cultural tradition of the Assamese people, touched them with a sense of national pride.

On the Maghotsav day, light refreshments were served at the venue of the function and usually all the Brahmos, irrespective of caste difference, sat and ate together. This itself was quite a deviation from the usual caste practices of the orthodox Hindus. For Bishnupriya, such an atmosphere was still somewhat unique. Having been brought up in a conservative Brahmin family with all its restrictions, she was still to adjust fully to such a strange situation. But as she was gradually learning to fit herself into this liberal set-up, her doubts and apprehensions were disappearing. However, she was yet to give up some of her earlier beliefs and practices. For instance, she had never taken food cooked by non-Brahmins. Maybe, if circumstances had compelled her, she would have given up this habit as well. But certain set-beliefs still prevailed amongst the members of the "Adi" Brahmo Samaj and these helped in preserving the old attitudes towards caste.

Although most of Gunabhiram's close associates were against such ideas, yet Gunabhiram himself had not as yet succeeded in fully accepting the new ideas of Keshav Chandra Sen. This was why he had not opposed some of Bishnupriya's beliefs.

15

Lakhi's wedding was to take place a few days after Maghotsav. Swarna was eagerly waiting for the day. She had, till then, not been to anyone's marriage and so, was curious to know what a wedding actually was like. Usually, Bishnupriya would give all the answers to Swarna's queries. But, she became reticent when it came to matters of marriage. Unable to get the answers she desired, Swarna would finally end up depending on the information given by the servant-girl.

Though Bishnupriya and Gunabhiram had attended a few Brahmo weddings in Nagaon, they had never been to a wedding at a Brahmin house. The old, traditional Brahmin families didn't invite them to their weddings because the Brahmos were looked upon by many as Christians. Gunabhiram was, therefore, a bit surprised with Panchanan Sarma's invitation. He thought about it and concluded that Panchanan Sarma, of late, seemed to have been somewhat affected by liberal ideas and because of this he had decided to invite them. Even then, he was somewhat apprehensive about sending his wife to the marriage. He wouldn't have thought so much had he been able to accompany her. But on that day he wasn't keeping well. He was down with cold and fever. Seeing the mother and daughter getting dressed for the wedding, he said in a slightly worried tone: "The carriage will be waiting for you outside Sarmas' house. If there is any problem, you can come back at once." Bishnurpiya looked at her husband in surprise. She didn't understand why all of a sudden he cautioned them in such a manner. Gunabhiram, however, did not say anything more. But as Bishnupriya placed a new gold necklace round Swarna's neck, a strange feeling of uncertainty came over her. Yet she didn't feel like asking her husband about it. Assuring herself that her husband would certainly have warned her if there was anything to worry about, she left for the wedding with Swarna. Swarna was wearing a pink silk frock which her father had brought from Calcutta and she was flitting about like a butterfly. Everyone in the family had told her that she was looking pretty in her new frock. Hence, her face and eyes exuded her happiness. Observing her daughter's innocent face, Bishnupriya suddenly felt sad. The girl to whose wedding they were now about to go was not very much older than Swarna. What did that girl really understand about marriage, she thought?

They were received warmly enough at Sarma's residence and several women led them towards a merdhara spread out hurriedly on the floor. This was followed by the offering of tamul-pan on a silver bota. Lakhi, who was sitting in her bridal finery in front of the morol, jumped up excitedly on seeing Swarna and embraced her warmly. Bishnupriya affectionately held her by the chin and then slipped a gold necklace onto her neck. Some girls came up and escorted Lakhi back to her place in front of the morol. Swarna too went and sat by her side. She found it difficult to believe that a girl's appearance could be transformed so much by a pair of silken riha-mekhala and the big red bindi on her forehead. Swarna kept on staring at Lakhi's face in wide-eyed wonder.

Meanwhile, the women had started singing the wedding-songs. The familiar strains of the songs evoked in Bishnupriya bitter-sweet memories of the past. She too was of Lakhi's age at the time of her first marriage. She faintly recollected her own wedding day though she didn't remember anything else except that she had almost fainted during the ceremony out of hunger, thirst and tiredness of having to be on a fast the whole day. She had no memories of what the groom looked like, what he was wearing, when he came to sit by her and how the marriage took place. She merely remembered the flames of the havan fire as she was woken up every now and then from her sleep by people pulling her around. She had never thought about her future at that time but had unquestioningly carried out whatever she had been asked to do. Even after her wedding, she had just obeyed orders at her husband's place. She was totally obedient to her husband, father-in-law, mother-in-law and all the others and her life seemed ever so peaceful. But, everything changed suddenly after the death of her husband, Parshuram Barua. When, as a widow with the responsibility of bringing up her two little daughters, she was almost reaching a breaking-point in her life, her husband's old friend Gunabhiram had offered her hope of a new life. She had been completely dumbstruck when he had first proposed to her and did not know how to react. But as Gunabhiram explained to her the teachings of Vidyasagar on the rights of the widow, her attitude changed completely. Before accepting him as her husband, she had known Gunabhiram as a family friend and guide. It was Gunabhiram who had first taught her to stand up against social injustice, not merely through debates and discussions, but through courageous action in one's own life. It appeared so strange to her now after so many years that she, being the weak, docile creature that she was at that time, had mustered enough courage to defy society and go in for a second marriage. Listening to the songs being sung by the women now, she seemed lost in her own thoughts. Just then she felt Swarna's little hand on her shoulder and woke up from her reverie with a start.

"What is it, Maisena?"

"Ai, it seems they have asked all the others in for refreshment. Why haven't they asked us?" Swarna whispered urgently in her mother's ears.

"Of course, they'll ask us. One shouldn't be so greedy, Maisena," said Bishnupriya with some irritation. But as she threw a quick look around, she noticed that almost all the invited guests had gone inside. From a distance she could see that the aunts of the bride were busy discussing some problem. The moment they caught her eye, they dispersed hurriedly. Gradually Bishnupriya started feeling uneasy. In the meantime, Debeswari, the wife of the priest, who had been sitting by her side, had also gone inside and returned to her seat. This time, however, she sat slightly apart from Bishnupriya, as if she was slightly apologetic about something. Bishnupriya, noticing this, signalled her with her eyes to come near. When Debeswari came near, Bishnupriya politely told her: "We have sat for quite sometime. I think we should take our leave now. Please go and call the bride's mother."

Debeswari opened her eyes wide and pretending surprise, said: "Baideu, if you leave like this without eating anything, the family will be really upset. Everyone here is so happy that you have come. Perhaps there is a little problem in asking you inside. You can't be seated with the married Brahmin ladies, nor can you be seated with the Brahmin widows because there is some talk about your religion. As you know, people are so very sensitive on these matters…"

Before Debeswari could finish what she was saying, Bishnupriya slowly rose from her seat. Clutching the end of her chador with one hand and firmly holding Swarna by the other, she started walking out from under the canopy. A commotion followed. Lakhi broke into uncontrollable sobs and the bride's mother and some elderly ladies requested Bishnupriya with folded hands to come back. But Bishnupriya refused. With great difficulty she controlled herself and told them politely that she had actually come to bless the bride and that it was not her practice to eat on such occasions. Saying this, she gravely advanced to her carriage. Only when the carriage started rolling down the road did she let go of Swarna's hand. All this while, she hadn't even noticed that she was clutching Swarna's hand so tightly that the girl was writhing with pain. But a stupefied Swarna forgot about this pain when she saw the flood of tears rolling down her mother's cheeks the moment the carriage started to move. She had never seen her mother cry like this before. She didn't really understand what had actually happened. But she had a feeling that all this happened because she was being greedy about the food at the wedding reception. She was therefore numb with grief. Holding on to her mother tightly, she said between sobs:

"Ai, I'll never want to eat at a wedding again. Please stop crying."

Hearing her daughter's words, Bishnupriya couldn't control her feelings any further. She buried her face in Swarna's hair, and said in a voice choked with grief:

"We'll never again come to such weddings, Maisena. We'll go to good weddings where everybody is treated as equals."

As the carriage stopped in front of their house, Bishnupriya remembered what her husband had said just as she was about to leave for the wedding. So, he actually knew that such a situation might arise! She confronted her husband now in grief and misery: "Why did you knowingly let me go to such a place?"

One look at his wife's face and Gunabhiram knew everything. His face revealed his deep anguish. With a sigh he said: "I was under the impression that the society was finally changing somewhat. Panchanan Sharma is an educated person. One expects enlightened behaviour in his house. That's why I had allowed you to go. But I have been proved wrong. In future you'll never go to such weddings. Swarna too shouldn't go. She'll be really hurt."

"The poor girl is so upset today. She has cried a lot without even understanding what is actually wrong. How much longer will we be able to hide the truth from her?"

"There's no point in hiding things from her. We have not done anything wrong. We've married according to the shastras and the prevailing law. Why should we have any feeling of sin? The more we are hurt by the narrowness of society, the stronger should be our self-confidence. When our children grow up, we'll explain everything to them."

"But will they accept what we have to say?"

"If we can hold up a correct ideal before them, they'll be able to distinguish between the right and the wrong in social practices. That's why we must give them a good education and bring them into contact with people with liberal ideas."

"But such people are so rare in our Assam. None of our own kin have accepted us so far. Even amongst our friends, apart from the Brahmo community, how many have tried to understand our position?" Bishnupriya spoke in a dejected tone. Gunabhiram was silent for a while. Of late, he had been constantly assailed by certain negative feelings which he did not dare to share even with his wife. He was aware that indulging in such thoughts was indicative of defeat. But now he shared some of his apprehensions with Bishnupriya:

"Actually, I too am worried that eventually we may be compelled by circumstances to choose a life of self-exile. The Assamese bhadraloks will never accept us and if we happen to die here, nobody would volunteer even to cremate us!"

Gunabhiram tried to smile. But in that smile Bishnupriya saw an image of the harsh truth. There seemed little possibility of the Assamese society undergoing any major change in the near future. In such a situation, even if not for themselves but for the sake of their children, they would have to move to such a place where there were lots of people who thought as they did. Bishnupriya and Gunabhiram had been talking a lot about Calcutta, as if that enchanting city was beckoning to them with open arms. But they were not as yet prepared to give up their deep affection for this land of theirs and respond to that call. They had not gathered enough strength of mind to finally sever their ties with the soil and snap their roots for ever.

16

When Tora went to Bilwa Kutir to give the news about her school results, everyone shared her excitement. She had come second amongst all the girls who sat for the examination in Nagaon. A girl from the Bengali school had come first. Bishnupriya called Tora to her side and blessed her affectionately. Tora had always been drawn by Bishnupriya's dignified personality and her affectionate manner of speaking. Though she looked upon the missionaries with great respect, yet she felt that somehow Gunabhiram Barua and Bishnupriya were always closer to her. In their presence she didn't have to feel conscious of what to say and how to behave. They seemed to belong to the same world as hers, not like the sahibs who appeared distant and unapproachable like the stars in heaven. Swarna ran to her father to give him the news about Tora's results. Gunabhiram called Tora over to his study and asked her about her future plans. Tora answered in one breath: "I'll study in a 'Normal' school so that I can go and teach in the school at the Baliram village."

Gunabhiram appreciated her decision and said in an approving tone: "If only all our girls had similar aims in life, then our society would have progressed fast. But we should blame ourselves for this. We bring up our girls so that they are fit only for household chores. We don't allow any other idea to enter their heads." Saying this, he carefully took out a book from the cupboard in his study.

It was an Assamese dictionary written by Miles Bronson. Opening the book, he wrote in his beautiful hand on the fly cover: "To dear Tora, with best wishes for a bright future—Gunabhiram Barua". Wrapping the book with a piece of paper, he handed it to Tora and said: "I can't give you a better gift than this. Hope you will be inspired by the ideals of the great individual who wrote this book and learn to work for the good of your people."

Tora accepted the gift respectfully. Though she was unable to realize the full worth of what Gunabhiram had said, yet the very atmosphere of the room and the presence of the older gentleman left a deep impression on her. She felt as if she wasn't like the other girls around her. Gunabhiram Barua, Bronson Sahib, Miss Orell Keeler—everyone expected something great from her. She would have to fulfill these expectations. That day as she was returning home from Bilwa kutir, her steps seemed heavier with some newfound responsibility.

There was a change in Tora's dress and manners after she joined the Normal School. She now began to wear a chador wrapped over the coloured mekhala and the cotton jacket, a sign of her growing up. The chador would be carefully held in place on her shoulder with a brooch. This manner of wearing the chador was introduced by the girls in the mission school. Unmarried Assamese girls usually wore the riha and the mekhala. Only married women would wrap a chador over their rihas while going out. The girls from the poor families didn't wear any blouses. They would tie the mekhala over their breasts and wrap a gamosa over that. However, Christian girls, even when they came from poor families, dressed differently. Most of the girls from the Mission School used to wear cotton blouses which they called "jackets" and they covered themselves modestly with chadors. They even wore sandals, a rare practice amongst ordinary Assamese women. But amongst all the Christian girls, it was Tora's dress which seemed to be the neatest. She wore her

ordinary cotton garments in such a graceful manner that passers-
by could not fail to notice her as she walked along the road. But
no one ever dared to tease her or to pass comments because she
held herself with such dignity and confidence. How many girls
of "good families" in Nagaon could walk like her through its
streets with head held high? Actually, most of the people from
the Assamese gentry had come to look upon the Mission school
girls as creatures from anther planet. That their own daughters
too could one day move around as freely as the Christian girls
was something which was beyond their imagination. They had
no sympathy for modern concepts like women's liberation which
were being raised by Gunabhiram and others. The women of the
lower castes, according to them, had been ordained by God to
lead a life of unceasing hardship. That was why they could toil in
sun and rain while their own wives were meant to stay indoors,
away from the public gaze, and follow the dharma of the family.
Any violation of such codes of conduct would lead to disaster
and chaos! Hence, the respectable folk of Nagaon discouraged
their womenfolk from mixing with the likes of Tora.

Tora's days filled with work which she loved doing. Going to
the Normal School in the morning, accompanying the missionary
women in their jenana-work in the afternoons, giving a helping
hand now and then to Miss Keeler in running her school, knitting
and sewing clothes for the poor Christian children—all these
were a part of her daily activities. Sometimes she would assist the
missionaries in their work of translating books into Assamese.
Tora was deeply inspired by the attempt of the foreigners to
learn someone else's language and then write books in it. Seeing
her eagerness to try her hand at translating a small booklet into
Assamese, the missionary men and women were thrilled, and
they encouraged Tora in all possible ways. Meanwhile, Bronson
Sahib's health was continuing to deteriorate ever since he lost his
second wife and a grown-up daughter. The Christian population

of Nagaon was overwhelmed by his efforts to keep up the work of the Mission despite his sick body and broken heart. Everyone wanted to somehow make things easier for him. Golapi suggested one day that since Bronson needed someone to look after him and also to do the housework and this was not possible for the missionary men and women, Tora would be the right person for this. At first Bronson firmly opposed the idea. He just couldn't agree to have Tora leave her mother and look after his needs. But seeing that his health was giving way with every passing day, the other missionaries urged him to accept Golapi's suggestion. Bronson really needed an intelligent and efficient girl like Tora to manage everything, from his papers to dispensing his medicines. At last, Bronson acceded to the demands of his well-wishers to allow Tora to stay with him. Tora felt depressed at having to leave her mother for the first time in her life. But Golapi's coming over to make enquiries almost every other day made it easy for Tora to adjust to her new situation. She started feeling proud of being entrusted with such a grave responsibility. Within a few days Tora learnt all the ins and outs of the sahib's household and, with her typical self-confidence, she started keeping an eye on everything. The missionaries were amazed at the sense of duty of this young girl. Bronson started loving Tora as his own child and allowed her to sleep in that very room which was crowded with his daughter's memory. In the beginning Tora was somewhat afraid to stay alone in that room. But her mother assuaged her fears saying that there was nothing to be afraid of in a house where a messenger of God such as Bronson sahib lived. Even then, feeling rather uneasy to sleep in Maria's bed, Tora made her own bed on the floor.

17

The Government English school at Nagaon did not have a boarding for the boys who came from distant towns and villages. So, many of them stayed as guests with the families of friends and acquaintances. A number of boys were accommodated in the bamboo and thatch huts which Gunabhiram had put up within his compound. They cooked their own meals, and the Barua household often supplied them with milk, vegetables and other eatables. The boys found Bishnupriya very affectionate and loving, but they were a little scared of the Hakim and maintained a respectful distance from him. Generally, whenever they caught sight of him they would lower their heads and try to run away. They even avoided using the front gate of the house for fear of confronting the Hakim, but used a separate gate in a corner of the compound. Gunabhiram, saw himself as a sort of a guardian to these boys and therefore kept an eye on them.

Among the students was a boy named Lakheswar Kotoky. He was somewhat different from the others. The son of a Brahmin priest from Kaliabor, the financial condition of his family was precarious. His father barely managed to eke out a living with his occasional earnings as a priest. Lakheswar was the eldest son of the family. He had always been good in studies and his father had, with considerable effort, sent him to school at Nagaon. His wish was that once Lakheswar passed his Entrance Examination, he would be eligible for a government job and the family's difficulties would cease.

Unlike the other boys, Lakheswar didn't try to avoid Hakim Dangoria when he saw him. He would always come forward and greet him with folded hands. His answers to Gunabhiram's queries would be polite and humble. It was his behaviour which eventually made him the favourite of Gunabhiram. Gradually, he started accompanying the older man on his morning walks. His companions were naturally envious of him and Lakheswar was rather pleased at this. When they teased him as the "Hakim's son-in-law", Lakheswar pretended to be angry, but actually he rather enjoyed this sense of importance. He was an ambitious young man and wanted to rise in life quickly. So he felt that his companions were unknowingly pushing him up the ladder to a higher rung than what he had expected.

During one of their morning walks Gunabhiram brought up his favourite topic about the achievements of the late Anandaram Dhekiyal Phukan and how during his stay in Nagaon he had, alongwith Gunabhiram, started the Gyan Sabha. He went on to describe the important topics that were discussed in the meetings of the Gyan Sabha. Lakheswar listened quietly for a while and then asked in a serious tone: "Why can't we start a similar Sabha now, Dangoria? If you show us the way, we the students can take the initiative."

Gunabhiram had been thinking of something like this for a long time. It seemed as if Lakheswar was just echoing his own thoughts. He started envisaging the Gyan Sabha with a new sense of zeal. The Sabha could be held in a classroom of the government high school. He himself would get the Principal's permission. Lakheswar at once undertook the responsibility of arranging the room and inviting the guests. It was decided to hold the first sitting on the following Wednesday. Gunabhiram himself prepared a list of the persons to be invited. Those included were

Miles Bronson, Rudraram Bordoloi, Padmahash Goswami, Ratia Koch, Phatickchandra Barua, Janakinath Sen, Ramlochan Sen and many other leading members of Nagaon's educated elite.

On one Wednesday at around three in the afternoon the Sabha met in the school classroom. It was well attended with students and eminent invitees from the town. Lakheswar and his friends had decorated the room as best as they could. The table was covered with a table- cloth borrowed from Bilwa Kutir and a vase of flowers had been placed in the centre. The students stood at the door welcoming the guests and ushering them into the room. Gunabhiram was unanimously requested to chair the meeting which started with a Borgeet sung by a schoolboy. This was followed by Rudraram Bordoloi, Padmahash Goswami and others speaking on the significance of the meet. Lakheswar read a self-composed essay entiled, "The Necessity of Education". Miles Bronson was requested by Gunabhiram to speak a few words. But as he was not well, he didn't wish to speak. He merely expressed his good wishes and hoped that the Gyan Sabha would continue to function for a long time. That he had come to the meeting despite his ill- health, made everyone feel grateful. The Sabha concluded with an inspiring speech by Gunabhiram which touched everybody. He referred to the ideals set by Anandaram Dhekiyal Phukan and recalled the contributions made by the people of Nagaon towards the cause of Assamese language and culture. Srimanta Sankardev himself was born in the district of Nagaon. What greater inspiration could there be for the people of that place? Gunabhiram's speech greatly inspired all those who were present that day. Everyone pledged to work towards fulfilling the objectives of the Sabha.

In the first flush of enthusiasm Lakhewar decided to hold the Sabha every Wednesday. But after a few sittings, it started meeting every fortnight. Then it became a monthly affair. Yet, the students learned a lot from the Gyan Sabha. Several of the students who attended its sessions regularly, later on became leading litterateurs of the state. Though Lakheswar couldn't become a writer, yet his association with the Sabha helped open up his own road to success. Gunabhiram started helping him in his studies in all possible ways and freely lent him his books and journals. Besides, whenever he ran short of money, he could always depend on the generosity of Gunabhiram and Bishnupriya. Thus, slowly and cleverly, Lakheswar succeeded in entering the family circle of Bilwa Kutir and he even won the respect of Swarna with his witty comments and his eagerness to impress her with his skill in fitting her books with new jackets and writing her name on them in his neat calligraphy.

At that time, Lakheswar was in the second standard of the high school. He would have to take the Entrance examination on reaching the first standard. So, he had started taking his studies seriously because only if he did well at the Entrance, was there any chance of his getting a scholarship to study in a college in Calcutta. And for a long time Lakheswar had cherished the dream of going to Calcutta for higher studies. Once he had raised the matter before his father. But his father had said with a sigh:

"Son, where will I get all that money to send you to study in Calcutta? The government scholarship is not enough. It would be better if you get yourself a clerk's job in a government office after doing your Entrance. People like us should not aspire for more than that."

But Lakheswar was not the type of boy to listen to such discouraging words. He had already made his plans. He would make Hakim Dangoria pay for his expenses in Calcutta. Meanwhile, he had, alongwith two other Bengali boys, arranged with the sahibs of the Mission to acquire fluency in English and in order to please the white missionaries, he had even evinced an interest in Christianity when he was in their company.

18

Though the journey time between Nagaon and Calcutta had been considerably reduced after the introduction of the steamer service on the Brahmaputra, yet it still took some nine to ten days to make the journey. But despite its geographical distance, Calcutta was not very far for the Brahmos of Nagaon. They would be posted with news about the metropolis, from the letters, papers and journals that kept coming from Calcutta at regular intervals. And, of course, there were the not too frequent visits from friends and relatives from Calcutta. Some pieces of news created great commotion in the Brahmo community and sparked off almost unending debates. Many, like Gunabiram, were saddened by the differences that had cropped up between the two most respected leaders of the Brahmo Samaj, Brahamananda Keshav Chandra Sen and Maharshi Devendranath Tagore. For the Brahmos of Calcutta the struggle between the guru and the disciples must have led to a consolidation of the different groups, each adding strength to itself. But, for those Brahmos who were scattered in distant lands, such differences and debates led to a crisis of their faith. In Calcutta, Keshav Chandra's fiery oratory and liberal views had attracted the support of most of the young Brahmos. His followers had such high respect for him that some of them even worshipped him as an avatar of God. Even in Nagaon there were a few such followers of Keshav Chandra. But Gurunath

Dutta and Gunabhiram did not support the tendency to worship one leader and denigrate the other. As such, in Nagaon till then there was only one Brahmo Samaj. It had not split into the Adi Brahmo Samaj and the Bharatiya Brahmo Samaj. However, cracks once again appeared in the Brahmo Samaj of Calcutta as the news spread that the same Keshav Chandra Sen who was a pioneer in the field of women's education and who differed sharply with Devendranath Tagore over the question of bringing radical changes in the Hindu marriage customs, had himself violated the Native Marriage Act which the Brahmos had been instrumental in getting enacted, and was preparing to get his minor daughter married. Not only that, he had selected the sixteen-year-old Rajkumar of the orthodox Hindu royal family of Cooch Behar as his son-in-law. Thus, from all angles, this marriage went against all the cherished principles of the Brahmos.

The Brahmos of Nagaon first got the news about the Cooch Behar marriage through a letter written to Gurunath Dutta by one of his friends. Having read the letter, a much-disturbed Gurunath rushed to Gunabhiram's place to discuss the possible consequences of the event. They discussed the matter and resolved that as there was a chance of the news being false, it would be best to keep silent for the time being. But how long can the truth be hidden? About two months later during the Pujas, the daughter and son-in-law of Radhanath Sen, a lawyer, came from Calcutta on a visit and spread the news among the Brahmo Samajis of Nagaon. Instantly, sharp differences arose between the followers of Keshav Chandra Sen and the others. When it was seen that a person of Keshav Chandra's stature did not hesitate to sacrifice his ideals for small gains, the entire Brahmo community started having doubts about the very ideals nourished by the Samajis. Realizing the gravity of the situation, Gurunath Dutta and Gunabhiram decided to call a meeting of the Brahmos. As soon as the meeting started, one of the Samajis stood up and started condemning Keshav Chandra Sen in a vehement tone. Immediately there was commotion. Several speakers got up excitedly to give their views. Gunabhiram Barua stood up and with folded hands requested everyone to calm down. When the audience calmed down somewhat, he began slowly:

"Friends, the Brahmo Samaj was established on the basis of truth and certain ideals. For a Brahmo, the only truth lies in Parameshwar, the all powerful, holiest of the holy, Creator of the Universe. The only two gurus or guides from whom we come to know about the Parameshwar, are Nature and the laws of Nature as they have been conceived by the human mind. Any one who has faith in these two gurus can never be shaken by temporal events. There is no greater error on this earth than to accept some individual as a Guru and to think that he is above all weaknesses and delusions. We often commit such mistakes. And because of it, we also get hurt. But if we understand the essence of the Brahmo faith, then we would never lose hope nor would we be confused."

He spoke at length on the guiding principles of the Brahmo religion. Many of those who listened to him that day felt that their courage and faith had been restored. Just as travellers in a small boat caught in a storm in the wide seas clutch at one another to save themselves, similarly it was imperative for this small band of Brahmos to live in close friendship and understanding and have deep faith in their religion. The only way to preserve their identity seemed to lie in resolving their differences and disputes in a spirit of brotherhood.

Though Gunabhiram had spoken that day in a voice that inspired confidence in others, yet when he returned home, he sat till late in the evening on a chair in the veranda, lost in his own thoughts. Even when Bishnupriya came to call him for dinner, he didn't seem to respond. So, drawing a chair close to him, Bishnupriya sat down quietly and said: "What you said at the meeting today has given strength to many".

Gunabhiram sighed: "Yes, it seems I have a lot to say which gives strength to others. But the trouble is that I have not been able to give strength to myself. If someone as wise as Brahmananda Keshav Chandra has finally succumbed to the pressure of blind customs, then how long will a person like me be able to keep on struggling alone? Moreover, the situation in Calcutta is so much better than Assam. If the enlightened people there cannot overcome their weaknesses, then what can we expect of others in a backward place like ours?"

Bishnupriya was silent for some time. Whenever she found her husband giving in to despair like this, she tried to present herself as extra strong in spirit. She was apprehensive that if she showed any sign of weakness, then her husband might break down completely. So, when she found him yielding to his gloomy thoughts, Bishnupriya said with a firmness she rarely displayed:

"We'll never get our Swarna married before she is fourteen, no matter what others may say. We have no place in the orthodox society here in Assam. So why should we be bothered about what that society thinks about us? If we give up our faith in our beliefs in fear of incurring the displeasure of such a society, then we'll lose both the worlds."

His wife's courageous words seemed to quieten somewhat the restlessness of Gunabhiram's mind. That evening both of them talked a lot about Swarna's future. They would put her in Calcutta's Bethune School. After that, they would marry her to an educated young man from a respectable family. He would have to be a Brahmo. Bishnupriya did not nourish any false hopes of getting a suitable Assamese Brahmin boy for Swarna. No Assamese Brahmin would ever dare to ask for her hand. Moreover, how many Assamese were there among the Brahmos? In Nagaon there were just one or two families. Even then, the Barua couple tried to convince themselves that evening that if Swarna grew into an ideal Indian woman in all aspects, then there would eventually be some boy from a liberal, upper caste, educated Assamese family who would agree to accept her as his wife. After all, Assamese society couldn't always remain the same.

Meanwhile a year had passed, almost unnoticed. Christmas was again round the corner. But, this time the festivities seemed to be marred by a feeling of sadness. Bronson sahib was very sick. Ever since he came to Assam, the family has been plagued by illness and death. After a fatal illness had claimed his wife and two daughters in quick succession, this unusually tireless worker seemed to have finally exhausted himself now, if not in mind, at least in body. The death of his wife and elder daughter, Maria, had totally broken his spirits and his health. When all the attention and prayers of the missionaries proved to be of no avail, they decided to send him back to America. Bronson, however, was unwilling to leave. He did not wish to go to America just to die there, leaving behind the land in which he had spent the greater part of his life, whose language and literature he had made so much his own and whose people were so close to his heart. Even then, he had finally to accede to the entreaties of his well-wishers who wanted him to go to America so that after recovering his health, he could come back to the place he so loved. This time it was Tora's turn to be stubborn. She insisted on accompanying Bronson to America. Else, who would be there to look after him on the long sea journey? Golapi looked at her daughter in disbelief and said:

"Tell me the truth Tora, is it because of your love and regards for the sahib that you want to go or is it to fulfil your wish to see America?"

Tora replied tearfully: "Believe me Ai, I have decided to go in order to look after Bronson Sahib. I always wanted to go to America. But if Sahib stays here, then I too will always stay here. Isn't he my father? When my real father was dying, didn't he sit by his side and look after him? It is my wish that I too stay with him and look after him till his last moments."

As she said these words, tears flowed from her eyes. Golapi didn't say anything more after this. She discussed the matter with the missionary women and prepared to send her daughter to America. Tora had never thought that she would go to America in such a manner. The idea of service had so inspired this girl, that she was left with no time to think of herself. When the date of the journey was fixed some two months after Christmas, Tora became busy arranging Bronson's things. She packed all his important papers in a big wooden box. After that, as directed by Bronson, she started packing his clothes, bedding, medicines, an easy-chair and other things that would be needed for the journey. Regarding her own packing, her mother took charge of everything with great care. From stitching laced jackets to embroidering handkerchiefs and gamosas, Golapi tried to do everything as best as she could. The missionary ladies too contributed to Golapi's efforts by paying attention to practical details about which she had no experience or knowledge. Thinking that Tora might find it difficult to wear the mekhala-chador while abroad, they got skirts and blouses and a coat for her. They taught her to use the fork and spoon so that she would face no difficulty while on board the ship or in America. During this time they also acquainted Tora with some of the customs and manners of the foreign land and told her about the matters on which she ought to be careful. On any other occasion, Tora would have been somewhat scared. But with Bronson Sahib there with her, she was not in the least frightened. She felt as if she was about to go on a preaching mission to a nearby place.

A lot of people came to say good-bye to Miles Bronson. Swarna, Bishnupriya and Gunabhiram Barua were also among them. Gunabhiram bade the old missionary a cheerful good bye, but in his heart of hearts he felt that this was perhaps their last meeting. He had always been struck by the tireless devotion of this missionary to his duties in the mission as well as in the society at large, ever since Anandaram Dhekiyal Phukan had taken up his duties as a government officer in Nagaon. It was difficult for him to think of the intellectual world of Nagaon without the inspiring presence of Bronson. Would it be possible for anyone else to fill up the place left empty by the man who had worked ceaselessly over three decades for the welfare of the people of Nagaon? Gunabhiram was yet to see a social worker like Bronson among the local people. As he was returning home from the Mission that day, his mind was preoccupied by a question—would the time ever come when the people of this country would learn to work for their own society with the same zeal and dedication of the Christian missionaries?

While her parents were saying good bye to Bronson, Swarna was busy inspecting Tora's new box full of the things that her mother had packed into it. Tora was visibly excited about the prospect of the journey and she tried to convey her excitement to her friend. But Swarna had her doubts. She had heard about the hazards of a sea-voyage. "Will the waves of the ocean obey Bronson Sahib?" Swarna asked in a low voice.

Tora's voice was full of confidence and faith in her master: "Yes, of course."

"Won't you miss your mother?" Swarna asked again.

At this Tora's voice quivered a little, "Jesus will look after her. I will always pray for Ai. I'll also pray for you, Swarna. I will write to you from America and you too should write to me."

"Will letters travel so far?" Swarna asked in wonder.

"They'll go in ships, just as we do," Tora replied with a smile. To Swarna every word that Tora said seemed like the ultimate truth. She felt that Tora, like her name, was really a heavenly star, so unlike all the other girls she knew.

20

Lakhipriya hadn't met Swarna since her marriage. But she missed her a lot. Whenever she remembered her wedding day, she would blush with embarrassment. She was very angry with her own people for what happened that day. Should invited guests ever be treated in such a manner? Even her young mind had felt the seriousness of the insult meted out to Bishnupriya on that day. How could they insult that lady who treated her as one of her own and who had given her a gold necklace as a wedding gift? She felt all the more upset because even after committing such as offence, none of her relatives felt sorry about it. Panchanan Sarma no doubt had scolded his mother and wife after hearing of the incident. For, the insult to Bishnupriya had ended his relationship with the Hakim sahib for all time to come. It seemed to Lakhipriya that if anyone regretted the shameful incident later on, it was more out of fear for the Hakim than out of respect or sympathy for Bishnupriya. She realized suddenly how selfish and cruel people could be. Sometimes she was gripped with the urge to rush to Swarna and explain everything to her. But her movements had become somewhat restricted after marriage. She couldn't go out now without being accompanied either by her mother or some senior person. Even when she went out, she had to wrap herself in a chador and shield herself from public view with a japi. It was only during the four days of the Durga

Puja that she could move about a little more freely. She could go every day to the Puja in the company of married girls of her own age who were staying with their parents and newly-wed daughters-in-law of the neighbouring families. That little bit of freedom would make Lakhi forget herself with joy. She waited eagerly to meet Swarna at the Puja-ghar, but her hopes remained unfulfilled. Only later did she come to know from Lakheswar that the Brahmos didn't participate in the worship of the Mother Goddess.

Lakheswar was an occasional visitor at Panchanan Sarma's house because Lakhi's husband happened to be a distant relative of his. He would call Lakhi "nabou" and get a lot of attention from the Sarma family. Initially, Lakhi was shy to come out and talk to him. But when she learnt that Lakheswar stayed in the Bilwa Kutir compound, she was always eager to talk to him about Swarna and her parents. At first Lakheswar tried to tell Lakhi about her husband. But when he did not succeed in rousing her interest in the subject, he started talking to her more about Bilwa Kutir. But Lakheswar was always careful not to talk about Bilwa Kutir in the presence of the other members of the family.

Lakhi had heard from others that Gunabhiram Barua and his wife had lost their caste. The elders of the house used to discuss the matter in whispers and would silence the children if they showed any curiosity on the matter: "You shouldn't hear all this. It's sinful even to listen to such scandalous things". Lakhi just didn't understand what sort of sin could have been committed by so amiable a lady as Bishnupriya and such a dignified, wise and accomplished person like Gunabhiram. One day, unable to restrain her curiosity any further, she asked Lakheswar about it.

"Don't you know that Barua became a Brahmo in order to marry a widow after the untimely death of his first wife? His present wife was earlier married to Parasuram Barua. She even has two daughters by her first marriage. They are both married."

Lakheswar almost whispered the words as if he was talking about something obscene.

Lakhi kept silent for a while, trying to understand the seriousness of the matter. Then she suddenly asked, "Well, would the Hakim have lost his caste had he married a Brahmin girl after the death of his first wife? He lost his caste because he married a widow, isn't it?"

"Undoubtedly so. Do you need to ask such a question? If he had wished, he could have brought a second wife home even while his first wife was alive. Moreover, it is an accepted custom of society that a man marries a second time if his wife dies. Hakim Dangoria messed up everything by marrying a widow." Lakheswar spoke like an experienced person. His tone was completely different from the low and humble voice with which he addressed the Hakim Dangoria. He was somewhat shocked by the next question which Lakhi asked. For, till then, he seemed to believe that his opinion was the accepted opinion of the entire Brahmin society.

"If there is no harm in a man marrying a second time, what is wrong if a woman does it?" Lakhi asked in all simplicity. She didn't have the slightest idea that this very question was creating such waves amongst the educated elite of neighbouring Bengal. Lakheswar opened his eyes wide and grimaced in obvious disgust: "Shame on you, Nabou, one shouldn't bring such words to one's lips. It is sinful. You must have been reading Barua's play *Ramnabami*. Such scandalous questions have been raised there."

"No, I haven't read it, believe me. What is there in that book?"

"You needn't know about those things. I have read it. It deals with how Brahmin widows get degraded. Girls like you from good families shouldn't allow such trash to enter their heads. If I had my way, I would have burnt all those books!" Lakheswar said vehemently.

Lakhi wanted to ask him as to how a woman gets degraded. Was Bishnupriya too a degraded woman? But she got scared at the manner in which Lakheswar was speaking and went inside without saying anything more. However, many issues remained unresolved in her mind. When she thought of Bishnupriya she couldn't find any trace of sin on her face or with her behaviour. Unlike one of her own aunts whose widowed life was full of suffering, Bishnupriya was leading a contented and happy family life. What sin could there be in it? Then all of a sudden another realization dawned upon her: suppose Gunabhiram Barua and Bishnupriya had never married, how would a girl like Swarna have been born? At this Lakhi became even more confused about social values: what was good, and what was bad? She could not make up her mind. But, about one thing she was certain: never for a moment could she think of Swarna and her loving parents as sinners.

21

Swarna had given up playing under the bilwa tree after Lakhi's marriage. She didn't like to play alone. She did play sometimes with her brother Karuna. But he didn't like playing at kitchen for long. Imitating his father's gait, he would say "I am going off to the kachhari now" and then run off. So Swarna would sit alone on the front steps and embroider a hanky or just watch the clouds in the sky. She loved watching the clouds change shape and mysteriously disappear in the deep blue sky. Sometimes as she stared at the luminous white clouds in the eastern sky, dark clouds from the west would suddenly cover up the entire sky in a moment. Then a cool breeze would blow soothing one's spirit. Swarna would never be bored watching the ever new and exciting face of nature. She never ceased to marvel that even black clouds could have so many shapes and tones.

Meanwhile, there had been a new birth in the family, another little brother for Swarna. Bishnupriya's elder daughter by her first marriage came to look after her mother during her confinement. Her name was Kalipriya. Swarna called her "Kali Baideu". But being much older than herself, Swarna found her to be more like a mother than an elder sister. She was good-looking like her mother and Swarna couldn't understand why she was named after the goddess Kali. Kali Baideu also had an infant son. Now, the house was always full of people. There were lots of visitors who came to see the new baby. Swarna felt lonely that she could not be near her mother. She would spend her mornings with her brother Karuna, picking sewali flowers from the grass and weaving garlands under the bilwa tree. The brother and sister would hang the small garlands of sewali on the bilwa-tree. Swarna loved that spot under the tree where she had spent so many happy hours playing with Lakhi.

Lakheswar was one day watching the brother and sister from a distance. He had passed his preparatory test for the Entrance examination and was now preparing for the crucial final examination. He would spend almost the whole day inside his small room and emerge occasionally when he got tired with his books. Seeing Swarna and her brother near the bilwa-tree, Lakheswar tried to pick up a conversation with the little girl: "It seems you are worshipping the tree! Good! Sometimes the Burha-Dangoria appears in this tree."

Both the children were perturbed when they heard this. They had heard about the Burha-Dangoria from the servants in the house. But when "good people" like Lakheswar talked about such things, then there was little scope for disbelief. Karuna held Lakheswar's hand and implored him to tell them a story about the Burha-Dangoria. But Lakhewswar was in no mood for stories. He wanted to talk to Swarna about something else. Drawing her aside he whispered,

"I suppose you know that Lakhi Nabou has celebrated her *shanti* marriage?"

Swarna gave him a blank stare and asked, "What is that?"

Lakheswar was somewhat taken aback by Swarna's innocent question. Looking at her childish face, he didn't feel like elaborating on the topic further. Instead he said in a sombre voice, "Ask your mother about it. I heard when I was home last week that my cousin, that is Lakhi Nobou's husband, will come in a month or two to take her away."

Swarna's eyes became moist with tears as she remembered the day when Lakhi broke down under the bilwa-tree as she gave her the news of her marriage. Lakhi's wedding had cast a shadow over her life. Why should girls be married at all? Why can't all girls be like Tora? Tora studied in school and went off to America of her own free will. She'll be teaching in a school after she comes back. No one ever talks about *her* marriage.

Swarna's spirits rose when she remembered Tora. She had read and re-read so many times the letter Tora had sent to her by post from America. Her father had looked at the water-mark and told her that the letter took almost two months to reach her. On a map of the world, Rajani Master, the school teacher, had pointed out to her the route taken by Tora's letter across the globe. Holding the letter in her hand, Swarna would try to imagine how it carved for itself a path through the blue and green patches on the map to finally reach her. The postage stamp on the letter seemed to carry the tidings of some mysterious land. In the letter Tora had written mostly about her sea voyage. How, once during a storm, the waves almost sank their ship, of her suffering from sea-sickness and being bedridden for several days till the ship's doctor treated her to recovery. After this Tora had written that the ocean waves listened to no one and that none but Almighty God could save human beings from the wrath of the cruel sea. She sent her regards to Swarna's parents and, saying that she really missed home, she hoped that she would be able to return home as soon as Bronson sahib recovered from his illness.

22

Lakheswar was preparing to leave for home after his Entrance examination. While taking his leave from Gunabhiram and Bishnupriya he repeatedly requested them to keep the Gyan Sabha alive after he left. Gunabhiram was moved by Lakheswar's modesty and sincerity. These are the qualities for which Gunabhiram had always given him a special corner in his heart. So, he wished the young man well and assured him that he would try his best to keep alive the Gyan Sabha. When he asked Lakheswar about his future plans, the young man replied with a sigh that he had given up all hopes of going to Calcutta for his college education. It would be impossible for him to manage in the hostel with a meager scholarship of ten rupees from the Government because there was no chance of financial help from his home. So, there seemed to be no way out for him but to get a job after passing his Entrance. At this, Gunabhiram protested loudly, "No my lad, please don't say such things as long as I am there. It is my desire that Assamese boys should receive higher education. The aim of one's life should not be confined to writing a few sentences in English and then settling for a clerical job. I shall always consider it my duty to help students like you to go in for higher studies. Don't worry about expenses. If you do well in the examination, I shall arrange everything for your study at Calcutta. I happen to know a lot of people there and arrangements could be made for your stay at a moderate cost. I shall meet all the expenses."

So, Lakheswar's worries were over. Bowing low to the Hakim Dangoria and touching his feet, Lakheswar took his leave. As he departed, the corners of his eyes were moist. The magnanimity of Gunabhiram seemed to have moved him genuinely, even if it was for a moment.

Just a few days after Lakheswar had left Nagaon, a great misfortune befell Panchanan Sarma's family. Lakhi was getting ready to leave for her new home and her trusseau had been prepared with great care by her mother and aunts. The wedding furniture, the brass utensils and everything else that the bride would need in her husband's home had been finally packed and made ready to be sent with her. Panchanan Sarma's house was in a festive mood on the morning on which Lakhi's husband Hariprasad was to arrive from Kaliabor. There was a sudden flurry of activity from early morning, getting a room ready for the new son-in-law and his companions to rest and be refreshed. Every little detail had to be attended to so that no one would be offended with the arrangements, this being the first visit of the son-in-law to the bride's place. Panchanan Sarma was, therefore, busy supervising everything. His son-in-law was expected around lunch time, as he was to have left Kaliabor almost at the break of dawn. Lakhi had been made to put on a new set of clothes and special care was taken over her appearance. But the vermillion bindi on her forehead and the gold ornaments she was wearing failed to bring any lustre into her pale face. Even at this rather tender age Lakhi had grown accustomed to suppressing her feelings in public. She held back her tears with great difficulty, but Panchanan Sarma and his wife understood her feelings at the imminent separation from her parental home. They couldn't look at their daughter's sad face without a sense of remorse. Sarma seemed especially conscious of the fact that he was doing some injustice to his daughter. He had not felt like this on the day of Lakhi's wedding because at that time he was wholly taken up with the thought of liberating himself from the bondage of having a daughter. Now, whenever his eyes fell on Lakhi's helpless face, his heart was wrenched by a feeling of sadness. Would this innocent twelve-year-old be able to carry out all the chores in her father-in-law's house? Will she be able to fulfil the expectations of being the perfect daughter-in-law? Panchanan would immediately reassure himself that after all every girl takes up these responsibilities after her marriage and for an intelligent girl like Lakhi it shouldn't be difficult to keep her husband and in-laws happy.

Meanwhile, lunch time had long passed and the sun was about to set, and yet there was no news from Kaliabor. At last, just before dark, two persons arrived at Sarma's place. They brought the news that Lakhi's husband had died after four days of high fever. Neither the traditional medicines nor those given by the kaviraj had had any effect. Lakhi hadn't eaten anything much the whole day and she was feeling tired and weak. When she saw all the people running out and wailing in grief, she too was about to get up and run outside to see what was happening. But just then her mother came rushing in and, holding her tightly, started crying loudly. Lakhi had no notion about the nature of the misfortune that had befallen her. But instinctively she let out a frightened shriek and held on to her mother. Meanwhile a group of women had entered the room and were referring to Lakhi as the unlucky, unfortunate and ill-fated one. Slowly the truth started dawning on her. But not a tear fell from her eyes. How could she grieve for a husband she hadn't met at all? Moreover, she was yet to be initiated into the travails of widowhood. Lakhi just sat by her mother and kept staring at her. The noise all around her seemed really unbearable.

Bishnupriya got the sad news about Lakhi from her neighbour

Krishna pandit's wife. She cast aside all bitter feelings of the past and left for Sarma's house in haste. Lakhi's innocent face kept coming to her mind and her heart was rent with sorrow. How would such a small girl face all this? Panchanan Sarma's house was already filled with neighbours and relatives when Bishnupriya reached there. Sarma was sitting in the courtyard, broken with grief. Inside, Lakhi was sitting like a stone near her mother. She had already been given a bath and her ornaments had been taken off. She was now draped in the white garb of the widow. The moment Bishnupriya saw her, she turned away her eyes. She felt that the women were especially cruel. They were scolding Lakhi because she wasn't crying and wailing. Pretending to share her grief, they were all the while trying to tell her about the fearful future which awaited her. But Lakhi appeared totally unmoved. With slow steps Bishnupriya advanced towards Lakhi and then sat down beside her. She put her arms round the girl and started saying slowly:

"You are not to be blamed for all this, my girl. Life and death are nature's laws. No one can change them. It is wrong to think that a girl's life comes to an end the moment she becomes a widow. Nowadays things are changing. You must find the means to live with honour. We are there to support you. So, you needn't worry, my child."

Though Bishnupriya had tried to sound unperturbed, yet her voice was shaking. Lakhi fixed her gaze on Bishnupriya's grief-laden face and then like a river bursting its dam, she broke into loud sobs. She didn't really know why she was crying. Maybe after all the harsh comments, it was Bishnupriya's soft, loving words which had such an effect on Lakhi.

23

Panchanan Sarma did not send his daughter to her in-law's house. Perhaps initially he had thought of sending her. But he learnt from the persons who had come to give the news of his son-in-law's death that Lakhi's in-laws were holding her responsible for the tragedy. She was being seen as the bringer of ill luck into the family. Sarma realized what Lakhi's fate would be if he sent her to her in-laws. He, therefore, decided that it was better to have Lakhi stay with him and share her misfortune with her own family. But coming to that decision was no easy task for Sarma. It was simply unbearable to see their daughter cook her widow's meal separately while Sarma and his wife continued to eat fish and meat. One day, as Sarma was about to have a meal of rice and curry made of the delicious pabha fish, he noticed Lakhi's face at the kitchen window staring at the food. Immediately, he pushed the dish of fish aside and his wife broke into sobs. How could they bear the pain of seeing their daughter eating bland vegetarian food when they knew that the girl hated a meal without her favourite fish curry.

Panchanan Sarma observed with concern how the customs and practices, the fasts and rituals which went with a widow's life were gradually shrivelling up his daughter's spirits. Earlier too there had been young widows in their house but he had never been upset at their observing their ritual fasts. For him all that had just been part of the monotony of daily existence. But now whenever he saw Lakhi, his heart seemed to burst with sorrow. He kept on remembering Gunabhiram's words. Though he could never support widow re-marriage, yet he was now realizing the import of what Ishwarchandra Vidyasagar had written about society's injustice towards its widows. What ordinary people could not accept without direct experience, the wise like Vidyasagar could envisage even from a distance and empathize with. Gunahiram Barua had told him about all this long ago. That was why circumstances once again pulled him towards Bilwa Kutir. And once again, Panchanan Sarma started spending his evenings in the Hakim's sitting-room.

Barua and his wife received Sarma with the same degree of cordiality which they had showed him earlier. For the first few days Sarma would say a word or two and then remain silent. Gunabhiram too didn't trouble him with unnecessary questions. But one evening Sarma himself started talking about Lakhi. He tried to share with Barua, in a hesitant way, some of his grief at his daughter's fate:

"No one can forestall the designs of fate and we have learnt to accept it. But, please advise me now how to save the girl from this suffering of hell. Widow marriage will not be accepted by our society. Even if that happens some day, we'll not live to see it. Unfortunately, there are hardly any gentlemen here with a liberal mind like yours. I wish there was a way out without going in for widow-remarriage. My girl is quite intelligent. In fact, she is more sharp than my sons. I noticed it during those few days when she had taken lessons alongwith Swarna."

Gunabhiram pondered deeply for a long time. He had developed a sense of bitterness against people like Panchanan Sarma who bowed so easily to social customs and prejudices. But Gunabhiram softened up when he heard the pleadings of a helpless father. He replied in a gentle tone:

"It all depends on your will. But for that you will need some courage. In Calcutta these days a lot of young widows are being sent to school by their parents. Some of my acquaintances have started a school named Bharatiya Mahila Vidyalaya. Moreover, the Bethune School is also there. If you wish, you could send Lakhi to any of these. I will make all the arrangements. If she stays there her mind will open up and she'll learn a lot from the good people she would meet there."

Panchanan Sarma could not give any direct answer to this. Educating a boy in Calcutta was a difficult proposition. But, sending a girl there all alone was something unthinkable for Sarma. Moreover, it would be an injustice to his two sons if he spent so much money on his girl's education. Therefore Sarma changed the topic by saying, "Well, we'll have to think about all this seriously."

However, Sarma had to take a decision about Lakhi's future sooner than he had thought. One day, having returned from the kachhari, Sarma was taking his afternoon nap, when quietly like a shadow Lakhi came into the room and stood by him. She had grown much taller. Even with the insipid vegetarian food her body seemed to be growing at the normal rate. Nature's laws made no distinction between widows and married women in this respect. Sarma asked his daughter to sit near him and affectionately asked her to speak about her problem. He then noticed that Lakhi's eyes were filled with tears. Sarma understood that she had been hurt over something and had come to him for help. Otherwise she usually avoided him. She seemed to be nourishing a deep sense of grievance against her father and when she spoke, her voice betrayed this feeling of hurt: "Pitai, do I really have to spend the rest of my life like this? What wrong have I done? I always did whatever you asked me to. And now my aunts always keep on accusing me that I am the unlucky one and that I am fated to suffer all my life.

Pitai, I implore you, please do something to save me from this tortuous existence."

Sarma was silent for a long time. Then with a deep sigh he said:

"Hakim Dangoria has said that you should be sent to school in Calcutta. But for people like us that is impossible. We shall be ostracized by society and you will face a lot of problems."

Lakhi's face had brightened up on hearing the first few words of her father. She felt that there was some light in the midst of all the darkness. In her excitement she didn't even hear the second part of his comment. Clutching his hands firmly, she said:

"Pitai, will you send me to Calcutta? I've heard that Swarna too is being sent to Calcutta for her studies. Both of us could go together."

Sarma became grave and said:

"Swarna comes from a rich family. She will finish her education and then get married to an eligible groom. What will you do by going to study in the city?"

"I'll be a teacher, like the memsahibs," Lakhi answered promptly. "Or I'll be a doctor. A girl named Sushila from Christianpatty went to study medicine in Calcutta and is now working in a government job somewhere near Dhubri. I will also work like her."

Lakhi finished speaking in one breath and then looked expectantly at her father. Seeing her enthusiasm Sarma felt somewhat relieved even in the midst of all the gloom. But, he continued in the same negative vein:

"But how will you be like the memsahibs and the Christian girls, Lakhi? Have you ever seen girls from Brahmin families like ours going to Calcutta for their studies? Moreover, girls like you—"

Sarma couldn't bring the word "widow" to his lips and stopped short. Lakhi, however, didn't notice anything. Her mind had already started racing through the open skies. It was after a long time that she was speaking without a break, just like her earlier self:

"Several Brahmin boys have gone to Calcutta. Christian and Brahmo girls have also gone there. Once I go, other Brahmin girls will also start going."

Sarma felt that his daughter was speaking just like the Hakim Dangoria. Looking at her face he tried to be convinced by her confident words. But he couldn't forget the immediate present while thinking of a golden future. He told Lakhi in a despondent tone:

"I don't believe that our society will change so fast. No one will give up the old customs so easily. Nothing will really happen just because a few persons are raising a hue and cry in Calcutta. Our Asom Desh will remain the same. If you are so eager to go to school, then let me enquire. I'll put you in the Bengali school here."

The Sarma household was in turmoil from the moment the question of sending a grown-up girl to school arose. The father and daughter were on one side and the entire family ranged on the other. Everyone condemned Sarma for attempting something which was totally unheard of in society. When Lakhi tried to plead on behalf of her father, one and all cursed her. But surprisingly, Sarma refused to budge an inch from his position this time. He stubbornly stood by his decision and discussed the matter with Charushila Sen, the Headmistress of the Bengali school, and fixed Lakhi's admission into her school. Keeping in mind Lakhi's age, she was asked to get admitted to a higher class in the lower primary school. Lakhi had already done some initial reading at home and she had finished learning the first book of Arithmatic. So, Charushila assured her that she would face no problems in coping up with the school work. However, she might take some time to learn the Bengali language. But after talking to Lakhi, the Headmistress didn't have any doubts that she would be able to pick up Bengali very soon. Lakhi developed a strong liking for her Headmistress Baideu. She was so different from the other women Lakhi had met so far. She possessed a broad and enlightened mind and her father had told her that she was a Brahmo, like Swarna's parents. Lakhi didn't know anything about the Brahmo faith. But she seemed to like every Brahmo she had met till then. When Charushila Sen saw her for the first time, she had nodded her head gravely and said: "The sad outcome of a child-marriage". But after that instance she had never made Lakhi feel that she was in any way different from the other girls. All the girls in the school were Bengalis. But everyone talked to Lakhi in Assamese. Within a few days Lakhi too picked up some Bengali, enough to speak a sentence or two. The two-roomed thatched school house brought immense hope into Lakhi's life and the horizon suddenly seemed to widen. Her life, which was like a sapling about to be stamped under feet, suddenly found new roots and started once again to grow luxuriantly.

24

✤

Lakheswar returned to Nagaon a few days after the results of the Entrance examination were declared. He was the only student from the Nagaon High School to have got a First Division. Gunabhiram Barua was greatly pleased with the news. He felt as if someone very close to him had passed with distinction. He immediately wrote to his friend, Durgamohan Basu of Calcutta to arrange for Lakheswar's stay with some good Brahmin family. He himself would bear all the expenses. He wrote something else too to Durgamohan Basu. A seat in the Bethune School hostel may kindly be arranged for Swarna.

Ever since the mishap at Panchanan Sarma's place, Gunabhiram had been in a disturbed state of mind. If the educated section did not try to do away with its evil practices, Assamese society would always remain the same. How would his own children adjust to such a society? He was particularly worried about Swarna because she was a girl. As she grew older, wouldn't the superstitions and evil customs of society gradually entangle her? Staying in a place like Nagaon it was doubtful whether he would be able to wage a war single-handedly against all the social evils. Thinking about all this, he decided that Swarna should be sent to Calcutta as early as possible. His decision to give financial assistance to Lakheswar to study in Calcutta was also not without another rather selfish motive. If Swarna was admitted to a school in Calcutta, it would be possible for Lakheswar whom Gunabhiram considered to be a member of his own family, to pay her a visit now and then. Not that he did not have friends and well-wishers in that great city, but Lakheswar was closer to him than they. If God wished, someday he could really become like a son to him. He had great faith in the young man and believed that Lakheswar would eventually grow up into an educated, enlightened person. And, of course, he had always been thinking about such a groom for his Swarna.

Lakheswar did not have to make any particular arrangements to go to Calcutta. He packed up his clothes and spent the rest of his time bidding farewell to relatives and friends. Hakim Barua arranged for virtually everything—from the steamer passage to his stay at Calcutta. Barua wanted to book first class berths in the steamer for everyone. But Lakheswar insisted that he be allowed to travel second class alongwith a friend of his who would also be going to Calcutta. It would look rather odd if he travelled first while his friend went by second class.

At the time of departure, Lakheswar's parents sought only one assurance from him, that he should not get married without their consent. Guessing the cause of his parents' apprehension, Lakheswar touched his mother's feet and promised that in matrimonial matters he would always abide by their wishes. Having received this assurance from Lakheswar, the Kataki couple blessed their son and bade him good-bye. His father fulfilled his filial duty by thrusting a ten rupee note into Lakheswar's hands just as he was about to leave. They didn't show any interest in knowing how Lakheswar would manage in Calcutta with just his scholarship money. They seemed sure that their practical-minded son would be able to find some way out. The Katakis didn't find anything wrong with their son accepting financial and other help from Hakim Barua without however developing any other sort of relationship with him. In Bilwa Kutir too, preparations were in full swing for the Calcutta trip. The entire Barua family would be escorting Swarna to Calcutta. Though Bishnupriya had finally consented to Swarna's education in Calcutta, yet she would feel relieved only on seeing her settled in her hostel. The very thought of sending a nine-year old girl so far away all alone brought tears to Bishnupriya's eyes. But she never cried in the presence of Swarna. Seeing all the arrangements, Swarna felt that as on previous occasions, they were once again about to go on a long journey. All that she had heard from her father about Calcutta seemed to evoke images of a dream city in her mind. She was still too young to be worried as to how she would eventually face that unknown city without the protection of her parents.

As the day of the journey approached, leave-taking of friends and relatives began. The Baruas had close links with several of the Brahmo families of Nagaon. They were also on good terms with a few respectable Assamese and Marwari families. To say farewell to Swarna, several of these invited the Baruas to afternoon tea or dinner. Everyone blessed Swarna and also gave her plenty of advice. A niece of Gurunath Dutta had left for Calcutta some two months back and was staying with her aunt at Bharat Ashram. The Bharat Ashram had been set up by Keshav Chandra Sen and his followers with the noble intention of bringing the Brahmos together as one family who would live, eat and pray in the ashram and also work sincerely for the spread of women's education. But Gurunath Dutta had come to know from the recent letters he had received from Calcutta that the condition of the Bharat Ashram was not good. Differences over approaches to teaching and organization of the school-curriculum had surfaced between Brahmanand Keshav Chandra Sen and Sibnath Shastri, one of the teachers of the girls' school in the ashram. As a fall-out of this, many of the more progressive Brahmos had left the ashram. It was with a deep sense of disappointment that Gurunath related these happenings to Gunabhiram Barua. But there was no sign of despondency in Gunabhiram's reaction. He told Gurunath that the Samadarshi Party set up by Sibnath Shastri and his supporters emphasized the need to keep pace with the changing times. There was a time when everyone unquestioningly accepted Keshav Chandra Sen as the sole leader of those who wanted some radical change in the society. But some of his recent actions had shown that even sages can sometimes go astray. A new group of Brahmos are now trying to carry society forward with modern ideas. There is no reason to be dejected because of this."

"But what about the rivalry and differences between the two groups over the question of women's education? Is this for the good of the samaj?"

"There's a lot of debate over the issue of women's education even in the advanced countries of the world. Many in the West seem to share Keshav Chandra Sen's view that women should not be given the same education as men. They feel that a woman should receive only as much education as would make her a fit wife for a person with modern views. On the other hand those like the Samadarshi Brahmos believe that in matters of education, there should be no difference between men and women. Just two years ago, two girls astonished us all by passing the Entrance Examination of the Calcutta University, competing equally with the boys. Therefore, we'll have to think afresh about women's education. The views of Keashav Chandra Sen seem to have become outdated."

After discussing with Gunabhiram Barua, Gurunath Dutta decided that Ranu too should be sent to the Bethune School. However, instead of staying at the hostel, she would stay with her aunt. Dutta suggested that Swarna too stay at Ranu's aunt's place. But Gunabhiram and Bishnupriya did not like the idea of keeping the girl with someone else. They wanted her to stay in the hostel under the supervision of good teachers. Though Dutta talked about problems of food in the hostel, the Baruas didn't give much heed. They seemed more concerned about the expansion of Swarna's mind rather than providing her with gastronomic delights.

Swarna didn't have anyone in particular to say good-bye to, except for Tora's mother. She hadn't seen Golapi for a long time. After her daughter left for America, she had been keeping herself busy with all sorts of outdoor work. Home was lonely without Tora. That's why she had accompanied the memsahibs to camp several times. She had also gone to the weekly markets at Raha and Phulaguri to spread the word of the Gospel. Golapi and the missionary women would set up a stall under a small tin shed in a corner of the market and start distributing pictures of Christ and small booklets written in Assamese. Occasionally, someone would pay for the booklets, but usually these were offered gratis. If they succeeded in drawing a small crowd, then the missionaries would tell a story from the Bible and follow it up with a short speech. Whenever they fumbled in their narrations there was Golapi to help them out with the appropriate Assamese words. Golapi, therefore, was left with little time to visit friends like Bishnupriya. Bishnupriya, however, remembered her quite often and when Swarna wanted to visit her, she eagerly accompanied her daughter to Golapi's house at Christianpatty.

It was a Sunday and Golapi usually stayed at home on Sunday afternoons. After returning from church she would write letters to her daughter, do some sewing, or just sit quietly all alone. When the Hakim's carriage drew to a stop in front of her house, for a while Golapi kept staring at it in surprise. Then noticing Swarna and Bishnupriya, she hurriedly went forward to welcome them inside. Her small sitting room was neat and tidy. The windows had frilled curtains like those in the bungalows of the sahibs. On the wall there was a picture of the Virgin Mary holding the child Jesus. Just below it on a table was a candle-stand and, by its side, an Assamese Bible. The table was covered with a finely embroidered cloth. Though the two chairs in the room appeared quite antique, yet one look was enough to reveal that they must have once belonged in a sahib's bungalow. Bronson Sahib had gifted the chairs to Golapi just before leaving for America. It was with great eagerness that Golapi listened to the details about Swarna's going to Calcutta. Though she herself had never seen Calcutta, yet she had heard a lot about that great city from her missionary friends. Basing her experience on this, Golapi offered bits of advice to Swarna and Bishnupriya. Bishnupriya concealed her amusement with a polite smile at Golapi's stressing on small points with the tone of a very experienced person. Golapi's face brightened up the moment Tora's name was mentioned. Tora was training to be a nurse in America. Though Bronson Sahib was much better, yet he would not be able to return to India soon. So, Tora would return in another two months along with another missionary family. The thought of seeing her daughter soon had erased the two years of loneliness from Golapi's mind. Bishnupriya could understand the state of Golapi's mind. She too would perhaps feel the same way when Swarna would return home from Calcutta for her holidays.

When Swarna and her mother took leave of Golapi,, Golapi asked them to wait for a while. She went inside and brought an embroidered pillow-case which she gave to Swarna and said: "Put this on your pillow when you stay in the hostel, my child. It'll help you remember us. I had embroidered this for Tora. But you too are like my Tora." Swarna thanked her politely and accepted the gift with an embarrassed smile.

25

The distance between Nagaon and Silghat was some thirty-two miles. By buggy it took about ten to twelve hours and one had to change horses twice. The Hakim's family started their journey early in the morning and reached Silghat late in the evening. Luckily, the steamer "Rajmahal" too had reached Silghat from Kokilamukh around this time. It docked at Silghat for the night and many of its passengers, both Bengali and Assamese, went ashore and got busy talking with acquaintances and friends. A few of them went off to their friends' houses nearby to spend the night there. But most of them stayed on board since the steamer was to set sail early the next day. Those who did not want to eat the food served on the steamer because of caste or other restrictions, had made themselves small bamboo and cloth enclosures on the sand and were busy cooking their evening meal on the river bank.

As soon as the Baruas arrived, Lakheswar told them that he had made all arrangements for Dangoriani Aideu Bishnupriya to cook her meal. But, Bishnupriya said with a smile: "Bopa, please go and take your meal with the other students. Mine will be taken care of by the Brahmin cook who has come with us".

Lakheswar had reached Silghat the previous evening, having travelled from home by bullock-cart. He was accompanied by another boy from Nagaon who was also going to Calcutta on a scholarship. They were travelling second class. When they boarded the steamer they met two other Assamese students. So, they were now four of them on way to Calcutta. The Barua family was travelling first and had a cabin to themselves. All the other occupants of the cabins were Europeans. Gunabhiram happened to know some of them and exchanged greetings. Bishnupriya, after feeding her sons and putting them to sleep in the cabin, went ashore for her own meal. Swarna had dinner with her father on board the steamer. She felt uneasy having to eat with fork and spoon, surrounded as she was with European ladies and gentlemen, but Gunabhiram had prepared his daughter to tackle such a situation. At home she had been taught for over a month to handle the fork and spoon. This was done with a view to help Swarna adjust to any situation in Calcutta. Just before dinner as Swarna was leaning on the railings of the steamer's deck and gazing intently at the hues of the setting sun over the Brahmaputra, a strange thing happened. An European lady struck by Swarna's fair complexion, shapely face and fashionable clothes, mistook her to be a white girl and started talking to her. A startled and embarassed Swarna hesitated for a few seconds and then ran to her father. At this, the lady recognized Barua and realized her mistake. As she passed Swarna's table during dinner time, she greeted Barua and said, "Your daughter is really pretty. My own daughter is also of her age. She's studying in England." Gunabhiram told the lady that Swarna too was joining Bethune School at Calcutta. Hearing this, she eagerly informed Barua that her friend, Miss Nichols was a teacher at Bethune's and if they so desired, she would write a letter of introduction to her. Gunabhiram was touched by this unknown lady's concern for Swarna and requested her for the letter. During the entire journey up to Goalando in eastern Bengal, this lady who was called Mrs Spencer, kept on offering biscuits and sweets to Swarna and her brother Karuna.

The steamer set sail early the next morning. Swarna and Karuna spent most of the day on deck enjoying the beauty of the Brahmaputra. As they neared the town of Tezpur, Gunabhiram and Bishnupriya started pointing out the landmarks on the banks to Swarna—the huge stone slab at Kaliabhumura, the Agnigarh Hill, Mahabhairav temple… she had heard her mother speak about these so often. Though Swarna was not aware of the memories which Tezpur might have had for her parents, yet for her, each of these places seemed to belong to some sort of a fairyland. She tried to relate the landmarks on the river-bank with the romantic stories about Usha and Aniruddha which her mother had told her.

The steamer halted for a while at Tezpur. The passengers cooked and ate their mid-day meal on the river bank. After this, they continued their journey to Guwahati. In the evening, just after sunset, the vessel reached Sukreswar Ghat. The sunset on the Brahmaputra which the passengers saw just before reaching Guwahati seemed to defy all imagination. Right in front was the beautiful river island of Umananda and reclining behind it was the magnificent Nilachal Hill looking up at the sky. At its feet lay the two giants in the form of hills, Kalapahar and Narakasura. The sun was going down into the mighty Brahmaputra in a dazzling pillar of crimson and all around it was the play of unending colours. The rainbow-coloured waves at the wake of the ship were gradually breaking up into a riot of myriad hues.

Most of the Calcutta bound passengers alighted at Guwahati and left for the homes of their relatives and friends. The Phukan family of Bharalumukh had sent a horse carriage to pick up Gunabhiram and his family from the ghat. For Bishnupriya this was her first visit to the Bharalumukh house after her marriage. Gunabhiram had grown up with this family after the death of his father. Gunabhiram would never be able to forget the love and affection that he had received from Anandaram Dhekiyal Phukan.

This was in sharp contrast to the indifference and neglect that he had faced from his step-mother and step-brothers. The moment he set foot in Phukan's house, Gunabhiram's mind was flooded with old memories. But for Anandaram's care and guidance, perhaps he would never have been able to reach his present position in life. He clearly recalled the day when he had brought his first wife Brajasundari who also happened to be Anandaram's sister-in-law, as a bride into this house. He had never been able to give any happiness to that unfortunate lady. Yet, he had tried to perform all his duties as a husband. Perhaps, fate itself had not ordained any happiness for Brajasundari. The familiar scenes of the house held so many bitter-sweet memories for him. Both Anandaram and Brajasundari had departed early from this world and for Gunabhiram the house was full of their memories. But everything seemed so new for Bishnupriya and the children. Anandaram's younger son, Annada, gave them a warm welcome when they arrived.

Of all the family members of the Phukan household, Swarna took an instant liking to Padmavati Devi. She was the eldest daughter of Anandaram Phukan and the wife of Nandeswar Kataki. Her beauty and grace combined with her zeal for knowledge left Swarna amazed. She could discuss matters relating to literature, religion or travel with equal ease. And, she could also cook delicious Bengali dishes for her guests. Thus, having spent the night happily, the Baruas returned to their steamer the next morning.

At Guwahati, several new passengers boarded the steamer for Calcutta. Most of them were business folk who used to bring goods from Calcutta and sell them in different districts in Assam. There were also some pilgrims who were returning home after visiting the Kamakhya temple. Most of these were Bengalis; there were a few Oriyas too. The Assamese passengers were relatively few. There was, however, a group of Assamese pilgrims headed for the Lord Jagannath shrine at Puri. As soon as the steamer set sail, the Assamese pilgrims started singing devotional songs to the accompaniment of khols and cymbals. Swarnalata was pleased to hear the singing as it wafted up from the lower deck. But a few British passengers who were on the upper deck appeared quite irritated with the singing. They called a boatswain and ordered him to go and stop the commotion downstairs. When the latter told them that the passengers below were singing devotional songs and to stop them could prove ominous, some of the white men grumbled and said: "Can't they pray to their god in silence?" Swarnalata realized that the tastes of the passengers in the ship clearly differed a lot. What was pleasing to one's ears was just noise and commotion for someone else.

As the vessel gradually took a southward course from Guwahati, the vegetation on both sides of the bank started changing. The hills were now replaced by almost endless tracts of river reeds and swamps. All around small and large sand banks appeared. The ship meandered its way between these sand banks, all the while trying to keep to the deeper part of the river. During the monsoons when most of the sand banks lay submerged, it was much easier to navigate the vessel. But in winter there was always the danger of it running aground in the shallow portions. Now as the steamer approached the town of Goalpara, the outline of a row of stone-houses could be seen through the haze. Pointing these out to his wife and daughter, Gunabhiram said: "There was a time when our trade with Bengal was conducted from here. This was a flourishing place then. One of our forefathers, Lakshminarayan Brahmachari, was once in charge of this place known as Hadira Chowki. It was from here that my grandfather, Parashuram Barua, learnt the tricks of the trade which helped him to manage the chowki so efficiently.

Gunabhiram had narrated this family history to Bishnupriya quite often. But that particular day as he leant against the deck railings and recounted the history of Hadira Chowki, Bishnupriya felt that she was being literally transported to the past. As Gunabhiram continued with his narration, very much like an eye-witness, about the historic battle of Hadira Chowki, Captian Scott's expedition into Assam and the miserable plight of the Assamese people under Burmese occupation, Swarna was prompted to ask: "Deuta, did you see the Battle of Hadira Chowki?" Gunabhiram replied with a smile: "Had I been some twenty years older, I might have been witness to it."

The steamer finally laid anchor for the night at Goalpara. Just as the Barua family was coming ashore, they met a Marwari gentleman whom they knew. He insisted that Gunabhiram stay at his place. Gunabhiram, however, was not willing to do so and decided to spend the night on the boat. So, the gentleman sent some home-made sweets for the children. Swarna and her brother had never tasted such delicious sweets at Nagaon.

Just as the passengers were about to retire for the night, there was a sudden commotion. The passengers knew that another steamer had laid anchor nearby. But nothing could be seen because of the darkness. The following morning they saw that the vessel next to the "Rajmahal" was full of girmitiyas, that is indentured coolies meant for the tea gardens of Assam. From their appearance, it seemed that most of them were Bhils, Santhals and Mundas from the northern and eastern regions of the country. Men, women and children were all crowded together in the steamer. They were not allowed to leave the steamer and go ashore. So, they hung on to the railings helplessly and kept staring at the passengers of the "Rajmahal". Just as the "Rajmahal" set sail, a person from the other steamer jumped into the waters. There was pandemonium all around. The passengers in the lower decks of both the vessels started shouting. The man who had jumped into the water swam towards "Rajmahal" in a frantic bid to overtake it. Luckily, someone threw him a rope to which he clung desperately. Finally with great effort he was hauled up by the rope and he collapsed on the deck. The passengers of the lower deck and the employees of the "Rajmahal" surrounded the man and started questioning him. But no one could follow the words he panted forth. Eventually, a Bengali gentleman started talking to the man in broken Santhali. At this, he responded amid sobs. He even fell at the Bengali gentleman's feet and implored him for help. The Rajmahal had meanwhile dropped anchor again. A European tea-planter from the upper deck started shouting instructions that the truant coolie be immediately put ashore. The Bengali gentleman retorted angrily that the man was seeking refuge because he was in grave danger. His wife and children had all fallen sick during the long journey and died on the steamer in which they were being brought to Assam. He too hadn't eaten anything since the previous day. That morning when he wanted to go ashore, the sardar had beaten him up. He did not want to go and work in the tea-gardens. The Bengali gentleman argued that it would be a grave sin to compel the man to leave the "Rajmahal" against his wishes. He insisted that the man be given refuge and taken to Calcutta. On hearing this, the white planter roared: " It is not our duty to give shelter to these lazy beggars. They signed an agreement of their own free will. Now it will not do if they try to cheat mid-way. This is the British Government's law. Let's see who dares to break it." These words, tinged with sarcasm, were obviously meant for the Indians. No one had the courage to accept the challenge openly. Meanwhile, Gunabhiram Barua also came and stood by the side of the European planter. He said in a placating tone in English: "Even without breaking the law one can be considerate to one's fellow human beings. Before we hand over the coolie to the sardar, we must be assured that he will not be treated harshly."

It was obvious that each of the gentlemen present there wanted to extricate himself from this tricky situation without, of course, doing much damage to his conscience. So both Europeans and Indians eagerly accepted Barua's suggestion and it was decided to warn the sardar to be more merciful towards the coolie. Meanwhile, the sardar had been running along the river bank and was almost opposite the "Rajmahal". He was waving his stick in a threatening manner and looked livid with anger. When the passengers of the "Rajmahal", particularly the white men, remonstrated with the sardar, he seemed to calm down a bit and accept what they had to say but kept on murmuring something to himself. He finally caught hold of the coolie and almost dragged him along the bridge to the shore. Every one knew only too well that the Sardar's assurances were of no value. But no one said anything even as the poor man was being handed over. The Bengali gentleman took out a notebook and wrote something. He said he would be reporting the whole incident in a newspaper published from Calcutta and he would also be writing about the plight of the tea-garden coolies of Assam. Lakheswar and his friends found out that he had come to Assam to collect facts for a Bengali newspaper named *Sanjivani*. Long after their vessel had left, Swarna kept standing near the the upper deck rails, looking at the shore. That so many grown up gentlemen had failed to protect an ordinary, poor man from imminent danger was something which hurt Swarna deeply. It was as if her faith in the world of the elders had suddenly taken a knocking. Later she asked her father in a small voice: "Deuta, will that fearsome person beat up the poor man again?' Not receiving any reply from her father, Swarna fell silent.

26

After stopping at Dhubri, Silamari and Sirajganj, the steamer finally reached Goalando. From there to Calcutta was just one night's journey. Having enough time at hand, the Indian passengers had a hearty meal of rice and a spicy fish curry at a shop run by a Bengali person. Gunabhiram's family, however, had food which was cooked on shore by their Brahmin cook. It was at Goalando that Swarna and her brother Karuna saw a train for the first time in their lives. The two children were totally awestruck by what they saw. The Barua family boarded a first-class compartment of which they were the sole occupants. The compartment was so much like a well furnished little room that when Swarna looked out of the train she felt that their house was moving! Ever since she left Bilwa Kutir, it seemed her life too was moving ahead at a strange speed. Swarna had never had time to reflect on the final destination of this journey of hers. At the moment, the only goal of her life was to travel, and travel and travel.

At last, the train moved into Calcutta's Sealdah station. There were quite a few people waiting on the platform to receive the passengers from Assam. Among them there were also some friends and acquaintances of Gunabhiram. A person sent by Rajaninath Ray had come to receive Lakheswar. He escorted Lakheswar to the house of a Brahmin family at College Square where arrangements had been made for his stay. But, Lakheswar had changed his plans during the journey and had fixed up his stay with some Assamese friends. For the time being, however, he would stay at the place arranged for him by Gunabhiram Barua.

A hackney carriage had been sent for the Baruas from Barrister Anandamohan Basu's house. Gunabhiram's friendship with the Basu family was an old one. During his visits to Calcutta, he would always stay with them. Anandamohan's younger brother, Dr. Mohinimohan Basu happened to be one of Bengal's leading scholars. As such, the Basu family was very much at the centre of Calcutta's intellectual world.

The journey by carriage from Sealdah station to the home of the Basus seemed to be out of the pages of a fairy-tale book for Swarna and Karuna. They watched with wonder the tall buildings, the endless rows of shops and the almost incessant flow of people. Everything about the great city appeared strange to them. The magic touch seemed to be everywhere—from the water gushing out of iron pipes into roadside stone tanks to the wonderful tram cars rolling down the rails. Watching the people hurrying down the roads Swarna wondered why everybody appeared to be so busy in the city. She had never seen anyone walk so briskly in Nagaon. Everyone there had plenty of time and one never walked past without exchanging greetings. This was the first bewildering impression that Swarna had about city life.

As the carriage came to a halt in front of the house, Anandamohan came forward and greeted Gunabhiram warmly by embracing him in a gesture of welcome. By then, the ladies of the house too had come out to receive the guests. Unlike typical Bengali women, they did not cover their heads with their sarees. Bishnupriya was surprised to find that the women were chatting away freely without veils in the presence of their husbands and other men, and even more surprising, they were also wearing sandals like their menfolk, something unheard of in the traditional

Assamese households. The women of the Basu household had not met Bishnupriya before. So, they welcomed her like a bride, with earthen lamps on a brass plate. Anandamohan's wife pushed a sandesh into Bishnupriya's mouth affectionately and then embraced her with a kiss. Though all this was done in fun and frolic, yet tears welled up in Bishnupriya's eyes. Perhaps she recalled that particular day when she had set foot as a bride in Parashuram Barua's house. But Bishnupriya didn't have much time for such thoughts. The warmth and affection of the Basu household made her forget the unhappy intrusions of the past. Meanwhile, Swarna, Karuna and the child Kamala were drawing all the attention. There was much praise for Swarna's complexion, the shape of her nose, her bright eyes and the texture of her hair.

Anandamohan's wife said in a lighter vein: "Now we know why our menfolk who go to Assam become sheep at Kamakhya and stay on!" Another lady joined in: "Now we are in for trouble. If Swarnalata stays on in Calcutta, in the next five years this city will be crowded with sheep."

Everyone had a hearty laugh. Swarna's cheeks had been squeezed by the ladies so often that they had already turned crimson. Now, hearing what was being said about her, she blushed hard and tried to cover her face with the end of her mother's saree. Karuna too was finding the goings on somewhat strange and so hung on to his mother. The baby Kamala burst out crying as the women vied with each other to cuddle him. Seeing the plight of the children, the good-natured hosts took pity and decided to leave them alone for some time.

When the family dinner was served, there were so many mouth-watering savoury dishes laid out before the guests that they didn't know where to start. Despite their protects, the ladies of the house started filling Gunabhiram and Bishnupriya's plates with different items. As Swarna and Karuna found the food too hot and spicy, sweets were served to them. Swarna, had never seen such large sweets before. One was enough to make a person feel queasy. Karuna almost cried when the ladies insisted that he eat two of them. Seeing their predicament, Bishnupriya, Gunabhiram and the hosts were much amused.

The guests stayed on the first floor of the house. The south-facing rooms with wide front verandahs were cooled by a refreshing breeze. It was difficult to believe that such a pleasant breeze could be enjoyed right in the centre of this noisy and crowded metropolis. Leaving aside the world of the elders, Swarna and Karuna leaned on the verandah railings and kept looking at the sights of the great city. The scent-laden southern breeze seemed to have swept away all their tiredness. The children were in a pensive mood. Suddenly, as if giving words to her thoughts, Karuna asked: "Baideu, will you like it here?"

Swarna had been trying to ask herself the same question. A few days' holiday with her parents at Calcutta would naturally be quite nice. But the very thought of having to stay on alone in a strange and unknown city amidst strangers made her feel quite uneasy. Yet, she didn't wish to disclose her apprehensions to her younger brother who had all these years looked up to her as his role model. So, she replied in a sober tone:

"Maybe when I live here, I'll come to like it as Deuta will keep coming every now and then. As it is, after some days, he will take me home for the holidays."

"Won't you miss home?" Karuna asked, his eyes full of sadness.

Swarna didn't say anything. Remembering their days at Bilwa Kutir, she was almost choked with sorrow. Tears rolled down her eyes and fell on the iron railings. Not knowing what to do, Karuna held her hand and stood silently. He understood that the situation was indeed quite grave.

27

Gunabhiram took his family around Calcutta before it was time for Swarna to leave for the boarding school. The Asiatic Museum, Fort William, Eden Park, Kalighat—he took them to all the places of interest. They shopped at Chandni Bazar, Bahubazar and even at New Market which had been set up exclusively for the European sahibs and memsahibs. Clothes and other necessities were bought for Swarna, but she seemed disinterested in them. As the day of her departure for the hostel drew near, she felt more and more upset at seeing all the new things that had been bought for her and, whenever someone from the Basu household found Swarna standing alone looking thoughtful, she would be pulled away to listen to the piano being played in the drawing room or to join the family members in a game of cards. Anandamohan's three young sisters-in-law, Labanyaprova, Hemoprova and Charuprova had, in the meantime, taken a strong liking to Swarna and were trying their best to make her feel at home. It was from them that Swarnalata learnt for the first time that her name was to be pronounced as "Shornolota" and not "Sarnalata" as most Assamese did. Swarna's shyness of strangers increased when she was thus made conscious of her faulty pronunciation and she became more hesitant than before of speaking to strangers.

Those days a lot of people belonging to the Brahmo fraternity of Calcutta would gather every evening at Anandamohan Basu's house. Debates and discussions on serious topics laced with witty comments and well-worked-out arguments marked these addas. A special feature of these sittings among the Brahmos was the equal participation of both men and women. Bishnupriya too participated in these discussions along with the other women of the Basu family. Though she did not speak much, she was an ardent listener. Swarna too sat by her mother during these evening sessions. Though she did not particularly enjoy the company of grown-ups, yet her parents wanted her to be with them. Aware of the imminent separation, they wanted to spend as much time as possible with Swarna.

One evening, Durgamohan Das, Sibnath Shastri and Manomohan Ghosh came with their families to visit the Basus. All three of them had at one time been the principal followers of Keshav Chandra Sen. Now, however, they were opposed to his views. Bishnupriya had heard a lot about Manomohan Ghosh's "modern" wife. Manomohan had created a sensation by sending his newly married wife to the Loreto School hostel to acquire the best English education available for girls in Calcutta. This explained the Western touch in her tastes and manners. She wore the saree like an English gown, after the new fashion introduced by the Parsee ladies of Bombay. Many Brahmo ladies of Calcutta had also started imitating the new fashion. The blouse with lace frills worn by Manomohan's wife and the pearl necklace to go with it also reflected Western taste. Manomohan Ghosh, too, was almost every inch an European in his dress and manners. Extremely polite in his manners, every comment he made bore evidence of his sharp mind. But Bishnupriya could not develop a liking for these Westernised individuals. The Brahmo Samajis were made fun of by everyone as "Christians" because their views and manner of worship resembled those of the Protestants. It was exactly because of this that both Gunabhiram and Bishnupriya had consciously tried to keep alive some aspects of the Indian tradition in their way of life. They had no reservations whatsoever in accepting all that was good in Western society. In fact, it was the beautiful synthesis of the Indian tradition and Western ideas in the Brahmo faith that had so attracted them to it. But foreign-returned Brahmos like Manomohan Ghosh had given up almost everything that seemed Indian. That was why, like many other brahmos, the Barua couple too found it difficult to accept them as their brothers and sisters in faith.

That particular evening's discussion was centred on the issue of women's education. It was Swarna's going to Bethune School which had sparked it off. Both Sibnath Shastri and Durgamohan Bose commented that the Bethune School syllabus as well as its teaching methods were far below those of the boys' schools. Manomohan Ghosh happened to be the secretary of the Bethune School. So, taking upon himself the criticism made of his school, he said that he had been trying to modernize the syllabus without displeasing the guardians. But, if a radical step was taken too suddenly then there was always the danger of many guardians withdrawing their wards from the school. "Actually our Indian males think that the sole purpose of women's education is to create some ideal housewives who would be able to cook delicious dishes and at the same time satisfy the aesthetic tastes of their husbands by reciting poetry. So, why should they encourage women to study mathematics or the sciences?" Ghosh commented wryly. After a brief pause, he continued: "From this year we are taking some new steps. Now that the Bethune College has started functioning, we'll have to raise its standard so that it secures permission to become affiliated to the University. For that, all the subjects taught in the boys' schools must be introduced both at Bethune school as well as the college."

Sibnath Shastri gave spirited support to Ghosh on this matter:

"You are right, Mr Ghosh. In matters of women's education some of our most educated persons turn out to be the most conservative. Don't you remember what Keshab Babu had once said to me—'What will girls do with Geometry? Some elementary knowledge of science should be enough for them'. It was because of his obsolete views that I quit Bharat Ashram."

"Don't speak about Keshab Babu," intervened Mrs Ghosh. "Miss Akroyd has told me that she is scandalised by the fact that such a leading social reformer as he has allowed his wife to remain a dumb, uneducated woman who is literally buried in gold ornaments. If his ideas couldn't influence his own family members, how could one expect others to be inspired?"

It was as if Mrs Ghosh had opened a Pandora's box! Instantly, everyone started talking about Keshav Chandra Sen's daughter's wedding. Each took turns at condemning Sen's betrayal of his ideals. Gunabhiram and Bishnupriya, however, did not take part in the diatribe. They couldn't bring themselves to use such harsh language against an individual whom they had once held in such high esteem. Once the emotions subsided, Gunabhiram returned to the question of female education and said:

"In matters of women's education, Keshav Chandra's views seem to conform with those of many others in England. Although the English are so much more advanced than us in matters of education, yet their womenfolk are still fettered to their old customs and traditions. Wouldn't it be a big step forward if our womenfolk who are living in virtual darkness, could be raised at least to the level of their Victorian counterparts?"

"Barua Mahashoy, you have spoken just like the Adi Brahmo Samajis. Amongst the British there is both good and evil. Should we be indifferent to the good and see only that which is bad? When we have before us the examples of women such as Mary Carpenter and Annete Akroyd, should we be attracted by the lives of the backward Victorian ladies? You have brought your daughter all the way to Calcutta to put her in a boarding school. You could have as well kept here at home where she would have learnt to draw, embroider clothes, serve food like an English woman, arrange flowers and become the perfect Victorian lady."

Manomohan Ghosh was saying this in such an ironic vein, gesticulating all the while with his hands, that Barua couldn't restrain his laughter which was joined in by others. But, the doubts in his mind persisted. Couldn't there be a synthesis of modern education and Indian tradition and culture?

Discussions that evening on diverse topics continued till late in the evening. Many of these topics were not new to Gunabhiram. He had kept himself informed about the debates in the Brahmo circles of Calcutta and had often discussed these issues with friends in Nagaon. But, in Assam he had never come across such a lively exchange of ideas as he had seen that evening. Those who used to visit him at Bilwa Kutir happened to be mostly listeners. He had rarely come across anyone in Assam who could debate with him on equal terms and dare to openly criticize his views. There he was a "wise man"; here in Calcutta he was one thirsting for knowledge. That was why he loved Calcutta so much. Each visit to this great city gave him fresh inspiration to live and work.

28

Jagadish Chandra Basu's sister, Hemaprova, and Durgamohan Das accompanied Gunabhiram and Bishnupriya when they went to put Swarna in school. Durgamohan had actively worked in setting up the Bethune School and was deeply involved with its affairs. It was he who introduced the Barua couple to the English Headmistress and the other teachers of the school. Everyone seemed both surprised and pleased that the Baruas had brought their daughter all the way from distant Assam to be educated at Calcutta. Looking at Bishnupriya and Swarnalata, the teachers repeatedly questioned them: "Do you really belong to Assam? Or have you gone from some other place and settled there?" Catching the slant of their questions, Durgamohan jokingly said: "You must admit after this that Assam is not a place of uncivilized races! We can also read about the grace and beauty of the women of Assam from the accounts of British writers."

The students and teachers of Bethune School showed a lot of affection for Swarnalata. Most of the girls in the boarding school belonged to the different districts of Bengal and Bihar. The girls from Calcutta usually commuted from their homes. Thus, most of the girls in the hostel came from muffusil areas or possessed a rural background. Calcutta was for them an unknown city. There were also a few married girls. Perhaps they had been sent to the school by their liberal- minded husbands and fathers-in-law.

Most of the girls were either Christians or Brahmos. They very easily accepted Swarna as one of them. Very few among them had actually heard of Assam. But, they surmised that it must be some remote district of Bengal.

Bishnupriya didn't say a word when she took leave of her daughter. She knew that the moment she would try to say something, her words would falter and, on seeing this, Swarna would surely cry. Gunabhiram blessed Swarna and said: "Ai, concentrate in your studies well and brighten up the face of the country. *Brahmakripahikevalam*".[3] When her parents left, a tearful Swarna kept looking on till their carriage disappeared down the road. Soon after, Mrs Nichols affectionately led her inside the school.

---

[3] A Sanskrit prayer meaning the mercy of Brahma is all that we seek.

Part II

1

Panchanan Sarma's house wore a festive look. Lakhipriya had passed the lower primary examination securing the first position in her district and all the teachers of the Bengali school were at Sarma's place to give him the good news. But even as they blessed Lakhi and had their share of tea and sweets, they somehow felt that neither Sarma nor his wife were that happy. The headmistress, Charusila Sen was quick to guess the reason but she pretended ignorance and asked Sarma:

"Well, Sarma Dangoria, I suppose you will allow Lakhi to continue with her studies?"

Sarma replied with a helpless smile: "Had my son done so well, I would certainly have given him the best education within my means. But hard luck! Lakhi has been born a girl and we don't have any schools for girls here. So, we must take it that her education ends here."

Charusila Sen had thought of her answer well ahead. Chewing her betel-nut all the while, she said: "I have been thinking of something. An intelligent girl like Lakhi cannot be allowed to go waste. The result of this could be quite bad. So, it would be best to put her in the boys' Middle English school. At least she should go upto the ME level."

"What? Are you really suggesting that I send her to a boys' school?" Sarma opened his eyes wide in disbelief.

"Yes, of course. Right now there seems to be no other way out because the government has not yet set up even a middle level school for girls. However, there is one option. She could go to the Mission School. But would you really agree to send your girl there?"

"No, not at all. That's impossible. We can't send our girls there," said Sarma decisively.

"Then why don't you put her in the boys' school? I have already talked to the Headmaster and he seems to have no objections. The government too should agree. Only if you ask Barua Hakim to put in a word, everything will be quite smooth. Moreover," she halted for a while hoping to remove the last bit of apprehension from Panchanan Sarma's mind, "Lakhi would be much older than the other boys of her class. For her, it would be like studying with her younger brothers".

Sarma did not reply. Lowering his head, he started thinking. He couldn't shut his eyes to the fact that the headmistress's arguments, which appeared so simple and straight, were, in actuality, highly explosive for the society he lived in. Since the Brahmos did not follow the customs and practices of the Hindus, it was often easy for them to give such advice. So, how could he expect them to understand the complex world of a man like him who was tied to the traditional bonds and beliefs of society? He reflected that humans couldn't live without their society and even the Christians had one of their own. Would they too ever be able to give up their own societies? As he looked up from his thoughts, Sarma was embarrassed to see a pair of eyes watching him from behind the curtains. He knew that Lakhi was eagerly waiting for his decision. In an instant, he took control of himself and, looking calmly at Charusila Sen, he said: "Let me think it over. I have been encouraged by your eagerness for the girl's education. If the others in the family agree, I shall have no objection."

Panchanan Sarma knew only too well what the others in the

family would say. Yet, he felt that it was safer to put it in that manner, rather than say yes right away and then end up by not being able to keep his word. Experience had taught him not to commit himself straight away. Charting the middle course had become a habit of sorts for Sarma and he kept thinking about this for a long time after Lakhi's teachers had left. He wasn't the least scared about the recurrence of a situation like what he had faced when he had first decided to send Lakhi to school. He knew that he had both the ability and will to impose his views on the rest of the family. But he wasn't too sure whether the step he was now about to take was really right. But he was certain that his conscience would never allow him to do anything that might harm Lakhi who to him was like a steady flame in the midst of all the wind and storm. He also knew that he would never forgive himself if he failed. Yet, he really didn't know how far he would have to go in order to do this. At this juncture, he desperately needed advice from someone and, as usual, his steps once again led him to Bilwa Kutir.

It was already some two months since Gunabhiram and his family had returned from Calcutta. They had in the meantime received the first letter which Swarna had sent from her hostel. She said she was fine, but was missing them a lot; that everyone in the school seemed to like her and she was concentrating on her studies. It was a short letter. Even then, both Gunabhiram and Bishnupriya's eyes watered when they read it—written in a child's hand, large letters carefully formed. Whatever appearances they had put on the outside, in their hearts they could feel how lonely the house had become without Swarna. Though their two little sons were with them, yet they missed Swarna's presence at every step. While Gunabhiram kept himself busy with his official world and his studies, it was Bishnupriya who missed her daughter the most.

The Baruas were thrilled to see Panchanan Sarma after all these days. It was Swarna's friendship with Lakhi that had brought Sarma close to them. Panchanan Sarma first enquired about Swarna and then gave them the news of Lakhi's results. Gunabhiram had already come to know of it at the kutcherry. A girl having come first in the district was news indeed and everyone was busy discussing it. The Barua couple heartily congratulated Sarma and asked him to convey their blessings and good wishes to Lakhi. Gunabhiram, however, didn't miss the opportunity to hold forth on his favourite topic of women's education and declared: "It is the sign of a civilized race to educate its womenfolk. If all the Assamese girls could be taught to read and write like Lakhi, our nation would really advance."

"But, Barua Dangoria, is it possible for a girl to study even if she wants to? Is there any middle or high school nearby where our Lakhi could study? Now I am left with no option but to put her in the boys' school," Sarma said somewhat agitatedly.

Gunabhiram kept mum for a while. Sarma's words seemed to prick him somewhere. Although he had raised the matter of setting up a middle school for girls before the District Magistrate. Some time ago, he had failed to follow up on it since he had been pre-occupied in arranging Swarna's trip to Calcutta. He now felt somewhat selfish that his concern for his daughter's future should have made him forget his obligation to others and he decided to bring up the matter before the authorities the very next day. But, knowing full well that such things invariably took time, he hesitated to offer any solution to Sarma's problem right then. He couldn't but agree more with Sarma. Though he himself was not in favour of sending Lakhi to a boys' school, yet there seemed to be no other option. So he said: "We have heard that elsewhere girls do study in boys' schools. It is, of course, necessary to have separate schools for girls. But since we don't have any, one will have to send them to boys' schools. It would certainly be a wrong step to stop educating the girls because there aren't any schools for them. Don't you worry. I'll write to the government for permission. As for Lakhi, you needn't lose sleep over her. She is a steady girl. She has also reached a reasonable age and will be able to manage herself."

"I too feel that way," said Sarma. "But I am a bit worried about what people will think."

"Will you abandon the right path out of fear of the public? Today people may condemn you. But tomorrow when the entire country will move forward, everyone will praise your courage."

"My weakness lies exactly there, Hakim Dangoria. Like you, I do not have the courage to lead all the others on. I am actually one who is used to following others," Sarma said with a smile.

Barua laughed and said, "Try to lead the others this time. If your steps falter, we are always there to help."

By then, Sarma had almost made up his mind. It was strange that whenever he came to see this couple, he felt that he was on the threshold of a new age. But once he returned home, his confidence slowly melted away. Today, however, he was decided. And, in order to give quick shape to his thoughts, he went straight from Bilwa Kutir to the headmaster of the boys' M.E. school and finalized everything about Lakhi's admission. He was told that once the approval came from the government, the admission would be done. Having thus finished his work, Sarma's immediate feeling was that of relief at a heavy burden being taken off his mind. In quick, light steps he hurried home to give the news to his daughter.

2

An old and experienced family servant named Bhodai was entrusted with the charge of escorting Lakhi to her new school. The earlier Lower Primary school that she went to was quite close to her home and her younger brother used to accompany her. Now, the old servant would follow her to the doorstep of the boys' Middle English school. On reaching school, Lakhi would fold her umbrella and hand it over to Bhodai who would leave instantly, to come back again just before school was over, to escort her back home. Every morning, on the way to school, Bhodai would faithfully walk behind Lakhi, all the while casting sharp glances at the boys. On their part, the boys used to observe the strange sight with amazement and curiosity, as though they couldn't believe their eyes. The invasion of a girl into the sacrosanct space reserved for boys was indeed a strange happening. On her first day in school, the Headmaster himself showed Lakhi her seat in the classroom. She was given a bench all to herself while the boys sat huddled together, five or six to a bench. The boys were too scared of the Headmaster to say anything about the new arrangement on the first day. But by the next day, they had become more bold. Some of the naughty ones shouted at Lakhi as she entered the gate: "Empress Victoria is here!" while the others giggled loudly. Old Bhodai charged at the boys with clenched fists. But, Lakhi quickly handed him her umbrella and said: "Kokai, please go home. I'll report this to Headmaster Sir." Then she went up to her classroom and kept waiting near the door, hesitating to enter because the boys were making all sorts of comments about her. And, as soon as the teacher came, she followed him into the class. As she sat down, she noticed a slip of paper held down with a small stone on her desk. It contained a note. The moment Lakhi glanced at it, her face turned red in shame and anger. A parody of a common folk saying was scribbled on it and it read: "The Brahmin widow is demanding attention because she too wants to be like all the others." Clutching the paper in her hand, for a few seconds Lakhi stared helplessly at the boys who looked back at her insolently, some of them trying to suppress a giggle. Suddenly, she was filled with rage. How dare these boys who were no bigger than her younger brother, insult her in this manner! She became livid with a helpless anger. All this while, their English teacher, Ajay Ganguli, had been observing her. From her expression, he could guess that something was really wrong. He stretched out his hand towards her and said, "Lakhipriya, please pass that chit to me." Once Ganguly read the note, he flared up in anger. "Uncivilized brutes! Who has written this? If you don't own up at once, I shall beat all of you black and blue!' He kept striking his table with his cane as he spoke. The boys had never seen their teacher so angry. Being new-comers to the Middle English school, most of the boys were not as yet accustomed to the moods of the teachers. As the boys cowed in silence, Ganguli rushed up to the front row of benches and freely used his cane on them. The brighter students of the class who were not used to corporal punishment usually occupied the front row. So, after just a few lashes, one of the boys burst out in pain: "Sir, it's not me. Girin has done it." Within seconds, the offender was dragged out by the teacher from the back-benches and given a sound beating. The boy didn't take too long to confess his crime: "Sir, I did it because a senior had asked me to," he cried out, "I'll never do it again." Ganguli now slowly walked back to his seat. He was exhausted by then. Before this, there had been many instances when he was angry with the students. But that was because they had been slack in their studies or had lied to him. But his anger that day was of a completely different kind. He seemed deeply upset by the symptoms of a deadly social disease among his young pupils and was convinced that if this tendency was not nipped in the bud, it would spread through society like a plague. So, he followed up the corporal punishment with a verbal assault:

"Boys! There is no point trying to acquire knowledge if your attitudes are so base and narrow. Today you have been so mean and cruel to Lakhipriya who is like your elder sister. Soon, you will make fun of your own sisters when they come to study in a school. You may think that education is your monopoly because you are all frogs in a well. But, go to Bengal, and you will see that women there are successfully completing their school finals and getting entry into colleges too. In all the civilized countries of the world people are trying to improve the position of girl. And here you are, trying to deny an unfortunate woman her right to education. If you persist with this, a day will come when your own grandchildren will condemn you for your despicable role and I warn you, even the goddess of learning will never forgive you."

Each word from Ganguly Sir was like a sharp jab for the boys, most of whom were too young to realize what they had done. All of them felt deeply guilty over what had happened and they asked Lakhipriya to forgive them. From that day onwards, no one ever taunted Lakhipriya and, learning of the incident, the boys from the other classes too started looking upon her with respect. Meanwhile, Lakhi didn't take long to prove her merit and won a place among the best boys of her class.

Although the obstacles at school were overcome for the

time being, yet Lakhi's struggle within the family and with her near ones wasn't to end so easily. Uncle Hari Sarma's house was situated on the way to Lakhi's school. Sarma was a peskar at the kutcherry. But more than his official work, he was occupied with jobs like tying the sacred thread, casting or reading horoscopes or ceremonially bathing the salegram when some family got polluted because of a birth or a death. Sarma's eldest son, Krishna, was in high school. His daughter Subhadra was two years younger than Lakhi. Though married, she was still with her parents because she was yet to reach puberty. Subhadra could neither read nor write but was good at memorizing things and could recite the "Lakhi Panchali" from start to finish. She could also roll out the do's and don'ts listed in the almanac. Hari Sarma believed that if the womenfolk knew this list well, then there wouldn't be any slip regarding the forbidden items of food on given days, say, the eating of potatoes on pratipad or of coconuts on the asthami day. So, he had not spared any effort to educate his daughter along these lines. Having heard that Lakhipriya was going to school, Subhadra too had once expressed her wish to study. But, when her father quoted the scriptures to show how dreadful the effect would be if women took to books, Subhadra never dared to bring up the topic again. Lakhi's untimely widowhood was seen by Hari Sarma as a vindication of his views. He repeatedly reminded the womenfolk of his family about how his prediction regarding Lakhi's married life had come true and used to quote from the scriptures to prove his point. But Hari Sarma's self-confidence was suddenly shaken when he saw Lakhi passing by his house every morning on her way to the primary school. He rushed to his brother Panchanan Sarma in an effort to save his simple womenfolk from such an ominous influence. And, when he failed to convince his brother with his endless arguments, Hari Sarma grumbled his way out, all the while casting doubts on his brother's state of mind. He decided he would never visit his brother again.

Hari Sarma had got the news of Lakhi's having come first in the district and securing a scholarship. He just couldn't accept the fact that a widowed girl could do so well when his own son, after all his efforts, had failed to make a mark. Finally, when he saw Lakhi going to the boys' school, Hari Sarma was simply flabbergasted. He just couldn't believe his eyes. One afternoon, unable to check his curiosity any longer, he stood by the bamboo stile gate in front of his house and waited for Lakhi's return from school. On seeing her uncle from a distance, Lakhi tried to quickly pass by the house using her umbrella as a shield to cover her face. But, her uncle shouted to her to stop. Even as a hesitant Lakhi slowed down her pace, Sarma asked her with a crooked smile playing on his lips:

"It seems nowadays you go to the M. E. school."

"Yes, I do", Lakhi calmly answered.

"Well, aren't you ashamed to study with all those boys? Where has one heard of such a thing? Panchanan Kakaideo must have lost his mind. To send a widowed girl out into the streets is in itself a sin. But to allow such a girl to sit with the boys in the same class! You all may not have any sense of shame. But you certainly don't have the right to spoil all the boys, understand?" Sarma had put some extra stress on the word 'right' as if he was dealing with some government petition. Usually, after such an outburst, few would dare to speak out. But Lakhi was very angry and agitated. First, Hari Sarma had called her father mad. Then, he was casting aspersions on her character. She looked straight into her uncle's eyes and said rather agitatedly:

"I haven't been troubling the boys in any manner. I am just studying in school, not indulging in any sinful activities."

"Ah! Leave it!" Sarma said with a contemptuous grunt. "How can the boys pay attention to their studies with a grown up girl sitting right in their midst?"

Each word spoken by Hari Sarma seemed to pierce through Lakhi like a barb. These days she had learnt to tolerate many things and whenever possible, she also avoided answering back. But that afternoon her uncle's words pushed her patience to its limits and the indignation and anger that had been pent up for a long time just burst forth. She suddenly saw her uncle as her main enemy. So, without thinking of the consequences, she gave him a steadfast stare and said in a fearless, composed voice:

"So what if they can't pay any attention to their studies? If I can study in the presence of all those boys, why is it that they can't, just because of me? It seems that the boys are weaker in mind than the girls. And, you have been admonishing me for being a widow. Was I a widow from birth? All of you got together to get me married. I never set foot in my husband's house. Yet I am not allowed to stay like an unmarried girl. Am I to blame for my widowhood? Of course, I will study. You have always maintained that girls who study end up as widows. But what do you have to say about widows who study? Maybe they'll have to rot in unending hell? But, I am not afraid of all that. I will go to hell if need be!" Lakhi's face was flushed red and her eyes were filled with tears.

Hari Sarma was simply dumbstruck. The courage of this wisp of a girl! To answer him right on his face like this! He shouted out in uncontrollable anger:

"What impudence! So, this is what your parents have been teaching you? Instead of keeping fasts and praying for the salvation of her husband's soul, this widow tries to show off through her studies! Well, will you be a clerk or a mohuri?"

"I have no wish of becoming either a clerk or a mohuri. I just want to be a human being. My husband died of dysentery. He did not die because of my sins. Thousands of people die of disease. No one dies because of the sins of others. Borkhuri also died of dysentery. But within a few months of her death, you brought another khuri. How many fasts did you keep for Borkhuri's soul?"

This time Hari Sarma couldn't control himself any longer. Holding on fast to one of the bamboo poles of the stile, he said with gritted teeth: "Will you disappear from here or not? Else I will give you a smart…" Before he could finish his sentence, poor Bhadai intervened with folded hands and pleaded:

"Dadaiti, please don't take Aijani's words too seriously. Grief has affected her mind. Come on Aiti…"

Saying this, Bhadai hurriedly led Lakhi away from the scene.

The moment Lakhi reached home, she rushed to her father and, in between sobs, narrated her experience. As he listened to his daughter, Panchanan Sarma was filled with a new sense of determination. Now that his brother had behaved in such a manner, he resolved to stand by his daughter at any cost. He decided that he just wouldn't care for the likes of Hari Sarma. He had always considered himself to be above people like them. Moreover, ever since he came into contact with Gunabhiram Barua, he was trying to see himself as one with a liberal outlook. And, now listening to his daughter's plight, of how she was accosted and abused on her way to school, Panchanan suddenly saw himself in the role of a social reformer. He felt that it was his duty to protect the helpless ones like Lakhi. Trying to console his daughter, he said:

"Ai, don't you worry. Think of Goddess Saraswati and go on with your studies. No one can harm you. I will go to Hari this evening and give him a piece of my mind. Who is he to accost and scold my daughter? From tomorrow give up that way to school. Take the one which skirts the pond. There is no point talking to anyone on the way. Keep quiet even if someone says something and don't enter into any arguments unnecessarily. There's no point complicating matters."

3

Swarna had spent a year in Calcutta. As her vacation approached, Gunabhiram went there to bring her home. Bishnupriya could not accompany him this time for she had become the mother of another baby boy. The newborn had been named Jnanadabhiram. But such a high-sounding name did not seem to match such a small creature. So, he was being called by commonly used names like Konbupa, Ponakan or Bhaiti-kon.

There was a lot of excitement over Swarna's coming home. Everyone was planning to welcome her in some special way. Bishnupriya got chira and akhoi made for her at home from the choicest joha rice and herself cooked Swarna's favourite fish, tenga aanja, to be served to her on the day she arrived. And, as the carriage drew up in front of Bilwa Kutir that evening, everyone—Karuna, Kamala, the cook, the servant girls—rushed out to greet her. Bishnupriya too came out to the verandah, carrying her baby. As she alighted from the carriage, Swarna looked all around her. The house and its compound were exactly as she had left them, with both the bokel and bilwa trees standing there in the front courtyard. But, strangely enough, it was she who now felt somewhat out of place. Her brothers Karuna and Kamala had grown a lot in the time she'd spent away from home. They too felt shy on seeing her and lowered their heads. Going up to her mother, Swarnalata gently uncovered the baby's face from the swaddle of clothes and gave him a kiss. She took an instant liking to her fair and chubby little brother.

In this one year, Swarna's appearance naturally had not undergone any marked change. Yet, Bishnupriya noticed that her daughter had thinned down a bit. She had also grown taller. But what struck her most was the change in her manner of speaking. Not having spoken Assamese for almost a year, it was quite natural for her to use a Bengali word every now and then. She, however, promptly corrected herself when her brothers laughed at these slips. In her one year at Calcutta, Swarna had picked up quite a lot of Bengali and could now speak it fluently. In the hostel, she spoke mostly in Bengali with her friends. In the classroom, however, the British teachers always spoke in English and insisted the girls do the same. During her first few days at home, Swarna spoke almost incessantly about life at school and in the hostel. She made everyone laugh by narrating some funny incident about her and would describe in detail the awkward situations that took place because of the mistakes she made while speaking Bengali. She told her parents how, on one occasion, seeing her running from shop to shop in search of a beji, the shopkeepers thought she was insane. It was only much later that she realized that beji which meant a needle in Assamese was actually a mongoose in Bengali!

Every day at meal time Swarna would talk about the hostel food. She narrated how everything there was so full of spices and how at first she could eat almost nothing; of how, only later on, the hostel superintendent learnt of her plight and started arranging for *ajhali* or spice free food for her; of how she would also occasionally send Swarna some white joha rice from her own share. The Bengali girls would, however, relish their parboiled rice with hot gravy and make fun of her white rice and bland curry by calling her a Brahmin widow. Swarna would also talk often about Miss Lipscombe and Miss Mitter and of how they would often invite her home and offer her cakes and pastries.

On Sundays, someone from the Basu family would come to take Swarna to spend the day at their place. It was there that she would be offered all sorts of nice delicacies to eat. Some would even be packed to be carried to the hostel where her friends would be eagerly waiting to share them. But, listening to Swarnalata's accounts of her hostel life would invariably make Bishnupriya sad. She felt that her daughter was not getting enough good food. But she knew she couldn't do much from such a distance. She kept on thinking if only some day she could go to Calcutta and stay with her daughter. But right then it was simply out of the question. She also had to think of her husband's job and of bringing up her young sons. So, she decided that it would be better to take care of her daughter and try to improve her health while she was at home.

Ever since she came home, Swarna was dying to meet Tora. It was almost three years now since they had last met. She had learnt from her mother of Tora's return from America and of how she was now quite grown up and accomplished. Having had to leave school mid-way because of her trip to America, she had now gone back to her studies. Moreover, during her spare time, she also helped in the morning duties of the mission's hospital, and her knowledge of nursing picked up during her brief stay in America was proving to be very useful.

Within a few days of Swarna's arrival, Tora turned up at Bilwa Kutir. Swarna noticed that her appearance had changed quite a lot. Instead of the usual mekhala–chador, she was now wearing a white saree with a blue border. She was wearing socks along with a pair of sandals with buckles. Since it was winter, she also had on a short warm coat, bought in America, over her saree and had walked alone all the way from Christianpatty to Bilwa Kutir. Just like in earlier days, Swarna kept on looking with awestruck eyes at Tora. She had hoped that with all her newly gained Calcutta experiences she would finally be able to match Tora, if not better her. But she had never imagined that Tora would mature so fast and already look like a grown-up lady. Thinking that Tora must also have grown wiser than her in the ways of the world, Swarna felt a bit sad. She was troubled by the feeling that perhaps she would never be able to match her. But within seconds of her arrival at Bilwa Kutir, all these doubts were dispelled. As in old times, Tora affectionately pinched Swarna's cheeks and said:

"You have grown a lot, Swarna. But all the Calcutta sweets have not been able to add any weight on you. Poor girl, you must be having awful food at the hostel. You know, Swarna, there is something unique in a mother's cooking and nowhere else in the world will you ever taste it. "

The two friends spent the morning talking of many things and trying to catch up with the happenings in each other's lives. Tora began by telling Swarna about her American experience. But Swarna felt that somehow Tora's earlier zeal for her foreign trip was missing and she no longer seemed as enthusiastic while talking about the white men and women. Eventually, when Swarna asked her which place she liked better, America or her own country, all of a sudden Tora expressed her true feelings:

"It is very nice to say there. Roads, vehicles, machines and so many other things. Compared to all that, our place is like a deep jungle. The people there seem to look upon our people as mere beggars. Even then, I like it here. Here all the people are like us. There are rich and poor, high and lower castes. Yet the people are the same. There I felt like a clown. The children would surround and stare at me in the streets. Some would clap their hands and shout "Nigger! Nigger!" It was only later that I came to know that nigger meant Negro, the black people of Africa. We are much fairer than them. Yet, in the eyes of the white sahibs we are all niggers."

"But, the missionaries aren't like that are they? They love you so much," Swarna asked in surprise.

"Of course, they do. Even there, everyone loved me a lot. But I couldn't help feeling that they actually only pitied us. Do you know what happened one day? Mind you, you are not to tell this to anyone, right?" Swarna nodded and Tora continued:

"One day at a church in Boston, there was a small congregation of young children after the morning prayers. It was here that a padre sahib made me stand up and, introducing me to the gathering, said: 'Here is a girl who has come from a village in India. It is a dangerous place covered by thick jungles. Our missionaries have braved strong odds to go there and spread the light of the Gospel among these savage people. Look at this girl. It is we who have given her the light of civilization and made her what she is today.' I was very upset at these words. I just couldn't keep mum and stood up and told the audience: 'Dear brothers and sisters. I am thankful to the padres for bringing me to this distant place. But please do not think that my town, Nagaon, does not have any civilized people. There we have lots of Hindus and Muslims and people of other faiths whose children are getting educated and marching ahead.' I told them about you too, Swarna—that you have gone to stay at a boarding school at Calcutta. But the missionary father later scolded me for what I said. He insisted that I had criticized their work. This really hurt me."

Hearing Tora's words, Swarna's face lit up with a smile. She was elated to know that Tora had spoken about her to all those children of a foreign land… She then began sharing some of her own experiences with Tora:

"Actually, people from outside have no idea whatsoever about our Assam. That's why they think that we are all uncivilized. The girls in my class often ask me: 'Which side is the district of Assam? To Calcutta's east or west?' Swarna broke into a laugh as she tried to imitate their manner of speaking."

"What else do they say?" Tora asked eagerly.

"The other day a senior girl came and told the class that the people of Assam do not wear any clothes and that they eat raw meat. I just cried out of anger. Later on, Miss Lipscombe gave the girl a good scolding."

That day, even as they kept talking, a new bond of friendship seemed to grow between the two girls. It was as if the two friends had finally come out of their adolescent dreamland into the world of hard reality. Stringing together the little bits of experience which they had picked up during the last few years, they seemed to realize that the real world was indeed a cruel and difficult one. But they realized that even within that, there was enough space to weave one's dreams. Swarna spoke out with childlike enthusiasm:

"I will write a book when I grow up. There I will write all the good things about our Asom Desh, so that no one can call us uncivilized. In that book I will write about you, your mother, my mother and Lakhi's story. Don't you know that Lakhi is now studying at the boys' M.E. school? She is a very brave girl. She visited us yesterday."

"I too met her the other day. She's become so beautiful. It would be really nice if some boy from a good family marries her. But unfortunately Brahmins never marry widows. Lakhi is such a good soul. When I told her that after passing my normal examination I would teach in a school at Baliram, she heaved a sigh and said that she too would like to work somewhere. She is very keen to be a teacher."

The two friends kept talking. From an adjacent room Bishnupriya heard bits and pieces of their conversation and reflected on how experience changes people. These two girls who had grown up in front of her eyes could now speak so wisely about the world, and of things which had never worried her when she was their age. Wasn't this, she thought, a sign of the changing times? All of a sudden Bishnupriya felt that Tora and Swarna were now her close companions. It was as if she had a lot to learn from them.

4

Lakheswar spent the first two years of his stay at Calcutta with some Assamese students at a Bengali boys hostel. The unfamiliar surroundings of the city, the change in lifestyle, the new type of food and the problem of communicating with others, had all forced him to keep a low profile during the first few months. Then, one day, having received a letter and a money-order from Gunabhiram Barua, he thought it would perhaps be proper to pay a visit to Swarnalata at her hostel. But, he was still unfamiliar with Calcutta roads. So, he requested one of his Bengali friends to accompany him. Haradhan Ghosh found the idea of visiting a girls' school quite attractive and immediately agreed. Ghosh, however, was a bit intrigued that a boy like Lakheswar knew someone at the Bethune School. As far as he knew, only girls from rich and aristocratic Brahmo families studied at Bethune. However, of late, a few girls from rich Hindu families had also started going to the school in well-covered horse carriages. But for the average Bengalis, these girls seemed to belong to some other planet. As such, like his other friends, Haradhan too had long desired to have a close look at the Bethune girls.

There arose a real surprise waiting for Haradhan when he reached Bethune School along with Lakheswar. On seeing Swarna, he felt that he was in the presence of a real fairy. He had never imagined such beauty and grace at so tender an age.

And, even a talkative boy like Haradhan whose spirits nothing could really dampen, was forced to put on a reserve when he learnt that Swarna was the daughter of the Chota Laat of Assam. And even as the two boys were trying to take in the unfamiliar surroundings and strike a conversation with Swarnalata, they noticed a well-kept family buggy coming to a halt in front of the school. A gentleman and a lady alighted from the carriage and from their very bearings Lakheswar and his friend could judge that they belonged to some rich Calcutta family. The style in which the lady was wearing her saree showed her to be a Brahmo. The couple signed the visitors' book and entered the visitors' room where Lakheswar and Haradhan were sitting. As they came in, Swarna gave them a bright smile and bowed and touched their feet. Meanwhile, Lakheswar and Haradhan kept standing awkwardly in a corner of the large room. But it was with great eagerness that Swarna introduced them to her Kaka and Kakima. Only then did Lakheswar realize that they were none other than the famous Calcutta barrister, Ananandaram Basu and his wife. Who among the educated elite of the city hadn't heard of them, thought Lakheswar. For, in those days one could actually count the number of Indian barristers on one's fingertips. Basu, of course, had other distinctions to his credit. Having secured a first class in his Mathematics Tripos, he happened to be the first Indian Wrangler at Cambridge. Anandaram Basu was also known as a leading Brahmo pioneer in the field of women's education. Therefore, Haradhan and Lakheswar considered themselves highly privileged to have met such a personality. Yet, somewhat over-awed by the presence of Swarna's elite guests, they thought it best to leave early.

On their way back to the hostel, unable to stem his curiosity, Haradhan kept questioning Lakheswar about Swarna. What was Lakheswar's relationship with Swarna's family? How did Swarna's father know Anandaram Basu? Lakheswar understood immediately that this was his moment of triumph. He just couldn't let this moment slip away. Seeing this to be a golden opportunity to prove to his Bengali hostel mates that he too came from a rich and well-known family, Lakheswar ended up telling a whole lot of lies. And, as he listened to Lakheswar, Haradhan seemed convinced that his father was either a big zamindar or some small rajah of Assam. Lakheswar told Haradhan that there were quite a few chota laats and barristers in his family; that even Swarna's father had stayed at their place and studied. He related how, later on, her father became a Brahmo and married a widow and was socially ostracized and how till date his people did not take a drop of water at Swarna's place. Lakheswar insisted that it was only because of his liberal convictions that he had kept links with that family.

By the time they reached their hostel from Bethune College, Lakheswar had fooled Haradhan completely. Had he heard all this on some other day or at some other occasion, an intelligent boy like Haradhan would not have believed Lakheswar's words. But on that particular day his experience at Bethune School, the meeting with Swarnalata and Ananadamohan Basu and everything else combined to cast such a spell on Haradhan that he unquestioningly took in all that Lakheswar said. And, from that day onwards, Lakheswar's position in the hostel improved perceptibly and the Bengali boys started keeping a respectful distance from the boroloker chele. On his part, Lakheswar re-inforced his boroloker status by buying a fine mill-made dhoti, a kameej and a pair of nice pump shoes with the money that Gunabhiram Barua had sent him.

Lakheswar's appearance underwent a remarkable change by the time he passed his F. A. examination and joined the B. A. class. He dropped his Brahmin's tuft and gave himself a modern hair-cut. He no longer wore his dhoti in the old style as at home but after the fashion of the Bengali bhadralok, with one end either held

by hand or tucked into the kameej pocket. In short, Lakheswar
was transformed into a complete bhardralok. And, as soon as he
became a graduate student, he shifted to another hostel where all
the inmates were Assamese and where, among other things, one
could always have one's pick of Assamese dishes like *khaar* and
tenga aanja made by an Oriya cook. Moreover, one could also
have the privilege of speaking only in Assamese and sometimes
have fun speaking wrong Bengali with the cook. All in all, the
inmates of this particular hostel had created a miniscule Assam
for themselves. As such, but for the time spent in commuting to
college or sometimes in shopping, these students managed to
spend their days without mixing much with the local population.
Staying in the city did not seem to affect the caste, village and
local identities of these young men who came from different
parts of Assam and they would often make fun of one another
by parodying their particular regional peculiarities of speech and
behaviour. Thus, those who were new to the city preferred the
place because it gave them a whiff of home, while the more
experienced ones came to stay here because of the camaraderie
and the secure feeling of staying with the flock.

Apart from these students, a number of visitors, stayed here
as guests of the boarders who in turn felt it to be their duty
to entertain a distant relative and show him around Calcutta.
The presence of these guests added to the homely atmosphere
of the hostel, with gossip from the different corners of Assam
adding to the excitement. It was for precisely these reasons that
Lakheswar had shifted here. At least here he felt quite sure about
his identity. In the mess where he had stayed earlier, he had often
felt somewhat inferior to his Bengali friends, especially when it
came to making conversation. He never could match the range
and depth of those few boys who had strong cultural backgrounds
whom Lakheswar considered to be his equals. Once, there was
a debate between two Bengali boarders over Chaitanya Prabhu.

One was an ardent follower of Sri Chaitanya, while the other was a Shakta, a worshipper of the Mother Goddess. While one tried to prove that Chaitanya and Nityananda were both avatars of Sri Krishna, the other insisted that Chaitanya was actually a devotee of Sri Krishna and hence couldn't be God himself. He argued that the bhakta or devotee could not be seen as God. To counter this, the Vaishnanva student recited freely from Chaitanya's compositions to show that one could really lose oneself in God and, in the process, become a part of God Himself. The debate went on like this for quite some time. The other inmates of the mess also joined in and arguments for and against flowed freely. Seeing that the Assamese boys were keeping silent, one of the Bengali boarders asked Lakheswar:

"Hey, Kataki. Who is the main Vaishnava guru in your part of the country?"

"A saint called Srimanta Sankardev preached Vaishnavism in our region."

"Could you tell us where his views tallied with those of our Sri Chaitanya?"

Lakheswar was now in a real fix. He had only heard the name of Sankardev. He hadn't read anything by the saint nor had he tried to know about his life. All that he had heard about Sankardev was from Gunabhiram Barua. However, unwilling to show his ignorance before his Bengali friends, he looked around and said with a smile:

"Both of them said the same things. Only their languages were different."

"That means Sankardev too spoke of attaining Krishna through Radha's love?" one of the boys asked.

"Yes, there are quite a few borgeets on this theme written by Sankardev."

Lakheswar had hoped that the other Assamese boys in the room would be equally ignorant on the matter and, as such, there would be none to counter what he had said. But Lakheswar's luck failed him that day. A boy from Sivasagar, Dharmakanta Barua, had been quietly sitting in a corner and listening to the discussion. Usually Darmakanta was reticent by nature and spoke little. Yet he never kept quiet when there was a point to be made. As soon as Lakheswar finished with his comment, Dharmakanta protested:

"Kataky, maybe you haven't read anything about Sankardev. Otherwise, you wouldn't say such things. From what little I know, Sankardev never gave any stress on the singara rasa as Chaitanya does. He has called the devotee a servant of servants, the truest being the Muktita Nishpriha or the one who is freed of all desire. You shouldn't have spoken about a mahapurush like this without knowing anything." Though clearly trapped, Lakheswar tried to lighten the matter by saying:

"Ah! Leave it Barua. Neither of us really knows anything about Sankardev. So, who will decide on who is right and who is wrong?"

This time, Dharmakant retorted angrily:

"Not to know about your language, religion and culture is no matter of pride, Kataky. All of us present here should be ashamed that we do not know about Sankardev and our literary heritage, and yet have come here to study English literature."

No one dared to oppose what Dhramakanta said. They knew he was different. No one would be able to stop him if he got angry. So, Lakheswar too kept quiet. But that very day, Lakheswar decided that, rather than suffer humiliation like this in front of his Bengali friends, it would be better to move into a completely Assamese hostel.

Dharmakanta, however, continued to stay at the Bengali boys' hostel. But the discussion left such a deep imprint on his mind that a few days later he turned up at the Assamese living quarters.

He was eager to discuss the matter with the other Assamese students. Expressing his resentment, he declared:

"We the Assamese boys do not know anything about our language and culture. Isn't it a matter of great shame? He who doesn't know himself, how will he know others? Like the small mulberry plant which tries to pass off as a giant banyan tree in a land where there are no tall trees, we too are filled with false pride and see ourselves as important people of our regions. We hesitate to talk to others, lest our ignorance is revealed. Just look at our fellow Bengali students who are so proud of their language and culture and who have such lively discussions. It is only we who shrink from discussing our own people. We come to know of the terror unleashed on the coolies in Assam's tea-gardens only from the Bengali papers. We wait to learn about our Sankardev from Bengali books."

Although a few of the inmates initially tried to make fun of Dharmakanta's excitement, most of the other boys listened to him attentively. His words seemed to leave their mark on them and one of the boys said in a thoughtful tone:

"If we have to know about Sankardev, then we'll have to go to the satras and find out the *carit-puthis*. There isn't a single biography of the saint written in simple Assamese language."

"It is we who must write," asserted Dharmakanta forcefully.

"Yes, but where do we have the time? Right now our time is taken up in reading the biographies of Keats, Byron and Shelley. We'll have to do something only after we finish our studies."

Dharmakanta became restless. He failed to understand this tendency of postponing things among the youth of his region.

"No, No! It will not do if one keeps pushing matters to others. It is we who must accept some responsibility and do something. A history of Assamese literature must be written, a list of all the writers, young and old, must be compiled and the biographies of the saints must be prepared. We also need a newspaper to highlight the problems of the people of our region," Dharmakanta said all this in one breath and even before he finished, another boy jocularly added:

"Well, Barua, do you wish to achieve all this at one go? But all this would require an age. Don't you worry, everything will happen in its own slow pace."

"I simply detest this *lahe lahe* attitude. This has made our people lazy. That which is to be done must be done in one night. Otherwise, it will never be done." It seemed as if Dharmakanta had said the final word

"You have spoken just like Lachit Barphukan did to his uncle. How many uncles will you behead if the work is not accomplished in time?" asked Nakul Goswami, a boy from Jorhat who could not gauge the depth of Dharmakanta's feelings.

"If need be, I will behead all my uncles," thundered Dhamkanta as he left the room in a huff. But some of his friends rushed after him and managed to bring him back for a cup of tea. From then onwards, the Assamese students started referring to Dharmakanta as Lachit.

Dharmakanta was very different from others. He did not have any close friends among the Assamese students and loved spending his spare time roaming the streets of Calcutta all alone. No one had any idea of where he actually went. He would bring back books and would be immersed in them. When he spoke, it was never about mundane everyday matters. When it came to discussing the country, its people and their history, Dharmakanta would get quite excited and go on for hours. But, the moment he realized that some people weren't really paying attention, he would promptly leave that place. Dharmakanta was quite popular with the Bengali students, for without him their adda wouldn't warm up. So, whenever some debatable issue cropped up at the hostel, Dharmakanta would be sought out and asked to give his views. On his part, Dharmakanta was a great believer in the power of reason and he would never be upset if someone refuted his arguments in a rational manner. But he wouldn't tolerate if anyone tried to make light of a serious discussion with silly remarks.

Dharmakanta was now a final year student of the graduate course at Presidency College and he was quite serious about his studies. So, it was natural that his teachers and fellow students expected him to do well in the B.A. examination. But not many knew much about his personal life. For, Dharmakanta rarely talked about home. All that his friends knew about him was that he belonged to some place near Sivasagar and that, having lost his father at a tender age, he had grown up with his uncle who worked in a tea garden. No one seemed to know that Dharmakanta's father, Lokenath Barua, was a close friend of Piyali Barua and had been convicted for treason by the British government and sentenced to life imprisonment in the Andamans during the trial of Piyali and Maniram Dewan. His father had died in the cellular jail in the Andamans after serving just about two years of his prison term. Dharmakanta was not yet born when his father passed away. Lokenath, along with other members of the Ahom aristocracy, had secretly met to devise ways of ousting the British from Assam and restoring King Kandarpeswar Singha to the throne. But the plot was discovered and the British were unduly swift with their punishment. Barely six months after Maniram and Piyali were hanged Dharmakanta was born in his uncle's house. The other freedom fighters were given long jail terms by the British. His uncle was then a head clerk in a European garden. Afraid of incurring the wrath of his employers, he had discouraged his family members of even uttering the name of his brother-in-law. All that Dharmakanta saw from his very early age was that his mother would break into sobs whenever he asked about his father. Only after he had grown up a little and

could understand things, did his mother make him sit by her side
and tell him about his father. He had been quite surprised at his
mother's attitude. Her whole face would brighten up whenever
she narrated incidents about her husband. In one such moment,
his mother had told him:

"Kakaideo has given us shelter. He is also taking care of your
education. We will never be able to repay our debt to him. All
these days I have kept quiet fearing that he would face problems
with his job because of us. Otherwise, I would never have hidden
from you the facts of life of a brave person like your father. He
didn't go to prison because of robbery or theft. It was for his
country that he went to prison and died. I only wish that you
too grow up with an independent mind like your father's. You
needn't be a servant of the English government which was your
father's enemy."

Listening to his mother's words, the young Dharmakanta
would be puzzled with many a conflicting thought. He thought
of taking revenge on those who were responsible for his father's
death. But he had no clue about the sahib who had sentenced
his father. Sometimes he would think about raising an army with
his friends to fight and drive out the British. All this eventually
turned Dharmakanta into a sort of introvert. He felt increasingly
isolated. He felt that he could never reveal to anyone the thoughts
that constantly troubled his mind.

It was his mother's strong desire which brought Dharmakanta
to Calcutta for higher studies. She met the expenses of his
education by selling off whatever little land was left them after
the government confiscated their property. When Dharmakanta
was a student at the Sivasagar High School, his teacher Gopal
Chandra Ghosh developed a liking for him. And it was from
him that he came to know about great personalities like Raja
Rammohan Roy and Ishwar Chandra Vidyasagar. He still
remembered clearly how Ghosh Sir kept telling them that the

British would never have been able to subjugate the Indians had the latter not fallen prey to various social ills and superstitions. Dharmakanta would also frequently recall how his teacher kept on insisting that only when people's minds were enlightened with modern ideas, would they be able to stand up against the colonial rulers. How inspired all of them were when Ghosh Sir had told them that the nation would grow strong only if it could build up mass movements against superstitions and prejudices of all shades

Apart from Ghosh Sir, there was also Gopal Babu from whom Dharmakanta learnt about the main tenets of the Brahmo faith. At that time there were quite a few educated Bengalis in Sivasagar who had embraced Brahmoism and they would meet regularly for religious discussions and prayers. Dharmakanta quite often would accompany Gopal Babu to these sessions. But ultimately, the Brahmo faith failed to attract him. For, even at that young age, Dharmakanta had developed an aversion to all forms of narrowness of thought whether they were caste prejudices or just simple gossip about others. So, it didn't take him long to discover serious limitations even within the apparently broad liberal framework of the Brahmo faith. Listening to them, Dharmakanta felt that the Brahmos seemed to look upon themselves as the only people on earth who were on the right path.

While in Calcutta, a major change occurred in Dharmakanta's life. The embers of revenge which he had long nurtured, gradually took the form of a new fire. He could now see that hundred years of British rule had not only made orphans of a few individuals like him, but had taken away everything from the thousands of tea labourers, jute mill workers and peasants who were being forced to work in the indigo plantations. He thought of his father who had been inspired by a high ideal to sacrifice his life and became a martyr. But these poor workers were being denied even that little satisfaction of dying for a cause; they were all dying a slow death, while their British masters were reaping huge profits out of their sweat and blood. It was from the Bengali journal, *Bharat Shramjivi*, that Dharmakanta first came to know of all this. He was gripped by the paper's inspired language and heart-rending portrayal of the life of the workers and decided that he would have to meet the editor, Sashipada Banerjee. Finally, he managed to trace the editor's address and went to see him. Banerjee's personality and sense of idealism left a deep mark on Dharmakanta. Here was a person who, without belonging to the Brahmo Samaj, was trying to bring about a social revolution. He and his wife had set up a school for widows at the Baranagar area of the city and, despite grave social opposition, got several of the widows married. A night school for the workers and a workingmen's club were part of his efforts, although most of his time was taken up in publishing the *Bharat Shramjivi* regularly. Dharmakanta was deeply moved by Banerjee's sense of self-sacrifice, his humanism and his endless capacity for work and he offered to collect stories for Banerjee Babu's paper. And so, when he went home for the holidays, he gathered many a poignant story about the lives of the poverty-ridden tea workers of Assam. The other Assamese students, however, were not aware of this aspect of Dharmakanta's life. They usually kept a respectful distance from him because of his quiet and thoughtful nature.

After Dharmakanta's outburst at Lakheswar's hostel about the ignorance of the Assamese boys, some of them felt that it would be proper to have a discussion group. Several years ago, Manikchandra Barua, Ganga Govinda Phukan, Jagannath Barua and others, who were studying in Calcutta, had started a Sahitya Sabha. However, once they left Calcutta, the Sabha too stopped functioning. The boys in the hostel now started planning a Sabha on the same lines as the earlier one. At first not all the boys were equally enthusiastic about the idea and some were clearly indifferent. But once they learnt that every now and then some important person from Assam would be requested to come and address the discussion group, they immediately agreed to help. For, none of them wanted to miss the opportunity of meeting people who might be of help in their future careers.

The students decided that Gunabhiram Barua who was Assam's Chota Laat and a frequent visitor to Calcutta, be requested to inaugurate the first session of the Sabha. Lakheswar was asked to contact Barua Dangoria as he seemed to know him quite well. Luckily, Gunabhiram happened to be in Calcutta at that time. So, along with two of his friends, Lakheswar turned up at Anandamohan Basu's place to meet Barua. The young students were at first overawed by their big mansion and their western style of living, but the politeness and courtesy of the family members soon put them at ease. Barua readily agreed to the suggestion and soon the details of the inaugural meeting were chalked out. Barua's enthusiasm knew no bounds. He was especially happy to see Lakheswar's love for Assamese literature. That very evening, Swarna too had come from her hostel to stay with the Basu family. She too joined in the conversation and offered her own suggestions. The two boys, Durgeswar Gohain and Nabin Saikia, who had accompanied Lakheswar, were both enamoured by Swarna's beauty and behaviour. They couldn't even imagine that Assamese girls had advanced so far in education. All these days they had been made to believe that girls exposed to Western education invariably went astray. They had been told that educated girls flirted with boys, had little respect for elders and were shameless and degraded in all possible ways. But they couldn't detect a trace of any of these faults in Swarnalata. Instead, her poise and grace coupled with her eagerness to learn made even these young students realize for the first time the importance of education for women.

That evening when they returned to their hostel, Durgeswar and Nabin tried very subtly to find out something more about

Swarnalata. Aware of his friends' curiosity, Lakheswar tried as usual to add to his importance and, just to make them envious, said:

"Hakim Dangoria has been trying to get Swarnalata married to me. But one can't take the risk of being socially ostracized by marrying a Brahmo girl. Moreover, Hakim Dangoria has himself married a widow. They should know that no young man from a respectable family would ever marry their daughter."

Lakheswar's harsh comments evoked a lot of sympathy for Swarnalata among the two boys and Durgeswar said with a sigh: "Well, our society is still too backward. Otherwise would there ever be any dearth of eligible grooms for such a girl."

"Why don't you try if you have the courage? Even if society ostracizes you, there will be much to gain," said Lakheswar in a lighter vein.

Irritated at Lakheswar's flippant remark, Durgeswar replied: "Kataki, if you really disapprove of Gunabhiram Barua because he is a Brahmo and because he has married a widow, then why do you go around trying to please him? Why do you talk to him about reforming society? Is it because of the money he sends you every month? If the Hakim Saheb is entertaining some false hopes about you, then you should tell him openly that you will be marrying a little nine-year old girl chosen by your parents."

It was perhaps the image of Swarnalata still bright in his mind, that provoked Durgeswar out of his usual reticence. Lakheswar was quite taken aback by the boy's anger and realizing that things had gone a bit too far, he made an excuse and quietly slipped away.

It was on a Wednesday afternoon that the discussion group met for the first time at the Assamese Boys' Hostel. While inaugurating the discussion, Gunabhiram gave a lucid account of Assam's ancient culture and civilization. His words excited everyone. Then came the turn of the students to speak. Most of them presented re-touched pieces which had already appeared in *Orunodoi* or in the Bengali papers. There were also a few translations of English articles. In the end, Dharmakanta rose to speak. He had no written presentation to make but he spoke fluently, without faltering. He began by discussing the lack of a proper atmosphere for literary studies in his province of Assam and regretted the fact that there was no history of Assamese literature or even a dependable Assamese dictionary. In contrast, there were so many journals and newspapers in neighbouring Bengal. In Assam, after *Orunodoi,* the only other journal called *Assam Bilasini* too had to shut down. Educated Assamese youth were not playing their part to develop their own literature. Dharmakanta also spoke on Assam's economic backwardness. The European tea planters were making huge amounts of money but the condition of the common people had remained the same. He went on to describe the plight of the tea-garden workers in heart-rending detail.

Gunabhiram Barua listened intently to Dharmakanta. The young man's intelligent face, his sharp and eager eyes and firm voice reminded Barua of his own youth. He too had once deeply wished to light the fire of reform and burn to ashes all the unwanted rubbish of society. But all these years he had not been able to achieve anything much. He couldn't help thinking whether pitting his own personal life as an example of protest against society's prejudices had really been of any help. After all, he had not yet succeeded in building up a social movement against these ills. Gunbhiram now felt that Dharmakanta's accusations seemed merely a reflection of his own conscience.

Once the meeting was over, Gunabhiram called Dharmakanta to his side and tried to find out more about the young man. Learning that he was the son of Lokenath Barua of Sivasagar, Gunabhiram praised him as the worthy son of a worthy father. For once, Dharmakanta did not have to face an embarrassing silence after giving his father's identity. Even though Gunabhiram Barua was a highly placed official of the British government, he didn't shrink on hearing Lakenath Barua's name. On the contrary, he referred to him as a brave son of Assam. Dharmakanta's regard for Gunabhiram Barua grew.

After this, Dharmakanta met Gunabhiram Barua several times and they talked of many things. It was on one such occasion that Gunabhiram Barua, while discussing the role of the Brahmo reformers of Bengal, bemoaned the fact that in Assam one didn't come across a single reformer after Sankardev and Madhavdev even though Assamese society was filled with superstitions and evil practices. Dharmakanta replied with zest to Barua's observations:

"There isn't anyone other than you who could lead such a movement in Assam. Plenty of people like me are looking up to you for such a move. Assamese society would benefit a lot if you could start a journal and through it spread the ideas of the new age."

Gunabhiram smiled sweetly and kept thinking. It was as if Dharmakanta's words were bringing back his self-confidence. Running his fingers through his beard, he said in a measured tone:

"I too have been thinking of bringing out a journal for quite some time now. Your enthusiasm has given me strength. But before us there have been several others who also thought of improving our society. For instance, people like Anandaram Dhekiyal Phukan, Maniram Dewan and others. It is with full respect to the efforts of these persons, that we must go ahead with our work. It is true that in recent times there has been no social movement in Assam. The main reason for this is the absence of knowledge. If we can give true knowledge of the sciences, the arts and literature to our people, then alone can we prove ourselves to be the true friends of Assam"

In the course of their discussion about the journal, Gunabhiram asked Dharmakanta about his future plans. Dharmakanta's mind was then filled with a thousand dreams. He was yet to fix his priorities. Somehow, the question of earning a livelihood did not figure at all in his plans. Gunabhiram did not wish to dampen the young man's zeal for social work. But, out of a fatherly sense of concern he told Dharmakanta that since he had decided against going in for a government job, he must think of some other means of earning a living. Otherwise, one could be forced to be dependant on others. And, this in turn, could compel one to give up one's beliefs and convictions. Gunabhiram followed this up with his views on starting an independent business like some of his acquaintances and friends in Assam who had started to deal with tea and timber. Some had even invested in river navigation companies. He told Dharmakanta that if he so wished, Gunabhiram would help him set up an independent business along with one of these friends.

Without giving the offer much thought, Dharmakanta agreed. The BA examination was still two months away so he was not overly concerned about a job just yet. But, soon after his return to Assam, Gunabhiram Barua wrote to Dharmakanta saying that the owner of the Tapatjuri tea estate near Nagaon, Devanath Barua, was willing to give him a job and so, he should come to Nagaon immediately after his examinations. In asking Dharmakanta to come to Assam, Gunabhiram had another purpose. He had hoped that with help from an enthusiastic young man like him, he would be able to begin his work on his journal.

Swarna too was occasionally present during Gunabhiram's conversations with Dharmakanta. After hearing about Dharmakanta's family from her father, Swarnalata was very curious to know more about this young man. But though Dharmakanta talked a lot about books and journals, about ideas and ideology, he rarely spoke about himself. Swarna noticed that whenever she gave an occasional comment while talking to him, Dharmakanta would pay a lot of attention to what she said and, unlike most other boys, wouldn't keep staring at her face. That was why Swarna came to like and respect Dharmakanta. She herself was then at that, critical juncture of adolescence and youth when each new relationship was bound to leave a deep impression. Later on, often, these early impressions change with experience. Nevertheless, they are never totally washed away. Swarna was deeply impressed by Dharmakanta's patriotism and idealism and she too quietly resolved to work for the good of Assamese culture and society. Though she hadn't read much of Assamese, as a first step of her new resolve, she now started writing to her parents in her mother tongue. This wasn't too easy for her in the beginning but encouraged by her parents, Swarna soon gained fluency in the language and, when she came home during the vacations, she took out the volumes of *Orunodoi* from her father's shelves and started reading them.

5

Compared to traditional Hindu festivals, those of the Brahmos were few and quite spartan. The two major Brahmo festivals of the year were the Maghutsav celebrated on the eleventh day of month of Magha, and the Bhadrutsav which commemorated the setting up of the new temple by Keshab Chander Sen. However, for the followers of the Adi Brahmo Samaj the Maghutsav happened to be the only major festival of the year. Both these festivals were observed in a solemn, simple and dignified manner and it was but natural for the Brahmo festivals to look lusterless when placed against the pomp and glitter of the Bengali Hindu festivals like Durga Puja or Kali Puja. Perhaps the initiators of the Brahmo faith were themselves aware of the fact that it would be very difficult for the average idol-worshipping Bengali to suddenly settle for the worship of a formless god. Even if this was possible for the first batch of Western educated Brahmos, they knew that in future if people were to be attracted to their beliefs, it would be necessary to introduce some glitter into Brahmo ceremonies as well. Otherwise, the time would come when the soft notes of the Brahmo Sangeet would eventually be drowned by the sound of dhaks of the Baghbazar Durga puja. It was perhaps keeping all this in mind that Maharshi Devendranth Tagore started celebrating the Maghutsav on a grand scale in the sprawling grounds of his Jorasanko house to which all the

Brahmo families of Calcutta as well as many other respectable citizens of the city were invited.

Ever since Swarnalata joined school in Calcutta, Gunabhiram had been planning to go to Jorasanko during the Maghutsav. But, the pressures of his government job always seemed to come in the way. Eventually, some three years later, he got an opportunity to go to the Maghutsav at the Tagores. He had known Devendranath Tagore for many years. Even as a schoolboy he had gone to the Tagores' Jorasanko house on several occasions with his guardian Anandaram Dhekiyal Phukan who was a close friend of Dwarkanath Tagore, a leading member of the Calcutta aristocracy. Thus, Gunabhiram knew the Tagores quite well since his student days at Calcutta when he was first attracted to the Brahmo Samaj.

Swarna too was very fond of the Maghutsav day. Even when she was at home in Nagaon, this particular day was always filled with songs and dances, plays and prayers. It had always been a very auspicious and happy day for her. She usually missed the Maghutsav festivities in Calcutta because it fell at a time when she was home for her winter vacation. But she knew from what she had heard from Charuprova, Hemoprova and Labanyaprova, that every single Brahmo family of Calcutta was mesmerized by Jorasanko's Maghutsav. All the members of the Tagore household, young and old alike would join hands to weave such a magic of music, lyric and rhyme that everyone in the audience would be left spellbound. Every year the leading artistes of Calcutta would glean fresh and exciting experiences from the cultural world of Jorasanko and one could hear the humming of new songs and tunes in the bhardalok circle of the city long after the Maghustsav was over. Among the Tagores Jnanendranath and Abanindranath were names that were frequently discussed. And, ever since she came to Calcutta, Swarna too had been hearing these names. She had also heard from her father about Maharshi

Devendranath. But, because she stayed at a school hostel, she hadn't had a chance to meet them. Moreover, so many families lived together at Jorasanko that it was often quite difficult to distinguish one personality from the other. But this time her father assured her that he would arrange for her to meet all the distinguished members of the Tagore household. Her father felt that now that Swarnalata was a grown-up girl, it was time for her to get acquainted with the intellectual world of the city. She, however, was particularly eager to meet one of the Tagores about whom she had heard so much. He was Maharshi Devendranath's son, Rabindranath. It was said that there was none in Bengal who could rival his poetry. Now, she wanted to find out for herself what sort of people these poets actually were.

Along with her parents, Swarna reached Calcutta several days ahead of the Maghutsav. As her school was yet to re-open after the winter recess, Swarna stayed with her parents at Anandamohan Basu's place. Bishnupriya had bought for Swarna a white Assam silk mekhala chador set to wear for the occasion. It had small flower motifs worked on it. When Swarna put on that dress, everyone in the Basu family was enraptured. Some of the ladies teased her by saying: "Just two wings would complete the beauty! Now she's like a fairy without wings." Swarna, along with Hemoprova and her friends, left a bit earlier than the others for the utsav in a separate buggy. The rest of the family followed in separate groups. By the time Swarna and her friends reached Jorasanko, there were dozens of horse carriages lined up in front of the huge mansion and the guests were being received by the different members of the Tagore family. Both the hosts and the guests were dressed in all their finery. But amongst them all, the women of the Thakur household stood out in their distinctness. There seemed to be an artistic touch in the way they wore their sarees or tied their hair or the ornaments they wore or the way they dressed. Each one of the Tagore girls was educated and it was some of these beautiful and accomplished young women who came forward to welcome Swarna and her companions. Everyone seemed to know Hemaprova, who introduced Swarnalata to Indira, Sarala, Protiva and the others. After this, all of them proceeded to pay their respects to Maharshi Devendranath Tagore.

Swarna had not seen the Maharshi before. Her head bowed in a natural act of obeisance when she saw this rishi-like person. Devendranath blessed them all but gave Swarna a somewhat surprised look, his eyes taking her in from head to toe. But before he could ask who she was, some other guests came in to greet him. Meanwhile, Swarna and her friends were taken into the house. As Swarna went in, Devendranath kept looking at her and seemed engrossed in some deep thought. Observing this, a gentleman friend of his commented as if to himself:

"She is just like Saraswati."

"Well, she could have been the best choice for the role of Rabi's Saraswati Devi. Isn't it? Whose daughter is she?"

The gentleman shook his head and replied:

"I don't know. I don't think I have seen her before. But with a little bit of effort, I can very well find out. From her dress it appears she is from Asam."

"Our Rabi too has reached marriageable age. We'll have to look for a good girl." It appeared as if the Maharshi was giving vent to his inner thoughts. The bhadralok understood what was in his mind and said in a low voice: "I will find out whose daughter she is."

The Maghutsav celebrations began with a prayer and a Brahmo Sangeet. This was followed by the community feast where the guests were offered a variety of home-made delicacies. Each member of the Tagore household saw to it that the guests were taken full care of. Once the feast was over and the dessert was served, the guests moved towards the tastefully decorated stage in front of which rows of chairs had been neatly placed. An attractive cultural show put up by the Tagores was always part of the annual Maghutsav festivities. And, on that particular year all attention seemed to be focused on the play, *Balmikir Pratibha* written by the Mahrashi's younger son, Rabindranath who had just returned from a tour of England. Hemaprova and her friends had already heard about this play. So, as they were waiting for it to begin, they started whispering among themselves:

"Do you know that Rabindranath has composed the songs and dances of the play and will be acting himself?" asked Charuprova.

"What degree has Rabindrantah earned in England?" Swarnalata asked softly.

"It seems he hasn't passed any exams. But he has come back highly enriched in poetry, music and plays," said Hemoprova.

"But would it really be possible to go through life only with that sort of knowledge?" asked Swarnalata somewhat naively.

Both the sisters were amused at Swarna's comment and replied in good humour:

"You don't know about whom you are speaking. The son of such a wealthy zamindar! Why should he worry about a job?"

Swarna couldn't help but feel a bit foolish. She kept quiet and just waited for the play to begin. Meanwhile, melodious notes on the piano and the violin could be heard and slowly the curtain rose on *Balmikir Pratibha*. The first scene opened with a bevy of Tagore girls appearing as maidens of the forest. The audience was simply captivated by the supple movements of the girls synchronized with the song that was being sung in a completely different and unfamiliar tune. And, when Rabindranath finally appeared on the stage as Dashyu Ratnakar, one could hear the murmurs of admiration from the audience.

Hemaprova whispered into Swarna's ears: "He is Rabindranath."

Swarna kept watching the play with a strange fascination. She had never before seen such acting. And, when the cruel dacoit king started singing "Keno Pran Kadere", with full emotion, Swarna looked on breathlessly. She did not even notice when one scene ended and was quickly followed by another. In the sixth scene, when Valmiki paid his homage to the Goddess Saraswati through a song, Swanalata was overwhelmed with emotion and her eyes welled up with tears. Seeing her wipe her eyes as the play drew to a close, Charuprova said with a smile: "So you have reached the stage when one can really fall in love with poetry".

The play over, the spectators waited eagerly to congratulate the actors. Protiva Devi's acting drew a lot of applause. So did Kshitindra, Surendra, Gaganendra, and Abanindra in their role as dacoits and the Tagore daughters as the forest maidens. But the loudest applause was reserved for Rabindranath. The moment he appeared on the stage, there was incessant clapping. Several leading musicians commented on the fine mix of Western and Eastern tunes in the play. Along with Rabindranath, his younger brother Jnanendranath was the focus of all eyes that evening. Swarnalata didn't hear Rabindranath's dialogues but, she looked on in fascination at the poet from a distance. Having changed his Valmiki's apparel, Rabindranth was now wearing a dhoti and embroidered kurta, with a neatly folded Kashmiri shawl draped around his shoulders. He was mixing freely with the audience and exchanging pleasantries. Swarnalata continued to feel that she was actually in a totally different world of dance, music and poetry. She was so engrossed with the poet that she didn't even notice that her parents were standing near her. She was quite taken aback by her father's voice:

"Come, Maisena, let's go and congratulate Rabindranath." Saying this, Gunabhiram was slowly making his way through the crowd. Rabindranath had met Gunabhiram before. He accepted Barua's congratulations with a shy smile. Just then, a bhadralok pointed towards Swarnalata and said:

"Rabi, she is Barua's daughter, Swarnalata. A little while ago your father had called her the Goddess Saraswati. In your drama this evening she would have been ideal for the role of the maiden goddess. What do you say?" Seeing that all eyes were now focused on her, Swarnalata's face flushed with embarrassment and she gently lowered her head. For a few seconds, the poet's intense eyes rested on her face. Then with a laugh, he said:

"Is it really possible to find the Goddess Saraswati in a play? So many poets have been frantically searching for her all their lives."

"But have you found your Saraswati?" someone jokingly asked.

With a smile, the poet replied: "I am still searching. Had I found her, I would not have been Valmiki!" Everyone joined in the laughter.

The celebrations drew to a close. Gunabhiram and the other guests took their leave. As they reached the front gate, Swarnalata turned and looked back at the group of people that was still surrounding Rabindranath. She could somehow sense that Rabindranath was looking at her. Their eyes met and she waited for a while. Then, following her parents, she slowly went out. On the way back, Swarnalata seemed preoccupied did not participate in the merriment of the group. Bishnupriya couldn't help but notice her daughter's absentmindedness. A fresh worry for her daughter, Swarna, now settled in her mind.

6

Swarna was just thirteen years old at the time. Usually in orthodox Brahmin families, girls never remained unmarried for that long. But according to a new custom among the Brahmos, a girl was considered to be of marriageable age only when she reached fourteen years of age. Among the many reform measures that the Brahmos had initiated under the leadership of Keshav Chandra Sen, this was one of the major ones. It was actually the Brahmos who had motivated the British to enact the Native Marriage Act which fixed the age of marriage of boys at eighteen and girls at fourteen. As a result, Brahmo marriages had to follow the Act if they were to be accepted by the law.

Gunabhiram Barua had legally registered his second marriage and wanted the same for Swarna. That's why, right then, he wasn't particularly worried about Swarna's marriage. The Barua couple had agreed among themselves that they would discuss Swarna's marriage only after she crossed fourteen. But, this time after the Maghutsav, Bishnupriya felt otherwise. The attention that Swarna had got on that day at Jorasanko seemed to fill Bishnupriya's mind with all sorts of old fears. She was filled with a sense of uncertainty about her daughter's future. Both her daughters by her first marriage had been married off when they were just nine or ten years old. At that time, she had never seen anything wrong in this. But, having come under the influence of

Gunabhiram, she had tried to adjust herself to modern ideas and had also succeeded in this to a certain extent. Even then, there were occasions when the old beliefs seemed to bear her down. Most people believed that girls should not be seen in public, for men's glances made them impure. But Bishnupriya never dared to speak openly about these beliefs to her husband. She knew that he would not tolerate such ideas. Still, as the day of their return to Assam drew near, Bishnupriya grew increasingly restive. She felt that even if she couldn't take Swarna home with her, it would be proper for them to at least fix her match with someone from a good family. Bishnupriya had always wanted a groom from a respectable Brahmin family for Swarna. But now she was gradually learning to accept the fact that no Brahmin family of her region would be willing to have marriage ties with them. She had suddenly become aware of this stark truth on the day of Lakhi's wedding. She could see that it was not just the Brahmins, but all the other upper castes too which did not accept widow re-marriage. It had become increasingly clear to her that apart from the Brahmos, no one else would accept their family.

As Bishnupriya was thinking of the leading Brahmo families of Calcutta, the Tagores of Jorasanko naturally came to her mind. She thought she would consider herself as highly privileged if Swarnalata could be married into that illustrious family. She knew her husband would be happy if such a match could be arranged. And, more than anything else, she felt she knew what was in Swarna's mind. She had noticed how unmindful Swarna had become since they went for the Maghutsav and of how she now spent her time mostly to herself, reading poetry. Quite often, she would forget herself while humming the tunes of the songs of *Valmikir Prativa*.

Finally, one day Bishnupriya told her husband of what was in her mind and asked him: "What do you think of a match between Swarna and the Maharshi's younger son, Rabindranath?"

Gunabhiram was initially taken aback by the suddenness of his wife's question and took some time to respond:

"Maisena isn't of marriageable age yet. Why have you brought this up now?"

It was as if Bishnupriya was ready with an answer.

"Only if we start negotiations now, would it be possible to have the marriage in time. But if we wait for Swarna to reach the right age, then they might fix the match with someone else."

Gunabhiram thought for a while and said:

"There might be good matches even outside the Tagore family. Why this hurry?"

It seemed as if Gunabhiram was trying to hide some apprehension of his from Bishnupriya. His wife was quite surprised and asked:

"Do you have any reservations about the Tagores? I feel that such a match would be ideal for Maisensa. Moreover, I too have been told by some persons that Rabindranath has agreed…" As she said this, Bishnupriya blushed like a teenager. Seeing this, Gunabhiram softened up and said with a smile: "If the boy and the girl seem to like each other, we might as well give it a try."

That very evening Gunabhiram broached the topic to Durgamohan Das. Durgamohan's response was swift. "Swarna and Rabindranath will make an ideal couple. It would suit a wise and talented young man like Rabindranath to have a beautiful and educated girl like Swarna. But the problem is with Maharshi Devendranath. It will not be so easy to get his approval."

"But the other day at the Maghutsav, he had enquired about Swarna. That means he has approved of her," Gunabhiram said with a sense of certainty.

Durgamohan was silent for some time. But his face showed that he was somewhat troubled. Then, without spilling the beans, he said:

"Things are not as you think them to be, Mahasay. Even then, I will try to find out through Lalbehari Ghosh. He is an experienced ghatak. Keeps close ties with the Thakurbari."

Following this, some days passed and Gunabhiram's leave was about to end. Yet, there was no news from Lalbehari Ghosh. Seeing that Bishnupriya was getting impatient, Gunabhiram sent a message to Lalbehabri and he turned up at their place. Gunabhiram had met him once before. He had then seemed to be quite a jolly fellow. But now his appearance was quite grave and there was no trace of a smile on his lips. At once, Gunabhiram knew that the news was not good. With some hesitation, Lalbehari said:

"Your proposal was eagerly accepted by all at the Thakurbari. Rabindranath too had agreed. But, I don't know why in the end Maharshi Devendranath didn't approve of it."

After this, Lalbehari Ghosh said many a thing to console the Barua couple. He took it upon himself to look for a good match for Swarna. But Gunabhiram was in no mood to listen anymore. Some unknown fear about his daughter's future seemed to fill his mind. Till then, he had never thought that even within the Brahmo Samaj there could be people who would be unwilling to accept them. Now, a storm began to brew in his mind. He didn't say anything to Bishnupriya but he went to meet his friend Sibnath Shastri to find out the reason behind Devendranath's objection. Shastri listened intently to all that Barua said, and then replied:

"There could be only one reason for this. Devendranath Tagore has never been able to fully accept the idea of widow re-marriage. You must be aware that though he appears to be a liberal in his outlook, his attachment to some of the rites and beliefs of Hindu society seems to be growing with every passing day. It is quite possible, however, that the younger generation of Tagores may not be with him in this. But no one at Jorasanko would really dare to go against Devendranath's wishes."

Gunabhiram nodded his assent, all the while looking blankly downwards. Finding him worried, Shastri tried to assure him and said:

"Why are you worrying so much, Barua? In the first place, being a member of the Sadharan Brahmo Samaj, why are you thinking of Swarna's marriage right now? Have you forgotten about our differences with Keshav Chandra Sen? Maybe, Devendranath will get his son married to a child of nine or ten. But if those of us who have been continuously struggling against child marriage for years, fail to apply our beliefs to our own lives, then this country will never see a social revolution. Let me assure you that there'll be no dearth of eligible grooms for Swarna. Now, please go back to your work with a free mind. Aren't we there to think about your girl's welfare?"

Gunabhiram was relieved to hear his friend's words. He was confident he could reassure Bishnupriya. Often, these days, Gunabhiram felt weighed down by a feeling of guilt towards his wife when it came to matters like Swarna's education or marriage. There was a time when he himself had told Bishnupriya that he would set a new ideal by helping Swarna to acquire higher education; that she would be the first Assamese girl to clear the Entrance examination. Gunabhiram had then been thrilled to hear that Sarala, the daughter of Kadambini and Durgamohan Das, was preparing for her Entrance examination from Calcutta University under the guidance of Dwarkanath Ganguly. Kadambini was the niece of Gunabhiram's close friend, Manmohan Ghose. He too had dreamt of making Swarna a graduate of Calcutta University like Kadambini. But a recent happening had wrought a major change in Gunabhiram's way of thinking. In spite of fierce opposition from the members of the Sadharan Brahmo Samaj, Dwarkanath Ganguly had married his student Kadambini who was then studying in the Calcutta Medical College. Dwarkanath was some eighteen years older to her. But, apart from the difference in age between the two, the leaders of the Sadharan Brahmo Samaj had little other ground to oppose the match. Dwarkanath was the most well known pioneer of women's education in Bengal. And, Kadambini was his protégé. Yet, many a Brahmo was unable to accept this marriage between a guru and his shishya. Gunabhiram too seemed to have been jolted by what had happened. At one time, he had differed with younger members like Durgamohan Das over the question of women's education. Like the older members of the Brahmo Samaj, he too had then believed that a woman should receive only that much education as was necessary to make her an ideal companion to a well educated modern man. The aim of women's education could never be to make the woman go after a job like a man. Subsequently, he had changed his views after coming into contact with Sibnath Shastri, Manmohan Ghose and others. It was then that he decided to make Swarna a graduate. But, now after the Dwarkanath-Kadambini union, many of the front-ranking Brahmos had started marrying off their daughters much before they finished their school education. Gunabhiram too had started to think that perhaps he would be carrying out his paternal duty if he could give Swarna's hand in marriage to an eligible groom. He tried to convince himself that the education Swarna had received till then should be enough for a girl like her.

7

When Lakhi passed her Middle English examination securing the first place in her district, she didn't have much cause to be elated. For, till then, she had withstood all the taunts and jibes from her relatives and had continued to study in a boys' school. But now it appeared certain that no one would allow her to be enrolled in a boys' high school. Moreover, she didn't see any hope of a girls' high school coming up in Nagaon in the near future. In a place where girls from well-off families were not even sent to lower primary schools, how could one expect a girls' high school? Still, Lakhi loved to imagine that one day she would pass her Entrance examination. Her teachers from the M.E. school had come to her house to congratulate and bless her for bringing glory to her institution. But, it was only Ajay Ganguly who told her that she should aspire to pass her Entrance. With a wry smile, Lakhi had asked him: "How will that be possible? I can't go to Calcutta."

"If there is a will, God will show you the way to achieve your goal. Nothing is impossible if one tries, Lakhi"

Lakhi was tempted to ask him that even if God showed her the way, would her fellow human beings ever allow her to go ahead. But thinking that such a question might be seen as an affront and could offend Ganguly Sir, Lakhi decided to keep quiet. However, as she was about to see off her teachers at the gate, Ajay Ganguly told her:

"If your parents permit, then you could try for the mission school. Nowadays, in Nagaon there is no way out but to approach the missionaries in the matter of girls' education."

Lakhi knew that the Mission's girls' school at Nagaon didn't offer high school education. As such, in order to avoid any unpleasantness at home, she did not tell anyone about Ganguly Sir's advice. But having stayed at home for some time, Lakhi's mind was gradually filled with despair. Now that there was no more school, for her the very purpose of living seemed lost. Occasionally, she visited Charusila Baideu and felt somewhat better. Charusila would lend her books and magazines to read. One day she gave her a new book she had brought from Calcutta. It was Bankimchandra's *Kapal-Kundala*. As she handed over the book to Lakhi, Charusila sounded a note of caution:

"It is a difficult kind of book. Read it alone. Your people might not like it if they see it."

At first, Lakhi was a bit surprised. What could there be in a book given by her teacher which her people at home would disapprove of? But as she finished reading it, Lakhi understood what her teacher had said. Really, she hadn't ever read such an exciting book. Some of the descriptions filled her with a strange sensation. She kept on reading the same lines over and over again and soon she knew them by heart. It was one particular sentence which Kapalkundala said to Shyamsundari that kept troubling Lakhi for a long time—"Had I known that for women marriage is slavery, then I would have never got married." Suddenly, Lakhi's mind too was filled with a feeling of revolt. She too wished to somehow stand up against all the injustices done to women by society. Ever since she stopped going to school, she had begun to feel that she was slowly sliding back to her earlier uneventful life of a widow. She now increasingly felt that the only way out of this for her was to find a workplace outside her home. And, as luck would have it, once while going to Charusila Baideu's place, she met Tora. After having shared her feelings with her, Lakhi requested Tora to arrange a job for her at the school run by the Mission.

Tora told the missionary women about Lakhi's sad life and of her eagerness to continue her studies. The women wanted to meet her. Without trying to hide her feelings, Mrs Moore, who had recently come from America, declared: "We need such girls. If we could make her understand, then one day she would surely accept the right path shown by Jesus."

Mrs Moore said these words with the best of intentions. She was new to the country and was over zealous about spreading the word of Christ among the Assamese people. But, having heard her, Tora suddenly felt depressed. Her eagerness to help Lakhi seemed to have been checked by the idea of conversion mooted by the foreign lady. For some days now, Tora was being troubled by certain doubts and questionings. She had been asking herself as to why couldn't people help others without any specific motive? Why should one use education or social service as a tool for religious conversion? Why couldn't one go straight to the people and talk openly about religion? While teaching the simple Mikir children, Tora had seen them only as human beings. She had never thought of using education as a bait. Somehow, she just couldn't agree with the missionary women on this count. Though they had come from across the seven seas and endured untold hardship in spreading education in far-flung, unapproachable areas in both the hills and the plains, yet now she felt that they wanted a price for spreading the light of knowledge. Maybe, their motive was right. But she felt that the moment one sought a price for service, it ceased to be selfless. Tora's mind was filled with confusion. Yet, she knew she couldn't discuss this with anyone.

Tora informed Lakhi of the missionary women's willingness to meet her. But, she kept her doubts to herself. And, one day she quietly took Lakhi to the Mission and introduced her to the inmates. Everyone was impressed by Lakhi's bearing and behaviour. They couldn't even believe that there could be such a girl in an Assamese Hindu family. The traces of revolt in Lakhi's language were enough to convince the missionaries that, with a little bit of effort, they would be able to bring her into their fold. That very day, Lakhi was offered a teaching job at the Mission's girl school for ten rupees a month. At the same time the padre assured Lakhi that she would be able to continue with her studies under their guidance and that they would try to secure special permission from the government for her to take the Entrance examination. Lakhi felt that heaven was within her reach! Without giving it the slightest thought, she readily accepted the offer.

While they were walking back home, Tora looked a bit worried and asked Lakhi: "Don't you think you should have sought the approval of your parents before accepting the job?"

"Had I asked them before accepting the job, my parents would never have agreed. But, now if I try to persuade them maybe, they will give in. A teacher's job for ten rupees a month is not to be laughed at."

Lakhi had guessed right. When she first broke the news, everyone was dumfounded. A teacher in the Mission school and ten rupees a month! An ordinary girl like her would earn so much, and that too on the strength of her own education? This was simply beyond anyone's imagination. To be able to teach the girls just as the white ladies did was in itself no small matter. Sarma's mind was filled with a quiet sense of pride. Though he pretended to show a bit of hesitation, yet it was clear that he would not oppose his daughter's decision. Others in the family too didn't have the courage to say anything because for them Lakhi now clearly seemed to belong to some other world.

On the first day of her job, Tora accompanied Lakhi to the school. She still appeared somewhat disturbed. After giving her small bits of advice, Tora said with some hesitation: "The memsahibs will also talk of religion with you. Would you really like that?"

"I always like listening to people talking about religion, whether it is mine or someone else's. But I don't like if anyone tries to force me into believing something. Ever since I was a child, I have grown up with religious rituals, fasting and prayers. But I have always done this only because others have asked me to do so. To be frank, I don't know what I really believe. Actually, I think that if one has to stay in society, then one should be of help to one's fellow beings, just as you have helped me. It is unwise to trouble God over such small things. His task is so much larger." Saying this, Lakhi smiled and tried to lighten the effect on Tora of what she had said. But Tora could very well sense the feeling of determination which marked her words. Tora could see that life's hardships had matured Lakhi well beyond her years and she would be able to take care of herself very well. So, there was no need to worry for her.

Although Tora was now quite certain about Lakhi, yet she continued to be burdened by some other thoughts. Her mother had been unwell for quite some time. But, she had not been able to take leave from her school at Beliram until a replacement was sent by the Mission. Eventually, when a Christian girl from the Nagaon Mission agreed to go there, Tora handed over the duties of the school to her and came home. When she saw her mother's condition, she cursed herself. This woman had endured so much suffering for her sake. She had spent the greater part of her life all alone. And, as she watched her ill mother still going about her daily chores, Tora's mind was filled with a feeling of guilt. She had all these years taken good care of others. But all this while, it didn't even strike her that she had some duty also towards her own mother. She resolved that from then onwards she would never leave her mother alone, whatever be the circumstances. Golapi, however, made a feeble protest saying that Tora should not neglect her duty at the Mission in order to look after her. But, Tora was adamant. And, the very next day after she reached Nagaon, she went to the Mission and expressed her feelings to the memsahibs there. Both Mrs Moore and Miss Keeler listened attentively to Tora's problem and seemed to realize that it wasn't after all good for her to spend too long a time all alone in an interior village. They had observed that for some time now her earlier unquestioning faith in the Mission was gradually showing cracks. The questions she had started to ask were a clear indication of the doubts that were growing in her mind. So, they felt that it was necessary to keep Tora near them in order to restore her feeling of faith. That was why they didn't object to what Tora said. They advised her to stay on at Nagaon and work wholeheartedly for the Mission. Tora was surprised to find the memsahibs agreeing so readily to her request. But she tried to convince herself that all this was the result of the warmth and affection which the missionaries had for the mother and daughter.

Once again Tora started her work in the familiar surroundings of the Nagaon Mission. Her work at the Mission was limited to teaching at the girls' school for three days a week and giving moral studies lessons to little girls in the Mission's Sunday school. But she used to do a lot of work at home. Apart from helping in the housework and attending to her mother, she would try to find some time to stitch garments and knit sweaters for the poor children. Her hands would busily keep on knitting even during those precious spare moments when she would sit by her mother and talk to her. Sometimes, she would sing a hymn in Assamese and passers-by would listen with halting steps to her melodious voice.

8

Unlike the other boys, Dharmakanta did not rush back home after taking his B. A. examination. The city held a lot of attraction for him because in the Calcutta of those days the winds of nationalism were blowing in new directions. Nationalist leaders were having regular meetings to draw up programmes aimed at giving a new focus to the grievances of the Indian people and the birth of the Indian National Congress was imminent. Dharmakanta did not wish to move away from such a situation. He was eager to attend the first session of the Congress at Bombay. He had met quite a few nationalist leaders at the office of Sashipada Banerjee's *Bharat Shramjivi* and had even debated with them on certain issues. Dharmakanta held the view that the goal of the Congress should be nothing short of complete independence from colonial rule. He felt that it was for the Congress to finish the task left incomplete by those who tried to liberate the country through an armed struggle in 1857. But Dharmakanta did not find any such hint in the speeches of leaders like Surendranath Banerjee and Anandamohan Basu. It seemed that they wanted to turn the Congress into yet another India Association whose activities would be limited to securing concessions for the Indians through petitions and memorials. It didn't take long for Dharmakanta to realize that none of these leaders were intent on freeing the country from British rule.

One morning two groups of students were having a serious argument at a tea-stall adjacent to Presidency College. The point at issue was a forceful speech given by Surendranath Banerjee at the College Square. One of the groups was led by Dharmakanta, while another student, Umacharan Banerjee, spoke for the other group. Umacharan, who had just graduated with a first class and was planning to go to England for higher studies, argued that the need of the hour was for all educated Indians to come together to fight for political reforms. His aim was to get through the Indian Civil Service and become a leading bureaucrat. Hence, it was but natural for students like Umacharan to be enamoured by leaders like Surendranath Banerjee who had qualified for the ICS but had casually given it up. Giving up a career in the ICS was seen by educated Indians as the ultimate in personal sacrifice. Dharmakanta, however, saw things quite differently. Initially, his arguments drew some support from the students who seemed quite impressed by his command over the language and the sharpness of his views. But it didn't take long for this positive response to turn into a stony silence, once Dharmakanta started advocating the overthrow of the British and full freedom for his country. No one was ready to risk their career by siding with such views. Even those few who seemed to accept the truth of Dharmakanta's arguments, thought it better to keep quiet out of fear of being spotted by intelligence agents.

In his hostel that evening, all to himself, Dharmakanta thought of many things. He had learnt a lot from the intellectual world of Calcutta. If he hadn't come to this strange metropolis, he would never have realized the strength of India's unity in the midst of all its diversity. It appeared as if he had found a part of himself in all those with whom he argued, fought and made friends within Calcutta's academic circle. It was Calcutta which finally helped him to order his tangled thoughts. But, having seen through many things, the greatest question which faced him now was: Which path should he eventually take? Had he so wished, he could have spent the rest of his life in Calcutta. Sashipada Banerjee and a few others had in fact asked him to stay on. But Dharmakanta questioned himself whether Calcutta needed him as much as he needed Calcutta for his intellectual satisfaction. Calcutta was never short of social and religious reformers and political leaders. But it was Assam which needed new ideas now. The debates in the tea shops of College Square no doubt had their own charm. Yet, what was really necessary for him was to go back to Assam and help the people prepare for the real struggle. That very day after the adda at the tea shop, Dharmakanta decided to return to Assam and build up his new *karmashetra* there.

His first thought was to go and meet the owner of the Tapatjuri Tea Estate, Debanath Barua. Gunabhiram had written to Dharmakanta suggesting that Debanath Barua was willing to offer a job to him in his tea garden and that he should meet him on his return from Calcutta. It was with this in mind that Dharmakanta had bought his railway ticket upto Guwahati. But, as he was about to begin his journey, he suddenly felt like going to Sivasagar. He hadn't met his uncle ever since he retired and settled in Sivasagar. He hadn't also seen his mother for quite a long time. So, he now decided to drop the trip to Guwahati and instead bought a ticket to Dikhowmukh.

Dharmakanta had always believed that when it came to new ideas, Assam seemed to lag behind. Yet, his stay in Sivasagar made him feel that the winds of change from the West were finally reaching even this small town. One day he was quite surprised when he visited an old schoolmate of the Sivasagar High School, Nakul Gogoi. A small meeting was on at Gogoi's home. The aim of the meeting was to build people's resistance to the new taxes that were being imposed by the British government. Nakul Gogoi was then teaching at the Sivasagar Government High School. The others present at the meeting were all educated young men.

Some of them were preparing for their Entrance Examinations while the others had to give up school because of financial problems and were now employed in minor jobs at the local kutcherry. Gogoi warmly welcomed Dharmakanta and, while introducing him to the small gathering, said: "We are coming forward to work for the people. Our aim is to set up a sabha on the lines of the Sarbajanin Sabha of Jorhat set up by Jagannath Barua. Could you please tell us, Barua, how effective such sabhas have been in Calcutta and its nearby areas?" Dharmakanta had never heard of the Sarbajanin Sabha and appeared quite embarrassed at his ignorance, but he was pleased to hear of such a sabha and asked Gogoi to give him the details. He felt that even though nothing really momentous had happened, yet the seeds of political awareness were beginning to sprout. That evening at Nakul Gogoi's place Dharmakanta spoke at length about his experiences in Calcutta and also informed the gathering about the preparations that were going on to hold the first session of the newly formed Congress. Dharmakanta was showered with questions relating to the Indian Association, Indian League, the Congress, whether their goals were different and which was the correct path and which was not. On each issue that was raised, Dharmakanta gave his views in a succinct and clear manner. In a determined voice he declared: "The days of submitting memorials before the British Government are finally over. The people should come out as one to snatch their rights from the British Government. Only if the Congress accepts this path, will the people be with it."

"I agree with you. Don't you remember the Phulaguri Dhewa? Can the people of Calcutta show such courage?" a young man in the audience asked proudly.

Dharmakanta stayed in Sivasagar for a week. During this period he interacted with his former teachers and schoolmates. People were eager to meet him after having heard that he had graduated from Calcutta University with a good grade. They were a bit surprised that this young graduate didn't have any airs and freely mixed with the people. They listened intently to whatever Dharmakanta had to say, be it something related to modern political thought or the Renaissance in Bengal or national awakening. He had so many things to tell them! And, they, in turn, found a new sense of hope in his words and started believing that, after all, some change was really in the offing.

Dharmakanta's uncle was quite upset when he heard that his nephew had opted for a tea garden job. He just couldn't understand why Dharmakanta, after studying so hard in Calcutta, didn't want to be a hakim and, instead, chose to be a clerk in a tea estate. Dharmakanta, however, was not inclined to argue with his uncle who had always shown him so much of love and affection. And, even now, his uncle's inability to understand him did not in any way affect the deep sense of respect and gratitude which he had always had for him. Trying to assuage his uncle's doubts, Dharmakanta said: "I am trying for a job in a tea garden owned by an Assamese precisely because I don't want to work under the British government. I am certain that one day all of you will be proud of me. I have been thinking of doing something worthwhile." Unlike his uncle, Dharmakanta's mother did not have any doubts about her son's decision. She understood her son's feelings and blessed him from the bottom of her heart. She had never wanted anything from her son and she was always convinced that he would never do anything which would discredit her.

The Tapatjuri tea estate was situated a few miles east of Guwahati. It was quite small compared to the British gardens, but because of the efforts of its Assamese owner, the garden was producing quite a lot of tea. Barua had succeeded in managing his garden with local Bodo-Kachari workers and hadn't brought in any girmitia coolies from outside the province. However, the garden did not have a factory of its own and the green leaf it produced was sent to Calcutta for processing by a Guwahati firm called Barua-Phukan Brothers. It was to look after the garden's financial transactions with this firm that the owner had employed Dharmakanta. On his part, Dharmakanta quite liked his job which gave him the opportunity to make frequent trips to Guwahati where he met and discussed political issues with many people. Even when in the garden, he didn't spend all his time with his files. Whenever he got the chance, Dharmakanta would slip out to the adjoining villages where, sitting in someone's courtyard, he would tell the people stories about other lands while never losing an opportunity of highlighting the disastrous effects of British rule. The simple village folk would listen intently to Dharmakanta and ask him endless questions. His replies would always fill them with surprise and wonder. That there existed a wide world outside the confines of their small villages and that the happenings of this outside world could have an effect on their own lives was something they had heard for the first time from Dharmakanta.

Dharmakanta kept in touch with Gunabhiram Barua through letters. It was from one of Barua's letters that he came to know that the work on the Assamese journal which he was planning to bring out was progressing well. The first issue of the journal, which had been named *Asom Bandhu*, was expected to hit the stands by the month of Magha. Gunabhiram had requested Dharmakanta to come over to Nagaon once the journal was out, so that he could help in its distribution. And, when the journal did finally come out, Dharmakanta applied for a few days leave from garden work so that he could go to Nagaon to help Gunabhiram Barua. The owner of the garden readily agreed because Gunabhiram was his friend. Moreover, the question of displeasing a powerful friend like Gunabhiram Barua just did not arise. Hence, it was decided that during the time of the Magh Bihu, Dharmakanta would go to Nagaon on a week's leave.

9

Bilwa Kutir was in a festive mood when Dharmakanta reached Nagaon. The inaugural issue of the *Asom Bandhu* had come from Calcutta and the educated elite of Nagaon were vying with one another to have a first look at the journal. The enthusiasm of young men like Satyanath Bora, Ratnakanta Mahanta and Hem Chandra Goswami seemed to infect everyone present. They were busy buying copies for themselves as well as for their friends. They also took it upon themselves to write a piece each for the next issue of the journal—maybe a poem or an article. There was no less enthusiasm even among the elderly. Gurunath Dutta, Padmahash Goswami, Panchanan Sarma and others heartily congratulated Gunabhiram's effort and offered their suggestions.

When Dharmakanta entered Bilwa Kutir, Gunabhiram made everyone feel as if the person really responsible for the publication of *Asom Bandu* had finally arrived. A bit embarrassed at Gunabhiram's effusive attention, Dharmakanta tried to deflect it by concentrating on the contents of the journal. "How do you like it?" asked Gunabhiram, who was looking over his shoulder to see his reaction. Unaware of this Dharmakanta raised his head, and saw that it wasn't just Gunabhiram but Bishnupriya and Swarnalata too who were waiting eagerly for his answer. Dharmakanta was in a fix. He just couldn't praise the journal unquestioningly. For, he was in disagreement with many of the views expressed in the introductory column. In spelling out the aims of *Asom Bandhu*, Gunabhiram had said that the journal would confine itself to issues relating only to science and knowledge and it wouldn't comment on matters of law, government and politics. But, for Dharmakanta there was little point in talking about scientific knowledge and humanistic values if one didn't struggle against ignorance, superstition and injustice. For him, the two seemed to be inextricably linked. Moreover, if the *Asom Bandhu* couldn't inspire the people to fight against injustice and oppression, than what sort of a "bandhu" or friend was it really?

Had he been his earlier self, Dharmakanta would have freely expressed is views. But, perhaps for the first time in his life, he restrained his tongue. He just did not wish to dampen the enthusiasm of the Barua family of Bilwa Kutir. So, with a courteous smile, he said:

"I have just skimmed through the contents. It appears that the topics are very relevant. There being such a dearth of newspapers and journals in Assam, this journal is sure to fill up a big void. But, it would have been nice had the print resembled the Assamese script. At least the alphabet 'ra' could have been Assamese!"

"I too have been thinking of that," Swarna joined in. "But the Calcutta printing presses do not have the Assamese 'ra'."

"But, how did they use it in the *Orunodoi*? Didn't the missionaries get their letter cases from Calcutta?" asked Dharmakanta.

"Don't talk about the Mission Press, Dharmakanta. Everything is so different with the missionaries. Browne Sahib had drawn the impress of the letter himself and then got it cast in lead by an Assamese artisan. They must have cast the letter 'ra' in the mission's own foundry. We do not have such facilities and are totally at the mercy of the printing presses of Calcutta," saying this, Gunabhiram seemed to sum up the discussion.

Dharmakanta, however, was not satisfied. He suggested that

the Assamese alphabets, "ra" and "wabba" could be made to order in a Calcutta foundry. If need be, he would get this done. Being unable to refute Dharmakanta's argument, Gunabhiram decided to write to Calcutta for a new set of letters. And, from the third issue onwards, the *Asom Bandhu* took on a completely Assamese face.

That one week at Bilwa kutir was a really hectic one for Dharmakanta. Complimentary copies of the journal were sent by post to each and every educated acquaintance from the different parts of the province. With each copy there was a letter requesting an annual subscription for the journal. Collecting addresses, writing them on labels, making packets and pasting the names on them and, finally, carrying the packets to the post office to have them weighed and get the stamps fixed—there were countless odd jobs to keep everyone occupied. Since Swarna had a nice hand, the job of writing the addresses fell on her. Swarna sent word to Tora and Lakhi for help. She knew that both of them would love to do this work. Moreover, it would provide an opportunity to the friends to come together. On receiving the news, Tora and Lakhi arrived at Bilwa Kutir straight after school. In a corner of the Barua's sitting room, Dharmakanta was busy wrapping the journals in small brown packets, while Swarna was writing the addresses and pasting the labels on them. Soon Tora and Lakhi too joined Swarna in her work. Swarna asked Lakhi softly: "You have come here straight from school without informing your parents, won't they mind?"

"They'll worry only if I am too late. Nowadays, my parents seem to trust me. They no longer send my brother or a servant with me," Lakhi replied with a smile.

"Why is it considered bad if girls walk unaccompanied in this country? Can one be a good girl only if one is dependant all the time on others?" asked Tora.

"That's exactly how people feel in our society. Those girls

who stay indoors with their heads covered, they are seen as the good ones. Girls like us are termed shameless. These days some even speak of women's independence. But these are the very people who refuse to let their girls out of the house," Lakhi added sarcastically.

All this while, Swarna had been working silently. Now, she put down her pen and said softly:"Our people think that way because they have not learnt the true meaning of women's liberty. What actually is modesty? It isn't surely covering one's head with an *uroni* and hiding your face from people. The meaning of modesty rests on one's fear to commit sinful acts. That person is really modest who keeps away from shameful acts and resolutely goes ahead with his or her own work. Those padre women who are doing so much good work don't cover their heads and they work freely with men. Yet, they have their own sense of modesty. This is actual freedom."

Both the girls were enamoured by Swarna's words. Placing her hand on Swarna's, Lakhi said emotionally: "You have given such a nice answer to something I have been thinking about all these days. From now on, I'll never shrink from doing my duty because of fear of what others might say. I'll try to show through my work that, even though I am a widow, a woman has a right to have a life of her own."

Dharmakanta was quietly doing his work and listening intently to what the three girls were discussing. On hearing what Lakhi had said, he now looked at her in surprise. Only a few minutes ago when Swarnalata had introduced him to her friends, he hadn't even noticed that the tall, slim girl called Lakhi was actually a widow. There weren't any signs of widowhood in her dress. She was wearing a muga mekhala and a green embroidered white cotton chador. But Dharmakanta should have known that a grown-up Brahmin girl without sindoor was usually a widow. He was now at a loss to understand how a Brahmin widow was a teacher in the Mission school. He suddenly wanted to know more about this girl.

Meanwhile, Tora and Lakhi had taken their leave and departed. After seeing them off at the gate, Swarna dropped into a chair on the verandah. Dharmakanta too had come out of the house. He pulled up a chair near Swarna and said with some hesitation:

"It was a real pleasure listening to the three of you. It is really good that you have been thinking seriously about the actual qualities of women. I think you should write out what you all discussed just now and send it to be published in *Asom Bandhu*."

Swarna wasn't aware till then that Dharmakanta had been listening to what they were saying. So, she said in a slightly embarrassed tone:

"Who will enjoy reading what we said?"

"Why? There'll be lots of people like me who'd appreciate it. Nowadays everyone makes fun of women's liberty. Your views will certainly help educate these people."

Both of them kept quiet for some time. Dharmakanta wanted to ask Swarna about Lakhi. But, suddenly an uneasy feeling seemed to fill his mind. Although he had always seen Swarna as his sister and had freely discussed matters relating to religion, literature and politics with her, yet when it came to personal matters, he was always quite reserved. Usually he kept away when people talked about girls. Moreover, this was an unknown field for him, for in his schooldays he didn't have any girls as classmates. Before he met Swarna, he was under the impression that girls somehow belonged to another world and they were inferior to men in intelligence and education. But after getting to know the Barua family, he had met some well educated Bengali girls and was struck by their intelligence and wisdom. And, now after meeting Lakhi and Tora, he realised that in Assam too there could be other girls like Swarnalata.

Swarna was so engrossed in her thoughts that she didn't

even notice that Dharmakanta was silent all this while. She had been dreaming of becoming a writer. Just as Dharmakanta had suggested, she was quietly arranging her thoughts so as to put them on paper. After a few moments, she exclaimed in an unguarded manner:

"If only if I could write like Bankimchandra!"

"Do you like his writings? What are the books you've read?"

"While in Calcutta, I had read *Durgesnandini*. Here I borrowed a copy of *Kapal Kundala* from Lakhi. What a strange book! One feels like reading it again and again. Lakhi has so many passages of that book by heart."

"Where did Lakhi get to read these books?" asked Dharmakanta in amazement.

"She gets them from Charusila Baideu. She has been encouraging Lakhi from her first day in school. One can't imagine what would have happened to her life without her support." Swarna heaved a sigh.

"Please tell me about Lakhi's life. It's so hard to believe how she has come this far in her education." Dharmakanta expressed his curiosity quite openly this time.

For Swarna it was quite natural for people wanting to know about Lakhi and Tora. They were so different from other girls. Swarna was only too eager to speak about them. She quickly drew a picture of Lakhi's life of struggle for Dharmakanta. It could be that at certain points she did exaggerate somewhat. But then, she had picked up this trait from her classmates in Calcutta. Who wouldn't want to embellish one's speech, especially if there was such an enthralled listener? Moreover, Dharmakanta was so spellbound listening to the details of Lakhi's life, that he naturally missed the exaggerations, if any. For him that day Lakhi had become the symbol of struggling womanhood and, without his knowing it, he seemed to be filled with lots of tender feelings for her.

During that period, Tora and Lakhi would come regularly
to Bilwa Kutir, for they had discovered a new joy in working
together. Gunabhiram too would occasionally join in and share
his plans for the future with them. Bishnupriya, while serving tea
and snacks would also throw in a suggestion or two. Even the
eleven-year-old Karuna seemed affected by the enthusiasm. As
soon as he came back from school, he would sit down and stick
postage stamps on the book-packets. The general feeling among
all those involved in the work seemed to be that something really
important was being done. On one such day, observing the scene
at the Barua household, Tora said with a laugh:

"It's just like working in the Mission bungalow during
Christmas. This is exactly how we work!"

"On the night before Bihu, often we the women of the house
keep awake, for there is so much to do. But, that could never
be as satisfying as this work. That work is for the pleasure of
self and family. But, this is for society, isn't it?" said Lakhi in all
seriousness.

"Well, if this small magazine could carry the light of
knowledge to the people of Assam, then all our efforts will be
really meaningful," said Gunabhiram as he ran his hand lovingly
over a copy of the journal. At that moment, Dharmakanta felt
that Gunabhiram Barua was some tall peepal tree and they were
all sitting in its shade and preparing themselves to meet the ups
and downs of life. He observed each one present in the room.
Bishnupriya too seemed to be a tree laden with flowers and
fruit—one that had weathered many a storm. Yet, she was always
the mother image of love and patience. As for Swarna, she was
like a rose that had just started to bloom and was untouched yet
by the harsh realities of life. For him, Tora appeared like a busy
stream that didn't have any time to wait for anyone. If only she
could put her unending energy to the service of the country,
thought Dharmakanta. And Lakhi? He couldn't really think of

anything to compare her with. She was so different from the other girls he had met till then. And, it didn't take long for him to realize that, after meeting Lakhi, he was no longer the same person. His private moments were soon flooded with thoughts about Lakhi. He was also somewhat worried that these thoughts could eventually force him to stray from his chosen path. Yet, he never considered thinking about Lakhi as something wrong or sinful. Thus, it was with many a confusing thought that Dhramakanta returned to Tapatjuri tea garden after about a week.

10

As the winter vacation drew to a close and the time of Swarna's return to Calcutta drew near, Gunabhiram and his wife started worrying about many things. They had resolved to get Swarna married off to an eligible groom within a year or two. So, they were not at all eager to keep their daughter in the hostel any more. On her part, Swarna was just not prepared to hear of leaving school. She was deeply upset when she saw that several of her schoolmates had been forced by their parents to abandon their studies mid-way and get married. She fervently tried to believe that her parents would not do the same, that they would allow her to read as much as she wanted to. And so, Gunabhiram and Bishnupriya, unwilling to hurt Swarna's confidence in them, decided to chart out an alternate course. It was agreed that Bishnupriya would stay in Calcutta along with her sons for a year or two and look after Swarna's education. Swarna was then in her third year at the high school and all her teachers were hoping that she would take the Entrance Examination after three years.

Meanwhile, Gunabhiram rented a spacious house at Calcutta's Maniktola Street for his family and then returned to Nagaon. A strange silence descended on Bilwa Kutir. Every month, however, at the time of the publication of *Asom Bandhu*, there was a great deal of activity. Being alone now, Gunabhiram spent most of his time in his study. Dharmakanta, however, would come to

Nagaon almost every month. Although the apparent reason for his coming was the *Asom Bandhu*, yet Gunabhiram couldn't help but notice that a serious sort of relationship was growing up between Dharmakanta and Lakhi. Though Gunabhiram thought of discussing the matter with Dharmakanta, yet he desisted from broaching the matter first, he being so much senior to them in age. He thought maybe he would talk about it if Dharmakanta brought it up. He seemed to have a deep sense of confidence in both Dharmakanta and Lakhi and didn't see any reason why they would do anything wrong.

In their Calcutta home, Swarna had, in the meantime, established herself as the guardian of her three younger brothers. It was Bishnupriya, however, who was finding it a bit difficult to adjust to her new situation. Although there were plenty of visitors who gave them company, yet when it came to the little things of everyday life, she had to totally depend on her daughter. Swarna could speak both English and Bengali quite fluently. So, whether it was managing the servants at home or writing applications in English to the school headmaster for her brothers, it was Swarna who looked after everything. She had suddenly discovered a new sense of fulfilment in doing all this. After having stayed away from home for such a long time, she now had an opportunity to re-discover her brothers. She got a lot of pleasure in getting them dressed, in arranging their books and looking after their lessons or in simply telling them stories. As for them, Baideu was the most beautiful and knowledgeable person in the world and they unquestioningly accepted whatever she said.

Her father had arranged a buggy to take Swarna to school. And, each day on her way to school, she would be captivated by the sights of the city. Maybe, she liked the city because it was filled with memories which had been cast in that delicate meeting point between adolescence and youth. Swarna liked Nagaon, just as a child likes her mother. But Calcutta's fascination was like that of a mysterious lover. Only those who had experienced the strange variety of its life could really understand this. Not to speak of the young, even old hearts would be roused by the city's southern spring breeze whose mere touch was enough to send many a dried up soul into the land of poesy. And, on those enchanting evenings, Swarna would stand by one of the south-facing windows of their house and try to recite Rabindranath. She hadn't had a chance to meet the poet after that particular Maghutsav evening; but she had learnt from her friends that he was now married to a young girl. The news had made her feel quite sad, for she had come to know from Hemoprova and her friends that that there was talk of her marriage to Rabindranath. But the match did not work out for some unexplained reason. That's why maybe she felt some mysterious kind of link with the poet. Swarna would sometimes miss a heartbeat while remembering that deep, pensive look of the poet on that Maghutsav evening. And that new song of *Mayar Khela*—"This spring filled with sadness…". Swarna felt that the poet had written that song just for her.

11

The *Asom Bandhu* was published regularly for about a year. After that it became clear that the journal was not in a position to survive any longer. There weren't the expected number of readers and many of those who had subscribed to the journal were now dropping out and not renewing their annual subscriptions. Gunabhiram wrote to several people requesting them to subscribe. But, barring a few, most of the people didn't reply. Dharmakanta went around Guwahati and Nagaon in search of new readers. He visited his acquaintances and friends, the latest issue of the journal always in his sling bag. While most of the people did not hesitate to buy a single copy, they were unwilling to pay for a year's issues, fearing that the journal would stop publication. Not to speak of the poorer section of readers, Dharmakanta was aghast that even those who were quite well off, came out with excuses to avoid paying the annual subscription of three rupees. While some said that they couldn't afford the sum, others criticized the language of the journal and hesitated to pay. In Guwahati, Dharmakanta even visited Lakheswar Katoky, since Gunabhiram had requested he do so. Lakheswar had passed his B. A. with a third class and had got a job on Gunabhiram's recommendation. But after that, he hadn't kept any contacts with Gunabhiram. However, he had written once to inform Barua that, as per his parents' wishes, he was now married to a

nine-year-old Brahmin girl belonging to the Goswami family of
Kaliabor. Dharmakanta had never approved of Lakheswar's ways
ever since their college days. It was only after coming to know
Lakheswar did Dharmakanta realize how little higher education
by itself could do to broaden one's outlook. Dharmakanta still
remembered the contents of an essay that Lakheswar had read
in their mess at Calcutta. In that essay entitled "Women's Real
Freedom", Lakheswar had argued against higher education for
women, saying that such a step would be disastrous for the nation.
He maintained that a woman's real qualities were revealed best in
their household work. There were many other such observations
in the article which Dharmakanta thoroughly disapproved of and
he now distinctly recalled how, on that evening in their Calcutta
mess, they had so heatedly debated matters. Dharmakanta now
remembered how he had pointed out the ideals of the Brahmo
religion in order to build up his argument. But he had then
noticed that Lakheswar too was not short of supporters among
the Assamese students.

Dharmakanta was now recalling all this as he proceeded to
meet Lakheswar. He knew that in order to keep the journal
going, one would have to seek help from all possible quarters,
even from people like Lakheswar. On meeting him, Dharmakanta
felt right from the first that Lakheswar was trying to make fun of
him. He showed no interest whatsoever in the *Asom Bandhu* and
after having enquired a thing or two about Gunabhiram Barua,
Lakheswar hesitatingly offered his three-rupee subscription and
asked:

"How will you run the magazine with donations like this?
When there are so many good Bengali magazines, who'll ever
read the *Asom Bandhu*? I gave up after thinking of all this."

"If educated people like you are so pessimistic, then Assamese
language and literature will never advance," Dharmakanta replied
with some irritation.

"Well, forget about literature. What about the other thing we have heard? Is it true?" Lakheswar asked in a low intimate voice.

"What is it?" Dahrmakanta asked in surprise.

"You are really sly! Even though we stay here we have come to know of your relations with the widowed daughter of Panchanan Sarma. But, do be a bit careful—though he looks a simple soul, Panchanan Sarma is quite a headstrong fellow. He will not spare you if anything goes wrong with that girl."

Thinking that he had finally floored Dharmakanta, Lakheswar continued with a wink: "Lakhipriya too is quite a girl. Once when I tried to hold her hand in a friendly gesture, she left in a huff, as if she was a sati-sadhvi."

At first, a sense of anger and surprise so overtook Dharmakanata that he couldn't say anything. It was only after listening to Lakheswar that he realized how people had misread their relationship and smeared Lakhi's character. He knew that it was futile to fight with low beings like him. Nonetheless, just to defend Lakhi's honour, he suddenly said something which he hadn't as yet been able to tell even to Lakhi:

"Kataki, you should not have said all this about my fiancée. After this, I will never be able to accept you as my friend."

"Your fiancée? Who? Lakhipriya?" Lakheswar asked in utter disbelief.

"Yes, of course. It is Lakhipriya. It may be impossible for low creatures like you, but not for me. For you, it may be just a game to spoil a helpless widow. For me, it is my sacred duty to give her a chance to live in society as a woman of honour. Good-bye."

Saying this, Dharmakanta walked out with firm steps, leaving a thunderstruck Lakheswar behind. As he left, he quietly resolved that during his next trip to Nagaon, he would formally propose to Lakhipriya. Till now, he had met Lakhi alone only on two occasions—once in front of the mission school and once when he had escorted her from Bilwa Kutir up to her house—a matter of a few yards. On both occasions, they hadn't been able to express their feelings towards each other. But, since things had taken such a turn, Dharmakanta resolved that to save her from society's cruel onslaught, he would have to marry Lakhi soon.

Dharmakanta narrated to Gunabhiram only a small part of the bitter experiences he had while trying to collect subscriptions for the *Asom Bandhu*. One day he said in quite a negative tone:

"Our Assamese people can never encourage anyone for trying to do something good. They just see faults."

"Well, but those who see the faults, do not themselves do anything," responded Barua. "If each one had learnt from the Bengalis to openly express one's feelings, then Asom would have progressed a lot. But our educated section is content with sitting around the kitchen fire and digging up the faults of others. They never write in the papers."

"It seems we'll have to eventually stop publishing the *Asom Bandhu*. You alone have been bearing all the expenses of the journal for the last few issues. It appears that apart from those who have been writing for the journal, there won't be any other subscribers. Is it possible to continue bringing out a journal like this? Moreover, even the number of contributors is steadily going down."

Dharmakanta's words were filled with anger and frustration. He felt that if the journal closed down, it would be like losing an intimate friend. It was through the journal that he had met Lakhi and had gained a friend like Tora, not to speak of the unstinted love he had got from all those at Bilwa Kutir. Now, if the *Asom Bandhu* was to cease publication, his ties with all these people were bound to snap. He had tried to give these ties some permanence by drawing Lakhi close to him.

In a small place like Nagaon, nothing could be kept hidden for long. But it was quite surprising that the family of Panchanan Sarma didn't have any inkling of Lakhi's growing relationship with Dharmakanta, even though people like Lakheswar had come to know of it in places as far off as Guwahati. Sarma had met Dharmakanta several times at Bilwa Kutir and was quite impressed by the young man's behavior and sense of idealism. But he could never have imagined that Lakhi and Dharmakanta had become so close to each other. That's why he was dumbstruck when someone in the market told him about their growing relationship. On returning home, he called his wife and daughter to their bedroom and shut the door. One quick look at her father's face and Lakhi could guess what the matter was. She knew that her parents would be shattered if she told them the truth. But, she had no desire to keep things hidden from them either. Only the previous evening, while walking along the bank of the Kolong, she and Dharmakanta had decided to disclose everything to Lakhi's father and then seek his blessings. At the same time they knew only too well that he would never approve of their match. So, before taking the final step and leaving home for good, Lakhi wanted some breathing space. But some "well wisher" had ensured that this was not to be. After drawing a long breath, Lakhi told her parents in clear terms that she had decided to marry Dharmakanta. Thunderstruck, Panchanan Sarma and his wife stood mutely for some time. They kept wondering how Lakhi had gathered the courage to take such an unheard of step! Panchanan Sarma kept staring at his daughter's face. It was that same face which had stubbornly insisted on going to school. Though now the eyes were lowered, yet he could well gauge their steady determination. Even then, making a rather half-hearted effort to enforce his authority, he said:

"According to which customs are you thinking of getting married? Inter caste marriages are not allowed by the Hindu religion. This is possible only if the boy is of a higher caste and the girl of a lower one. But, in your case it is just the opposite. Moreover, widow marriages are not accepted in our part of the world. No one approves of them. Therefore, such a marriage is simply impossible."

It was a tone not of anger but of helplessness that Lakhi noticed in her father's words—as if he wouldn't be really unhappy if the matter were made possible. Lakhi knew her father better than anyone else. She could see that there was always an unending struggle in his mind between his love for his daughter and his beliefs in the accepted norms of society. Till now, the father's love had triumphed. But, she asked herself, would it triumph on this occasion too?

It was a firm unwavering answer that Lakhi gave to her father:

"We'll marry according to the Brahmo rites. There are no barriers in that."

"Will you be really able to give up your religion? Do you realize that along with your religion, you will also have to give up your society? You will have no one to fall back upon in your times of distress."

"The Brahmo faith is not a separate religion. It is just a different form of the Hindu religion. People often mistake it for Christianity because its rites are different. But even if society gives us up, we'll continue to work for its good. And, some day that very society will once again welcome us back."

Pachanan Sarma just gave a sigh and shook his head. Meanwhile, Lakhi's mother had started sobbing inconsolably. She said: "Hakim Barua has finished you! Oh! Why did you have to go to their place?"

Lakhi was deeply moved by her mother's plight. She suddenly felt as if her mother was much younger than her. Her mother had not learnt even half of what she knew of life at her age. In certain respects, she was just like a child. Lakhi embraced her mother and pushing her head into her shoulders, she said:

"Ai, the Hakim Baruas do not know anything at all about this.

Please don't blame them. I am to be blamed for my own fate. Don't you feel sorry for me, Ai? Just bless me that I'll never hurt you all by committing any sinful act."

Lakhi's mother didn't understand a word of what her strange daughter was saying. What was a sin for the mother was not at all so for the daughter. Even then, she laid her hand on her daughter's head for a fleeting second and then collapsed on her bed. Seeing this, Panchanan Sarma quietly left the room.

As if to relieve him of his sorrow, he started walking towards Bilwa Kutir. On reaching Gunabhiram's house, Sarma straightaway asked the Hakim Dangoria as to why he had kept such an important fact hidden from him all these days. Caught somewhat unawares, Barua took some time to respond and kept sitting quietly, his eyes fixed on the floor. Then, in a self-accusing tone, he slowly said:

"Well, I should have warned you about this. I had noticed it quite some time ago but had never thought that it would go this far. Dharmakanta hasn't told me anything about it. I too haven't asked. Actually, for some time now I have been so taken up with Swarna's wedding that I haven't had the time to think of anything else. Her marriage has been fixed with a young doctor named Nandakumar Roy. He is from Dacca and has recently returned from London."

"You are indeed a lucky father to be able to give your daughter in marriage to such an accomplished groom. There is none as unfortunate as me in this world," Sarma said with a deep sigh.

"Sarma, no one really knows what fate has ordained for us. Dharmakanta may not be a Brahmin. But he comes of a good family. Believe me, I am yet to come across a more intelligent and upright young man. How many young men would really dare to marry a widow? Believe me, it would be difficult to find such a young man even in Bengal. I feel that if the two of them are serious about getting married, all of us should be really happy. Let me tell you that the Hindu shastras have nothing against widow marriage. In fact, the sage Parashar has approved of it. Otherwise, how could Vidyasagar quote the scriptures and build up such a strong argument in favour of widow marriage? Didn't I once give you a book by Vidyasagar to read?"

"Yes, you did. The name of the book is *Bidhaba Bibah Pracarit Hua Uchit Ki Na?* (Is it proper to allow Widow Marriage?) I have read it and found, that everything that is said there appeared to be true. But would our society here accept those arguments? Even if Lakhi gives up our religion and becomes a Brahmo, there'll be a lot of turmoil. We'll be ostracized."

Gunabhiram kept mum for a while. He felt that Sarma was right. For, in the eyes of the conservative Brahmin society, there was little difference between a Brahmo and a Christian. The Brahmos had the unsavoury reputation of not believing in caste differences and of eating forbidden food. Over and above all that, the social reformers who had married widows were invariably Brahmos. As one who had done this, he himself was quite apprehensive that he would be ostracized by society once he retired from his high post in the government. Even then he tried to assure Panchanan Sarma:

"Well Sarma, being a Brahmo does not mean giving up being a Hindu. The Brahmos have, in fact, accepted the oldest and purest form of the Vedic religion of the Hindus. So, you can be certain that Lakhi and Dharmakanta are not straying away from their religion. Moreover, if you decide to stand up for what you believe in, then you will also have to be prepared to face society's scorn. Don't be afraid. Even if others boycott you, at least we won't."

Gunabhiram added the last words in a lighter vein. Sarma too tried to respond with a smile. Listening to Gunabhiram, he felt somewhat relieved. But something still seemed to trouble him and he asked Barua:

"Does the Brahmo Samaj accept inter-caste marriages?"

"The Adi Brahmo Samajists led by Maharshi Devendranth Tagore had refused to accept such marriages. All these days, I too have been supporting that stand. But by arranging an inter-caste marriage, Keshav Chandra Sen created a furore in the Brahmo Samaj. Nowadays there have been several such marriages among the members of the Sadharan Brahmo Samaj. In fact, several of my friends have also gone in for such marriages".

"What about you? Will you accept Lakhi's wedding?"

Gunabhiram was quite unprepared by Sarma's pointed question. He paused for a while and then said:

"One's way of thinking is bound to change along with the circumstances of life. I have great affection for both Lakhi and Dharmakanta. So, even if I happen to disagree with their views, my blessings will always be with them."

12

The otherwise quiet and placid atmosphere of the Nagaon Baptist Mission was suddenly surcharged with a new enthusiasm. A new sense of urgency seemed to affect all its inmates and almost every day they would get together to draw up plans to ensure the success of the ensuing golden jubilee celebrations. The small town of Nagaon was preparing to pay homage to Nathan Browne and Oliver Cutter, two pioneering missionaries who, having come to Assam some twenty-five years ago, had endured endless hardships for the spread of the Gospel in this part of the world. Missionaries of the entire eastern region were now gathered in Nagaon to take stock of their work and envisage future plans. There was yet another reason for holding the golden jubilee celebrations. For this could very well provide the opportunity to strengthen the bonds of brotherhood amongst all those who were engaged single-handedly in the spread of both education and Christianity in the remotest corners of the region.

It was during one of the weekly meetings of the "Young Friends Meet" that Tora first came to know of the jubilee celebrations. This group would meet every Wednesday in the mission bungalow and the proceedings would start with some young man or woman reading out a particular episode from the Bible. After that, all the other members would give their views on the subject. In the end, the padre present at the meeting would elaborate on the real significance of that particular Biblical event. On that day, Tora was reading out from the story of Mary Magdalene. While describing how Mary washed Jesus's feet with her tears, Tora's voice was choked with emotion. There were then some twenty to twenty-five young people in the room, most of whom were from in and around Nagaon. The only guest who had come from a distance was Henry Thomas who was there to spend a few days at the Nagaon Mission. Though his name seemed foreign, yet he belonged to an Assamese family from Sivasagar. He had been named Ahina by his parents. But after having lost both of them while still at school, someone brought the child to the Mission. And, since then, he had grown up at the Mission as a Christian. It was the missionaries who named him Henry Thomas. The young man had worked for the Mission in the Garo Hills, and was now being transferred to the Naga Hills.

During his school days at the Sivasagar Mission, Henry used to frequently meet a Naga Christian convert named Subanmeren and it was through him that he had come to know the Ao Nagas. Subanmeren was quite popular with the missionaries and Reverend Clarke, who had learnt a lot about the Naga Hills from this Ao Naga, was especially fond of him. Henry's acquaintance with the Naga Hills had begun when, as a schoolboy, he used to accompany Gadhula Kakati of the Sivasagar Mission on his many proselytizing trips to the bachelors' dormitories in the nearby hills. Gadhula Kakati could speak the Ao language fluently and, having stayed with him, Henry too had picked it up. But after he went to the Garo Hills he lost his fluency owing to lack of practice. But his fascination for the Naga Hills always remained and boyhood memories would often draw him there. At one time he had hoped to begin his missionary life among the Aos. But that didn't work out because the Mission had other plans for him. However, later on when Clark Sahib started a mission near Mulumingsen in the Naga Hills, he asked Henry to join him.

Initially, the mission at Tura refused to relieve Henry. Ultimately, just before the jubilee celebrations, it allowed him to come to Nagaon to meet Clark Sahib. But before taking up work at the new mission, Henry took a few days break at Sivasagar. And, when he realised that he would not be able to come for the jubilee celebrations once he left for the hills, Henry decided to extend his stay there.

Henry had no memories of his days before he came to the Mission. Sometimes he felt that he was sent to the mission by his relatives who wanted to deprive him of whatever land and property his father might have had. Otherwise, he seemed to tell himself, how was it that there was no one in the village to bring him up? As far as he could remember, the sahibs and memsahibs of the Sivasagar Mission used to love him a lot and Henry soon began to feel that there could not be any other work than that of the mission for him. It was as if he was born to work for the satisfaction of the missionary men and women and his greatest offence would be to displease them.

Perhaps because he had spent most of his life with the missionaries, there was sense of orderliness and discipline in the way Henry carried himself. This was partly because from a very young age he had learnt to suppress his natural feelings and be a good boy and earn the praise of the mission people. At a time when the village children of his age would wallow in the mud wearing a gamosa and jump into the ponds for a quick swim or climb mango trees to taste the unripe green fruit, Henry would be going to school or saying his prayers dressed neatly in a clean shirt and a pair of white shorts. Moreover, being an inmate of the Mission did not give Henry much chance to acquaint himself with the outside world which seemed quite mysterious to him. Often, while passing by an Assamese house, the young schoolboy would stand in front of the bamboo gate and keep staring at it for a long time. He would be strangely attracted by the ordinary happenings in the lives of the people living in these houses. It was as if he could hear the faint notes of a familiar, distant song. But he could never gather courage to go inside one of the houses and talk with the occupants there. For, the authorities at the mission had prohibited him from visiting any non-Christian house without their permission. Hence, the world outside his Mission was like a forbidden one for him.

When Henry reached Nagaon from the Garo Hills, the jubilee celebrations were already in full swing. Reverend Moore and his wife, who were in charge of the mission, entrusted Henry with the responsibility of conducting the hymns in Assamese. Tora was asked to help him in this. At first Henry was a bit reluctant to take upon himself such a heavy responsibility in a place which was quite unfamiliar to him and where he had come just for a few days. But having seen Tora's flair for work and her efficiency in managing everything smoothly, he was both amazed and relieved. Moreover, ever since he came to Nagaon, certain thoughts were troubling his mind and he had not been able to concentrate on anything. But working with Tora seemed to make a lot of difference and gave Henry a strange feeling of openness. From the very first day itself, he had taken a strong liking to Tora and was enamoured by her love for work, sincerity and self-confidence. He realized how even a reticent and unusually grave person like him could learn to laugh and converse freely just by being with Tora. He was quite surprised at this change that had come over him. Actually, a feeling of change had been taking place in Henry's mind for quite some time. All these days his world had been small but well organized. There was no place in it for doubts, uncertainty and skepticism. The missionary folk were always there with answers to his queries. And, if he didn't get a correct answer to some question, he would simply push it out of his mind. He had learnt from an early age that in matters of religion, unquestioning faith was the sign of the true follower.

But this time the moment he stepped onto the steamer bound for upper Assam at Silamari, he felt that the world under his feet was getting strangely unsteady. It was as if an unruly gust of wind had ruffled his well groomed head of hair. Yet, till he had boarded the ship he had never even thought for once that such winds of change had started blowing in the world. Perhaps because he was thought to be a missionary, Henry was given a seat in one of the special cabins of the ship. The other passenger in his cabin was a Bengali gentleman. The moment Henry entered the cabin, the person said to himself, "Thank God!" As was his usual practice, Henry responded with a soft "Amen" and started arranging his things in the cabin. As always, he was hesitant to begin a conversation with an unknown person. But the Bengali gentleman was of an open nature. He came forward and shook hands and introduced himself.

"I am Rajnarayan Chattopadhyaya. I teach at the General Assembly College of Calcutta. I was a bit scared when I first heard your name. You know very well how difficult it is to travel in the same cabin with a feringi. I am very pleased to meet you. How far are you going?"

"Up to Silghat. And what about you?"

"I will get off at Guwahati. My brother is a government servant there and he has been inviting me to visit for a long time. So I thought let me go and have a darshan of Maa Kamakhya. You are a Christian. Otherwise, I would have asked you what other temples and holy places there are at Guwahati," said Chattopadhya.

Henry just smiled and did not say anything. Meanwhile, Chattopadhyaya opened a packet of sweets and offered Henry some sandesh.

"Please have some. I never thought that one could get such nice sweets at your Silamari."

Henry picked up a sweet with a lot of hesitation and then thanked the gentleman. Chattopadhyaya popped a sandesh into his mouth, took some water from a glass and then said with a smile: "Where are you from, Mr Thomas?"

"Well, I am from Assam."

"Is your mother tongue Assamese? In that case, you should be able to speak Bengali too? I have heard that the two languages are very similar."

Till then the conversation was going on in English. But Chattopadhayaya spoke the last sentence in Bengali. Henry didn't know Bengali well. So, he replied in English:

"Though there is an apparent similarity between the two, actually they are quite different. I can follow a bit of Bengali but can't speak it. You can speak to me in Bengali and I'll respond to you as much as I can."

Following this, they talked of many things, one of them speaking in fluent Bengali and the other using a mix of Assamese, Bengali and English. It was Henry's usual practice not to speak with strangers while on a journey but Chattopadhaya was such an amiable person that within a short while he started speaking with Henry in an intimate manner. Henry too gradually shed his reserve and stated telling him things about his own life. After questioning Henry about his work in the Garo Hills, Chattopadhyaya suddenly asked him:

"Well, Mr. Thomas, when you go on your mission to spread the Gospel, why do you ask the people to accept Christianity?"

"Because this pure religion shows the path to salvation for mankind," Henry replied instantly.

"Don't other religions too show the path to salvation?" Chattopadhyaya was clearly trying to test Thomas.

All these days, Henry had always avoided any discussion which could plant the seeds of doubt in his unshakable faith. He was ever ready to answer any question relating to God and religion put to him by ignorant people. But he was never prepared to indulge any educated individual who might try to shake his faith. So, he replied to Chattopadhyaya's question in a firm manner:

"I believe that it is only the Christian religion which can show people the path to salvation".

Chattopadhyaya lowered his head and kept quiet for some moments. Seeing this, Henry started flipping through the pages of his *Pilgrim's Progress*. As a schoolboy, he had read an Assamese translation of that book in the *Orunodoi*. It was only now after reading it in original English that he was able to enjoy the book. Meanwhile, holding on to the steamer's railings, Chattopadhyaya was enjoying the natural beauty of both the banks of the Brahmaputra. After some time, he came and sat beside Henry on a bench and asked in a serious tone:

"You must have been offended my question." Henry looked at him in surprise and the gentleman continued:

"Actually my intention was not to cast doubts on your faith. I should not have asked such a question to a person like you who is engaged in religious work. But some time ago I had met a really great seer in Calcutta. His name is Ramakrishna. People call him Pagal Thakur or the Mad Seer. After listening to him, I have been quite disturbed. That's why I asked you that question. Ramakrishna has said, "Jato Mat, Tato Path", there are as many paths as there are faiths. It is we who follow different paths to reach the same god. But ultimately, all these paths end at the same destination."

A somewhat puzzled Henry kept on listening to all this and then asked: "Isn't the seer a Hindu?"

"Yes, of course. But it is said that he has prayed in churches, mosques and temples and got the same sense of peace and fulfillment. After meeting Ramakrishna, I too have begun to feel that all religions are equal, their goal being the same."

Listening to Chattopadhyay, Henry observed that there was something philosophic about the man. He would have loved to prolong the discussion because in his presence he felt like a small boy looking through a crack in the wall at the forbidden world outside. Strangely, as he talked with his new acquaintance, Henry increasingly sensed the presence of an unknown world. But, he couldn't enjoy his new sensation for long. For, in the meantime, the steamer had already approached the outskirts of Guwahati. Chattopadhyaya looked at the Nilachal Hills in the distance and greeted them with folded hands. Then he got busy in arranging his things.

Most of the passengers from Calcutta disembarked at Guwahati. Those taking the journey to upper Assam would board the vessel the next morning. As for Henry, he went over to the nearby Baptist Mission to spend the night. There he met several old acquaintances. For, during his trips from Sivasagar to Tura, he would usually spend a few nights at the Guwahati mission which was a meeting point for missionaries from different parts of Assam. Athough the centre of missionary activity was Sivasagar followed by Nagaon, yet Guwahati was always important because it was well connected. Dedicated workers were routinely sent to Guwahati and, in turn, others went frequently from there to Nagaon. Henry was quite surprised to see that the wife of a local worker, Kandura, was managing the girls' school at Guwahati quite efficiently. Prior to this, the school had been run by foreign women like Mrs. Danforth, Mrs Ward and Mrs Scott.

When Henry arrived at the Mission, hectic activities were going on there in preparation for the jubilee celebrations. Reverend Bardett was busy preparing a report on the Guwahati Mission which he planned to read at the jubilee conference at Nagaon. In the midst of all this activity, Henry suddenly felt quite lonely. Just as he was learning to feel at home in Tura, he had to leave it and go to the Naga Hills. In Sivasagar too his earlier friends and acquaintances had all left. However, he had been taught as a missionary to always try to accept his workplace, wherever it may be, as his home. But in Guwahati that day, he seemed to be rather tired. As he was about to retire that night, he remembered what Chattopadhyaya had told him. Could it really be that, even among those whom he had all these years looked upon as heathens, there were people who were following the right path? If, as his fellow traveller had said, the goal of all religions was the same, then where was the harm in knowing about them? Thinking of this, he couldn't sleep for a long time.

The next morning he got up slightly late. Rushing to the ferry ghat, he found that the steamer was about to leave. He had left his belongings in the cabin of the ship. But having reached it, Henry discovered that the cabin had been cleared of his things. When he asked a khalasi as to why his belongings had been removed from his cabin, he was told that a British couple had boarded the steamer at Guwahati and the cabin had been given to them. He asked Henry to find some other place. Unable to do anything, Henry collected his belongings and went down to the lower deck where he found a seat at one end of a bench where there were already quite a few second class passengers. Dharmakanta was sitting on a bench just in front of him. Though he hadn't heard Henry's exchange with the khalasi, yet he could guess what had happened. He was quite angry with Henry for having meekly accepted the injustice without any protest. And, the moment Henry moved up to a seat near him, Dharmakanta asked him:

"Don't you hold a first class ticket? You should have got a place in the cabin on the upper deck."

"Yes, you are right. I had come in the cabin from Silamari. It's only now that I had to give up my seat to a British couple. It won't be much of a problem, though. It is only a day's journey to Silghat," Henry replied with ease.

"Whether it be for a day or for an hour, you should not have given up your berth so easily. You were already travelling in that cabin as a bona fide passenger. If there were no berths, tickets should not have been issued at all to the English couple." Dharmakanta's voice was somewhat raised in excitement. Henry replied calmly with a smile, "What to do? There was no way out. The rights of the Englishmen supersede ours."

An old anger suddenly caught hold of Dharmakanta. Addressing his fellow passengers, he spoke as if addressing a public gathering, "This is how we Indians have been surrendering our rights. Today it is a seat in the train or the steamer, tomorrow it is the house we live in, and the day after tomorrow it is our country that we have handed over to the foreigners. The foreigners have fattened themselves on our resources and looted our property and yet we are not aware of our rights. If we go on like this, one day we will lose everything."

Henry was amazed at Dharmakanta's words. He was a bit scared too. He had never heard anyone say such things so openly. Henry had learnt from a young age to look upon the white memsahibs with respect. In his estimation, there weren't any other people as loving and as wise and efficient as them. He had never thought that the British were looting the country's wealth and he couldn't even imagine that anyone could think in that manner. But, on that particular day, his illusions were shattered. Some of the fellow passengers nodded their approval at what Dharmakanta had said. One of them addressed Dharmakanta:

"We have heard that in Calcutta, Bombay and other cities many of our educated persons are coming together and forming a committee to speak for the people. Is it true?"

"You are right. Last year at Bombay there was a conference held by a body called the Indian National Congress. This time the meeting took place at Calcutta. Several persons from our region also attended the conference. Gradually, this association would be able to work for the good of the people of the entire country." Dharmakanta's words were filled with conviction and enthusiasm. Listening to him, several of the passengers were touched by a feeling of hope—as if some change was really in the offing. Henry was at first quite uneasy listening to Dharmkanta. He was somewhat worried that the unwanted discussion was sparked off because of him. He never nourished any ill will against the British. But now he had come to know from Dharmakanta's words that there were plenty of people who thought quite differently. Normally, he would have easily come to terms with the anger and frustration which he had felt on being evicted from the cabin. But that day Dharmakanta had made him conscious of the real person that was in him. He suddenly felt deeply ashamed at his inability to protest.

13

The moment Henry landed at the Nagaon Mission, all sorts of worries assailed him. Although he was committed to carry on with his duties, yet somewhere he felt that he was losing control over his will. Earlier, there had been only a single path before him, straight and clear. Now, he suddenly realized that he had all these years not even noticed what lay on both sides of this road. Somehow, he felt incomplete. Ever since he had met Tora, this feeling of uncertainty had only deepened. He had been attracted towards her from the very first day. But faced with her self-confidence and deep involvement in her work, Henry felt rather incomplete and weak. One day Tora jokingly asked him:

"Mr. Thomas, why are you always so grave? When I am with you, I feel I am frivolous."

Somewhat taken aback, Henry had replied:

"I have always been like this. Being a missionary, one had to be somewhat reserved."

"Aren't missionaries also human beings? Humans will always laugh and joke. Not always, though. But sometimes."

"When I am with you, I also feel like relaxing," having said this, Henry suddenly became conscious of himself. But quickly recovering his usual sombre poise, he said: "Actually, these days I have been a bit depressed. There are plenty of worries. I can't tell you all that."

Later on, however, Henry confided a lot about his life to
Tora. He also gave her an idea of his newly formed doubts and
confusions. But he hesitated to tell her all this in clear terms, lest
she misunderstood him because of her religious nature. One day,
while returning to Tora's home after the common prayer of the
jubilee function, Henry suddenly said:

"Tara, do you know we have no roots?"

Tara gave a surprised look and responded: "How can human
beings have roots?"

"Of course, they have. Clark Sahib, Gurney Sahib, Moore
Sahib, all of them have deep roots in their homeland. But where
are our roots?"

"Why, they are in our country, in our religion," Tora firmly
retorted. But Henry shook his head and said:

"No, not at all. Even if we have roots, they are but superficial
ones. They don't go that deep. Say, what is our link with this
country? We have denied its religion, culture and music as evil, as
the creations of the Devil."

"But what about our religion?" Tora asked helplessly.

"Religion too does not grow in a vacuum. It also needs roots
to survive."

Tora kept silent. She too had faced many a doubt, many an
apprehension. But she hadn't considered it necessary to indulge
these doubts. Whenever she talked with Swarna, Dharmakanta
or Lakhi, she realized that the culture and beliefs of those whom
the missionaries had described as unbelievers, was not something
which could be dismissed so easily. If Henry was to be believed,
these people had strong roots in this country. There seemed to
be a big difference between what they wanted to do for their
country and what the missionaries intended. Though Tora had
never seriously considered these matters, yet they were always
there in some corner of her mind. As if to assure Henry, she now
said in her usual confident tone:

"Henry, we too belong to this country. Our roots are also in its soil. We could find them just with a little bit of search."

After the jubilee conference, Reverend Clark somehow did not insist on Henry's going with him to the Naga Hills. Having observed the growing closeness between Henry and Tara, he must have felt that perhaps Henry would want to spend some more time at the Nagaon mission. Henry too didn't disclose his mind to Clark as he himself wasn't too sure of what he really wanted to do. He needed some more time to think things out. That way, the padres of the mission seemed quite sympathetic. They seemed to believe that if Tora and Henry eventually got married, the couple would work with even greater zeal for the Mission.

Henry would go quite often with Tora to see her mother Golapi and he soon developed a liking for their neat and ordered house. One evening as both of them were sitting near Golapi and describing to her the details of the jubilee function, Golapi suddenly caught hold of Henry's hand and said in a voice choked with emotion: "Son, I am really worried about Tora. I am so scared to think of what'll happen to her when I am dead and gone. Will you look after her?"

Henry was a bit embarrassed. Though the two of them liked each other, they had never discussed the idea of getting married. Now caught quite unawares by Golapi's question, Henry lowered his eyes and said with a shy smile: "Tora can take care of herself very well. Who am I to look after her?"

Golapi gave Henry a surprised stare. With a shaky voice she asked: "That means you will not marry Tora?"

Henry immediately realized that Golapi had misunderstood him. Hastily trying to correct himself, he said: "No, no, I didn't mean that. I will consider myself really privileged and lucky to marry Tora. But she must have her own views."

Tora was quite amused at Henry's predicament. Taking control of the situation, she gave him a naughty smile and said: "Ai's wish has been fulfilled, is it not? Now let's see who takes care of whom."

A contented smile lit Golapi's face. But Tora and Henry could see that that they were about to face a host of problems. Just getting married wouldn't do away with these challenges. That day, sitting on the front lawn of Golapi's house, both of them made a lot of plans about their future. It was not just to be near Tora that Henry had given up going to the Naga Hills. There were certain other reasons which had prompted both of them to give up their work at the mission. Having seen the white missionary men and women from close quarters during the jubilee conference which had ended just a few days ago, they suddenly realized that there was an almost unbridgeable divide between the native Christians and their foreign counterparts. Although the foreign missionaries who had travelled great distances to attend the jubilee meet had treated them with a lot of politeness and brotherly affection, yet Tora and Henry could see quite well that all this reflected only one side of their personalities—much like the moon which shows the earth only one side of its face. The jubilee celebrations revealed to Tora and her friends the other rather mysterious side of the personalities of their foreign mentors; especially when they made hearty conversation among themselves. Somehow Tora and her companions felt left out when they talked excitedly about their homeland America or about some mutual friend. These were times when they felt quite helpless, although the foreign missionaries generally avoided doing this in their presence. However, this caution on the part of the foreigners made matters even more complicated. For even as Tora and her friends picked up scraps of conversation from a distance, they could see that it was something more than just religion that had brought these men and women from distant shores to risk their lives in an unknown land. They realized that the white men and women drew their strength from their own culture and civilization. Seeing this, Tora and Henry decided that till they finally made themselves equal in all aspects for the task given them, they would stay out of the mission and work among their people and would try to know and understand their own country. Since she had taken a course in nursing while in America with Bronson Sahib, Tora now decided to try for a nurse's job at the government dispensary. As for Henry, he wanted to go to Calcutta for his graduation and had already discussed the matter with Dharmakanta. Actually, he had virtually given up studies after passing his Entrance examination from the Sivasagar High School some years ago. But now, spurred by Tora's encouragement, his interest in resuming his studies grew and he wanted to begin life anew as a student. Gunabhiram Barua encouraged him by saying that he was eligible for a special scholarship set aside for Christian students. With that he could go to Calcutta and stay at a Christian students hostel there and attend college. It was with this hope that Henry started preparing for his new life.

14

Wedding preparations were yet to begin in the rented house of the Baruas in Kolkata. Unlike traditional Assamese weddings, this one didn't call for silk garments to be woven at least six months in advance; nor was there the need to arrange for komal chaul, curd and pots of molasses to entertain the guests. One also wouldn't need green betel-nuts and paan, the sarai and the sarai covercloth that are so mandatory for wedding invitations. There would be no need for the brass pot, the donari or the ghot to draw water from the river in order to give the bride her ceremonial bath. Nor would they need to keep the saloni and the bamboo fan to welcome the guests during the juroon. This wedding would be solemnized according to Brahmo customs and apart from the Vedic rites to be carried out by members of the Samaj, there wouldn't be any other rituals. In such a situation, there was not much for Bishnupriya to do and she should have been happy to have such an ostentatious wedding. Instead, as she recalled Kalipriya and Damayanti's weddings when the happiness of being the bride's mother made her forget the almost endless hassles, she now felt a sense of strange incompleteness. She couldn't reconcile herself to the fact that they couldn't find a good Assamese match for this girl of theirs who was so much more beautiful and accomplished than her two other daughters. Thinking of this, every now and then Bishnupriya, unseen by anyone, would heave a deep sigh. She had always wished to see Swarna married to a boy from a respectable Assamese family. But Bishnupriya's illusions were shattered when she found that even a leading Brahmo of Bengal like Maharshi Devendranath Tagore had refused to accept Swarna as a daughter-in-law. She realized then that there are times when even highly educated people shrink from adopting a liberal approach. That's exactly why Bishnupriya was so grateful to the young man who had come forward to marry Swarna. Nandakumar Roy stood out both for his handsome appearance as well as his many qualities. Not to speak of Assam, even in Bengal there were just a handful of persons who possessed a medical degree from England. Everyone who heard of the wedding in Calcutta had called it a unique match and had warmly congratulated Bishnupriya and Gunabhiram. In reply to all these good wishes, Bishnupriya would respond with a smile:

"Please bless her so that her wedded life is happy. What else does one want?"

Just a month was left for the wedding. Gunabhiram had already taken leave and come to Calcutta. He wanted return to Nagaon with Bishnupriya and the boys, after the wedding for there was little point their staying on in Calcutta after Swarna left. Morever, his own service with the government too was ending. However, he had plans of building a house in Calcutta and settling there after his superannuation.

It was Gunabhiram's habit to do a round of the book shops selling second-hand books whenever he came to the city. Though he would often pick up a book or two, it was actually the hope of meeting old friends and acquaintances that drew him to that area. And, invariably, he would come across someone he knew. But the person he met on that particular afternoon was special. Though much junior to him in age, Gunabhiram had a lot of regard for this young Assamese whom he considered to be among the front-ranking scholars of Bengal. He had first met this young official when he was an Assistant Commissioner in Nagaon. At that time the two of them had discussed Assam and the state of the Assamese language and their hopes and aspirations had taken new wings. But they lost contact with each other after being transferred to government posts in different places. Now, having suddenly come across this old friend at Adya's bookshop, Gunabhiram promptly invited him home. Introducing his guest to his wife and daughter, Gunabhiram said: "May I introduce you to none other than the magistrate of Noakhali and a Fellow of Calcutta University—Anandaram Barua. He is the first I.C.S. officer from Assam". Bishnupriya and Swarnalata greeted their guest with respectful namastes. Introducing his daughter to the guest, Gunabhiram said with some tinge of pride: "This is my daughter, Swarnalata. At present she is a student of Bethune College." Anandaram, who had till then not really noticed Swarnalata, gave a slightly embarrassed look. Having immersed himself in books for most of his life, this rather quiet person had had little time to spare for other attractions. But, having seen Swarna that morning, he felt a sudden change coming over him, something which he couldn't really understand. Quite surprised with himself, Anandaram continued looking at Swarnalata for a wee bit longer than usual. He couldn't recall having seen such beauty and grace before. Swarna, unable to face the evidently enamoured look, lowered her eyes. Anandaram realized that he was embarrasing the girl and he quickly asked her:

"Lots of girls study in Bethune College these days, don't they?"

"The numbers have certainly gone up. But most of the girls leave midway through their studies," Swarna replied shyly.

"But why do they leave? Is it because the school isn't that good?" Anadaram asked in surprise.

"No, that isn't the case. Most of them are married off before they can complete school." Saying this, Swarna glanced at her mother with lowered eyes. Anandaram kept on looking at Swarna's flushed face for sometime. Meanwhile both mother and daughter went inside to make arrangements for tea.

That afternoon, the two friends had a long conversation. Their topics ranged from the backward state of education in their province of Assam to problems of Sanskrit teaching and the drawbacks in the administration. Anandaram gave his host an idea of his grandiose plans. He told Barua that once he had finished with the commentary and notes to the *Amar Kosh*, he would start work on an enlarged version of the Sanskrit Grammar. Ten of the twelve volumes of this work had already been published. But he hadn't had the time to start work on the two other volumes. He mentioned how difficult it was to do this while carrying out the duties of a senior government official at the same time.

Bishnupriya and Swarnalata could not take part in the scholarly discussion which stretched into the evening. Nevertheless, they considered themselves lucky to be able to listen. Swarna had heard a lot about Anadaram earlier. But now, listening to him, she could not imagine how a scholar of his stature who had won the Gilchrist Award and had qualified for the Indian Civil Service could be so polite and unassuming. That evening, Anandaram too seemed to slide into momentary spells of absentmindedness. It appeared as if his quiet, settled world had been suddenly shaken by an unexpected gust of spring wind.

Later that evening, sitting by the window of his room in the Great Eastern Hotel, Anandaram stayed awake late into the night, engrossed in certain sweet thoughts. Even his favourite *Amar Kosh* lay unattended on his bedside table. On other days he would work till late on the book. But this particular night the flickering gas lamps of the city seemed to draw him into a golden dream-world.

Two days later, Anandaram's friend Sivaram Bora approached Gunabhiram with a marriage proposal. Even as Sivaram spelled out the details, Gunabhiram heaved a deep sigh. With tears in her eyes, Bishnupriya said: "If only such a proposal had come just two months ago! This is called fate." Gunabhiram told Sivaram with folded hands: "Please tell Barooahdev that I have been deeply hurt at having to disappoint him. Had I known of this before, no one would have been happier than me. But now all arrangements for my daughter's wedding have been finalized. What can I do? My only appeal to you Borah Dangoriah is please find a suitable match for Barooah. We'll all be overjoyed to see a person of his qualities settle down to a happy family life." Sivaram nodded with a faint smile: "I have little hope that he will again agree to marry. It was after many years that he had expressed such a desire."

Swarna's wedding day drew near. In the midst of all the wedding preparations, Giunabhiram and Bishnupriya kept trying to forget Anandaram's proposal. Swarna, of course, did not have any inkling of all this, for her parents had intentionally kept her in the dark. Not being sure of her feelings, they were careful not to hurt them. But, although Swarna occasionally recalled Anadaram's lingering gaze, yet she didn't feel the same as she did when her eyes had momentarily met Rabindranath's on that particular evening which they had spent at Jorasanko. Whenever she thought of those fleeting few moments, she invariably missed a heartbeat! As for Anadaram, though he was quite young in age, somehow Swarna placed him with her father's friends. All her father's friends seemed to fit into a common pattern—they were all scholars, well-placed officials and leaders of society. Swarna felt that such people could command only a deep sense of respect, other feelings being simply out of question. Her fiancée, Dr. Nanadakumar Roy, was also a highly educated person. But for Swarna, he was a completely different soul. A very articulate person, he could sing quite well and also recite poetry. She had never earlier met a person with a greater jest for life.

Swarna's was quite an ostentatious wedding. Although all the Vedic rites were performed, yet since a lot of accompanying rituals were done away with, the actual wedding ceremony was over in just about two hours. Most of the invitees being Brahmo Samajists from Calcutta, there was a fine mix of the best in Western and Eastern cultures. Rabindranath was also there to represent the Tagores of Jorasanko. He was accompanied by his young wife, Mrinmoyee. Who knows what thoughts might have passed through the poet's mind when he saw Swarna decked in all her bridal finery that evening? When Swarna greeted him with a shy smile, Rabindranath reciprocated with a polite namaskar. But did Swarna's resplendent beauty strike a forgotten chord in the poet's heart? Perhaps he remembered a particular evening of songs and dances, memories of which seemed encrusted in some corner of his heart, like the sadness-filled fragrance of the jasmine.

Quite a few Assamese students of Calcutta had also come to the wedding. The handsome young man who was busy ushering in the guests happened to be Bishnupriya's uncle. His name was Lakshminath Bezbaroa. The youth must have caught the eye of many a guest on that wedding day, for the idea of arranging a match with such a handsome young man for the daughters of one's relatives and friends was, as always, an attractive one. That evening itself Gunabhiram introduced Lakhsminath to Rabindranath Tagore and though they had met for the first time, the two of them were quite comfortable in each others company.

To add glamour to that enchanting evening, there was another bright star among the guests. Every Assamese, including the host Gunabhiram, vied with one another to pay attention to him. As for the Assamese youth of Calcutta, they had naturally heard a lot about Anandaram Barooah. But for many, it was their first opportunity to meet him in person. Anandaram walked up to the bride and with a tinge of embarrassment, placed a small decorated jewellery box in her hands. It had in it a pair of beautiful gold ear-rings. It was as if he wanted to say something to Swarna but left without a word. Many saw this silence as an expression of his rather shy personality. But for a fleeting moment Swarna saw a touch of sadness on his face and her woman's intuition could sense it all. This quiet and self-contained person left for Noakhali just a day after Swarna's wedding. Who could then have guessed that just three years later this great soul would pass away in Calcutta?

Among the wedding gifts that Swarna received, there was a delicately embroidered table-cloth with fine flower motifs on it. Tora had made it herself and sent the gift with Henry who was now a student in a Calcutta college and stayed at a hostel meant for Christian boys. Golapi had passed away barely two months after he had married Tora. Though she had lost her mother, yet Tora insisted on Henry's going to Calcutta for his studies and, to keep herself busy in his absence, she had started a boarding arrangement for some girls from the Mission school at her own house. Earlier, these girls used to stay with a Christian couple. But after the sudden death of Bapuram's wife who was their matron, Tora took upon herself the task of looking after the girls. Meanwhile, the Mission too was going ahead with its plans to build a hostel where girls from far-flung areas were to be accommodated when they came to Nagaon for their schooling.

Once Swarna's wedding was over, Henry paid a visit to Gunabhiram to express his gratitude to the person who had made it possible for him to come and study in Calcutta. He had already picked up quite a few friends and acquaintances in that great city. He also went to the Assamese students' mess and met some of the students there. He found each one of them deeply engrossed in making new plans and programmes for the improvement of their language and literature. He was so impressed by their commitment that in his letters to Tora he would frequently mention their names and these included Lakhshminath Bezbaroa, Satyanath Bora, Rajanikanta Bordoloi, and Hemchandra Goswami.

15

Dharmakanta and Lakhipriya's wedding sent shock waves throughout Nagaon. The marriage of a Brahmin widow with a boy of the Kalita caste was enough in itself to cause a lot of excitement. But what was even more surprising was that the wedding was held, in the absence of the families of the bride and the groom, at the house of their teacher, Charusila. It was solemnized according to the "Naba Bidhan" rites of the Sadaharam Brahmo Samaj which meant that there was no h*avana* or the mandatory seven steps around the fire for the bride and groom. After this, however, the marriage was duly registered as per the law.

The day before the wedding, Charusila came to take Lakhi to her place. It was difficult to imagine the situation in Panchannan Sarma's house on that day. Even a death in the family could not have produced such gloom. Lakhi's aunts had thrown out the cooking utensils from the kitchen and were crying out loud, while her mother had gone without any food and was crying incessantly, sprawled out on the mud floor of her bedroom. As for Panchanan Sarma, he had left home early in the morning and was yet to return. In such circumstances, Lakhi thought it best to quietly leave for her teacher's house without any leave taking. However, she did go up to her mother and touched her feet to say good-bye. Though along with the other members of the family, her parents too had publicly disowned her, yet she seemed to understand them. She knew that her mother did not have any views of her own and was used to accepting whatever was told to her. She also knew that her mother had a great deal of affection for her and she felt guilty for having inflicted such pain on her. As for her father, Lakhi was convinced that he not only understood her but had even secretly approved of her action. She realized that a person like her father couldn't go beyond that, for that would mean a total break with tradition for him.

As the bullock-cart carrying Lakhi creaked slowly towards Charusila's house, she knew that she was finally leaving her past behind—a past she had been trying so hard to forget. And, when at last she dried her tears and turned her face away from the direction of her house and looked forward, then the lush green fields on both sides of the road seemed to welcome her into a new future. She now started thinking of Dharmakanta who it seemed had come into her life with a message of that freedom which she had been yearning for all these days. His endless optimism, enthusiasm and idealistic way of life had made her believe that the world was finally changing. It seemed as if the earth itself was discarding its worn out garments and putting on a fresh green pair.

Not all the Brahmo families of Nagaon came to their wedding. Among the absentees was Gunabhiram Barua and his wife. Dharmakanta was slightly offended at this, although Barua was away on official work and had sent his good wishes in advance. He concluded that the Baruas must have had some reservations about the wedding or else at least Bishnupriya would have come. He, however, did not know that Bishnupriya had avoided coming because of her earlier experience at Lakhi's first wedding. Nonetheless, Dharmakanta continued to believe that the Baruas were yet to free themselves totally from the prejudices of society and hence couldn't freely accept their marriage. He felt that even for someone as wise and courageous as Gunabhiram, it was not easy to fully overcome the narrowness of society, though he did suffer from severe pangs of conscience because of this. He had even noticed of late an element of indecisiveness in Barua, especially when it came to matters relating to the internal differences within the Brahmo Samaj. All this, however, did not affect Dharmakanta's innate respect for Gunabhiram whom he continued to see as the symbol of a changing age. He still admired this man who had stood up all alone against the in-built prejudices of a deeply conservative society. And, if at all he didn't appear to him as strong as before, then the time had come for people like Dharmakanta to take over and start working for change. How far would they be able to go?

Some time after their marriage, Lakhi and Dharmakanta started preparing to leave Nagaon for Dibrugarh in upper Assam. Because of his growing rift with the owner of the Tapatjuri tea garden Dharmakanta had given up his job a few days before the marriage. It seemed that the owner, Debanath Barua, did not approve of Dharmakanta's mixing with the labourers and talking politics with them. Although he had never directly said anything about this to Dharmakanata, yet he dropped enough hints to suggest that being too friendly with the workers would make it difficult for him to control them. Compared to the "girmitia" coolies of the British gardens, the local workers of Tapatjuri were much better off. At least here they were not treated like slaves. They came to work in the garden from the nearby villages and had the luxury of returning home every evening. Unlike in the British gardens, they did not have to stay in the coolie "lines". Dharmakanata would visit these nearby villages and try to explain to the people how the British had made life miserable for the common man by increasing the taxes. Quite often, he would bring tears to the eyes of the common folk by plaintively singing the songs about Maniram Dewan and would describe how Maniram had to give up his life for trying to drive the British out of Assam. He would also try to tell the people what independence really meant. Some of this had naturally reached the ears of the owner of the Tapatjuri tea garden and one day he told Dharmakanta:

"It is not that I do not think about the welfare of the people. But I surely don't want to be seen as a traitor to the king."

"Well, for you it is important who is the king. But for me the people are the king. So I don't think I am committing treason but actually serving the people," replied Dharmakanta.

Barua kept quiet for some time. He had always respected Dharmakanta's idealism. But, he wasn't prepared to take any step which might jeopardize the interests of his tea garden, to set up which he had taken so much trouble. Patiently he tried to reason with Dharmakanta and said:

"You may be right, Dharmakanata but I have a business and a family to look after. If I displease the government, it will hurt my interests and yours too. I am saying this for the good of all. Please give up all this and concentrate on your work. I can't see an honest upright young man like you destroyed."

Dharmakanta realized that it was meaningless to argue with Debanath Barua, for their views were poles apart. Yet he knew that Barua was, after all, his well wisher and not his enemy and he did not want their relationship to worsen further. So, one day he resigned from his job. On receiving his resignation letter, Barua called him and said:

"So, you want to leave? Have you fixed up a job somewhere else?"

"My friend from Dibrugarh, Krishan Kakati has a small printing press there. The two of us are thinking of bringing out a newspaper."

"But will there be enough readers for a newspaper in Assam?" Barua had asked in surprise.

"Well, someone must try sometime. Will we allow our people to live always in poverty and darkness? People will surely read if one writes about the truth in plain and simple language," Dharmakanta said in a determined tone.

Lakhi knew that to survive, at least one of them should have a stable job. She was not too sure if the job in the press would be able to sustain them. She was worried about their uncertain future when she suddenly got a piece of good news. Ajay Ganguly, her teacher at the primary level, informed her that one of his relatives was setting up a lower primary school at Dibrugarh and he needed a good and sincere teacher. Lakhi immediately wrote to the school authorities at Dibrugarh and received a reply just a few days before their marriage. She was told that if she agreed to take up the job, then all arrangements for her stay would be made by the school. The pay was to be ten rupees a month.

When Lakhi broke the news to Dharmakanta, he smiled and said:

"So, you will set up house after our marriage and I will stay there as a drone bee."

Lakhi had replied with a naughty smile: "Only then will we see whether you are a drone or a worker bee."

At this, Dharmakanta turned grave. He suddenly felt responsible for Lakhi and said:

"Who knows? You may eventually be put off by my manner of work. Like the others, I have no intention of settling down and becoming a good family man."

"Who has asked you to be one?" Lakhi had teasingly replied. "I will manage the home and you work for the country. I will never be an obstacle to you in your work."

Quietly holding her hand, Dharmakanta kept staring at Lakhi for some time. The inspiration he got from her seemed to double his resolve.

The day before they left for Dibrugarh, Dharmakanta and

Lakhi visited Bilwa Kutir. Bilwa Kutir seemed to have come alive after the return of Bishnupriya and her three sons. As they approached the house, the two of them sensed that there was a festive atmosphere there. And, just as they were about to enter, Swarna's brother Kamala informed them that Maisena Baideu and Bhindeu had arrived from Calcutta the evening before and that, in their honour, their father had arranged for a singing troupe from Hajo. The young boys seemed quite excited and were eagerly waiting for the chokra-chokris to arrive. Lakhi knew about Barua's interest in the singing troupes and how, whenever they came to Nagaaon from Hajo or Dergaon, he would invariably bring them over to his house and invite his relatives and friends to the *gaan* sessions. When invited, Panchanan Sarma too would come to see the *gaan* but he wouldn't bring his children along. As such, Lakhi had never had a chance to see the performance. However, she remembered her father once bringing her over to Bilwa Kutir to enjoy a puppet dance.

Initially, Dharmakanta was a bit hesitant to enter the house. Not because he had come uninvited but because he wasn't at all eager to face the Assamese society of Nagaon. He was sure that wouldn't be able to hold himself back if someone passed some snide comment at Lakhi. Even as he was deliberating on this, Kamala ran inside and announced their arrival and, in no time, Swarna and Tora came out to receive them. Lakhi was somewhat taken aback on seeing the two friends together after such a long time. How different they were from each other! She was meeting Swarna for the first time after her marriage. She had, however, gone to Tora's wedding, much against the wishes of her family. Tora looked just the same, her striking personality standing out even in her workaday clothes. Compared to Tora, Swarna in her gold ornaments and her Banarasi silk saree, seemed the epitome of grace and beauty and Lakhi felt that there couldn't be anyone more happy than her. Then, all of a sudden it seemed to her that a wide gap had grown between her and Swarna. She thought it was but natural that there should be a social divide between her and a magistrate's daughter, the student of Bethune school and now the wife of a London returned physician, Swarnalata. But when Swarna welcomed her with a warm embrace, all her doubts evaporated in a moment.

Meanwhile, even as Gunabhiram Barua himself took Dharmakanta inside, Swarna caught hold of Lakhi and Bishnupriya's hands and pulled them towards the bilwa tree.

"You know, I really like this place. Lakhi and I cooked so many play meals here, remember?" Swarna turned and asked Lakhi.

"Of course," said Lakhi even as she caressed the tree trunk. "We laughed and we wept so many times right here."

"When I first saw Swarna playing under this tree, I had thought that the Hakim's daughter must be really proud," said Tora as she broke into peals of laughter.

Suddenly, all the three girls became quiet and pensive. It was as if the bilwa tree had become the connecting link between their past, present and future. Whereas their own lives had changed so much, the tree had remained the same. Staring at the tree, Swarna said in a philosophic tone:

"People change so much. But the trees seem to remain the same."

"But in reality, the trees change much more than us. Every year new leaves come, there are flowers and fruits, and then they wither away." There was no complexity whatsoever in Tora's words. They were always straight and simple, from the heart as it were.

"Well, some ten years later when we meet under this tree again, then we'll see that this old tree will still be here. But who knows what will happen to us?" There was a tinge of sadness in Lakhis's words. Swarna tried to lighten the moment by wrapping her arm around Lakhi's shoulders and saying:

"It is okay. We needn't think of ten years hence. The three of us have come together after such a long time. So, let's have some fun. As it is, tomorrow Lakhi will leave. We too aren't staying too long and who knows when we'll meet again. Come, the music party must have arrived. It's been quite some time since we heard Assamese songs."

Even before the sentence was finished, the three friends had already reached the house. Having heard Swarna talking of Assamese songs, Dharmakanta commented: "Why are you calling these Assamese songs? Though the singers are from Hajo, they will be singing Bengali songs. And such Bengali pronunciation! Dr Roy will not be able to understand a word. Swarna would have to translate them into the Bengali spoken in Calcutta."

"Not the Bengali of Calcutta; it would have to be the Bengali of Dhaka," Swarna answered lightly, adding " There is not much of a difference between that Bengali and the Assamese-Bengali."

Thus, with a lot of fun and banter the evening drew to a close. Who knew that the three of them would never be able to spend a similar evening ever again? Seeing the tears in the eyes of the three friends as they were about to leave one another, Dharmakanta and Henry had a hearty laugh while Dr Roy said:

"Women can cry over nothing. There is Dhaka, here is Nagaon and Dibrugarh. Seeing your state, people would think that you are about to leave for a distant foreign land or maybe for exile in the Andamans!"

Part III

1

Five years had passed. Five years is not too long a stretch of time. Many people don't even realize how five years of their life pass by. Only those whose lives have reached stasis, continually keep looking back to the past. These days Dharmakanta was too busy to think of the passage of time. For, the fire of revolt was slowly spreading from one end of Assam to the other. The government had crippled the people with new taxes. Commissioner Ward had raised the revenue in the old settlements so much that now it was almost double the earlier rates. The people were obviously getting restive and in the namghars and masjids, *raij mels* or people's assemblies were being held. The story about the Phulaguri revolt was on everyone's lips. While young blood was on the boil once again as people recalled the heroic fight put up by the peasants against the colonial masters some twenty years ago, the old too did not lack in enthusiasm. For them the Phulaguri 'Dhewa' was a recent happening and they were ready to go out with lathis in hand to confront the administration.

The paper brought out from Dibrugarh by Dharmakanta was called *Dwigvijay*. He used to write a lot about the travails of the common people in his paper. But he always felt that the very people whose difficulties he was trying to highlight were iliterate and so could not read his paper. And those who were literate, would avoid reading the *Dwigvijay* out of fear of falling into the bad books of the administration. Since his Calcutta days, Dharmakanta had realized that almost all those young men who received English education invariably became loyal followers of the colonial masters. And most of those who had joined the Congress actually did so to derive concessions from the British, not to drive them out. As such, Dharmakanta felt that it was entirely useless to make these people read his paper. But unlike him, his friend Krishna Kakaty seemed quite hopeful. He believed that although it took some time to prepare the land for the crops, once this was done, the harvest would obviously come in. Kakaty had a quiet composed appearance and was not restless and impatient like Dharmakanta. Yet, because of his deep love for his country and his unswerving commitment, he was prepared to make the ultimate sacrifice. Hence, Dharmakanta left the task of running of the paper to Kakati and spent most of his time travelling and meeting people in order to organize them.

Dharmakanta met with success in several places. The people themselves organised assemblies and discussed the issues affecting them in detail. The earlier rate of revenue, five sikkas, had broken the backs of the people and now it had become impossible for the poorer peasants to pay their revenues. The peasants of Kamrup, Nagaon and Darrang were especially agitated. Since the Ahom days, the people of these regions were known for their militancy and were referred to as the "king chasers" of Nagaon, the ones who had driven out the king. Dharmakanta had observed that in the peoples assemblies in these areas, the peasants didn't even wait for the village elders to conclude their arguments before deciding to go out and fight. This sort of militancy often unnerved Dharmakanta. What would happen if these people were aroused and could not be kept under control? What if these poor peasants ended up becoming the targets of British cannons as in 1857?

Dharmakanta was no emotional and impulsive revolutionary. He certainly wouldn't take advantage of the people's distress to push them into the jaws of death. That's why he had drafted a petition against the notification on increased revenue rates issued by Ward Sahib. He wanted the people from all the districts of Assam to sign the memorandum and then send it to the Indian member of the Imperial Council, Rashbehari Bose. With that in mind he was travelling through the Upper Assam districts and had now reached Nagaon. From Nagaon he would go to Darrang via Kamrup. Having come to Nagaon after quite a long time, the first thing he did was to go to Bilwa Kutir to enquire about Gunabhiram Barua. Almost two years had passed since Gunabhiram, while sending him the subscription for *Dwigvijay*, had written to him saying that he was about to retire from government service and after that he would be moving to Calcutta with his family. Dhramakanta hadn't had any news about Gunabhiram since then. He had been far too busy to keep track of the Baruas.

Dharmakanta came and stood in front of Bilwa Kutir. There was no sign that anyone was living in the bungalow. The front garden was in a state of neglect. A few cows were grazing under the bilwa tree. Just as Dharmakanta was about to go to the bungalow, a person who looked like a chowkidar came from behind the house and told him that Gunabhiram and his family had left Nagaon for Calcutta immediately after his retirement from service. Dharmakanta was surprised to hear this. Gunabhiram Barua had told him that after his retirement he would build a house in Calcutta and move to the city only after that. He could not understand why he had left so suddenly.

Having come out of Bilwa Kutir, a somewhat forlorn Dharmakanta stood for a while holding onto the wooden gate in front of the house. Bilwa Kutir held so many memories for him. The house had been a sort of sheet anchor to him in his life's journey till now. He would never be able to forget Bishnupriya's warmth, Swarna's uninhibited friendship and Gunabhiram's encouraging and inspiring words of advice. Thinking of the Baruas, he suddenly remembered Tora and Henry and soon he was walking towards Christianpatty. Tora's house looked the same but, on entering it, he noticed some changes. Along with new chairs and a table, there was a bookshelf in one corner of the sitting room. Glancing at the top row of books, Dharmakanta could see some plays by Shakespeare and copies of Milton's *Paradise Lost* and Bunyan's *Pilgrim's Progress*. There were also some bound volumes of *Orunodoi* and a few religious booklets brought out by the Sivasagar Mission. What, however, surprised Dharmakanta was the neatly arranged books adorning the middle row of the shelf. These included *Durgesnandini, Kapal Kundala, Kamalakanta, Neel-Darpan, Religious Thought and Life in India,* Mill's *On Liberty* and Darwin's *The Origin of the Species.* All these days Dharmakanta had thought Henry to be a loyal, God-fearing and rather meek individual. But seeing the range of books he saw on Henry's bookshelf, he changed his opinion. He couldn't gauge the reason behind this radical change and kept wondering if it was because of Henry's exposure to Kolkata or the effect of the winds of change that were blowing across the country.

Tora wasn't at home when Dharnmakanta dropped in. Ever since she had taken up duties as a nurse at the hospital, she had little time to spare. He was received instead by Henry who was busy feeding his two-year-old son. Henry welcomed him warmly and after asking him to make himself comfortable, went inside to finish feeding the infant. Although there was a maid to take care of the little one, yet whenever he was home, Henry tried to give his son as much time as possible. He was now a graduate teacher at the Nagaon High English school and though initially the Mission people weren't happy with Henry's decision because they wanted him to be a preacher, yet they soon decided to leave him alone and not to interfere with his life.

When Henry returned after the child had been fed,

Dharmakanta who was casually flipping through the pages of a copy of *Jonaki* which lay on the table in front of him, asked him: "What's your son's name?"

"Naren," replied Henry. Noticing Dharma's surprised look, Henry continued with a smile, "Naren Michael Thomas."

"Why Naren?" a puzzled Dharmakanta asked.

"Actually, while in Kolkata, I happened to see Ramakrishna's disciple, Naren. I can still visualize his pure and handsome appearance. Maybe, if I am lucky, some day I will have the chance to hear him speak."

"How is it that being a Christian, you are speaking about a disciple of Ramakrishna?" Dharma seemed confused. Henry then said with a composed smile:

"Why, what's wrong in that? Am I retracting from my own faith? Ramakrishna has said that all religions have the same goal. I too have started believing in that."

Dharmakanta did not have much of an interest in arguments centred on faith and religion. Because of this indifference, his friends would quite often make fun of him by saying, "Barua, you should change your name". Though he did not consider himself an atheist, yet religion had never attracted him. He seemed quite relieved when a little later, Tora arrived. She was looking really smart in her nurse's dress. On seeing Dharmakanta, she quickly made some tea and snacks and came and sat beside him to enquire about Lakhi and the kids. Then, with a deep sigh, she told Dharmakanta of how on the very day he retired, Gunabhiram had received the telegram informing him of his son-in-law Nandakumar Ray's death. It was as if Bilwa Kutir was struck by a sudden bolt of lightning. Even a well disciplined and collected person like Gunabhiram had broken down in grief on that terrible day and the numerous friends and acquaintances that had come to offer their condolences seemed completely dumbstruck and had nothing to say. As for Bishnupriya, she kept blaming herself for her daughter's tragedy. Tora's eyes welled up with tears as she described the events of that day to Dharmakanta. Gunabhiram left for Kolkata the very next day and was followed by Bishnupriya and the children a few days later. That was the last time Tora had seen them. Later on, she came to know that Swarna and her two daughters were now living with her parents in Calcutta.

Dharmakanta was stunned by what he heard. He kept recalling their last evening together at Bilwa Kutir. He was mystified at the speed with which everything had changed. Who could have imagined that evening that a person as healthy and strong as Nandakumar Roy would leave this world so very suddenly? How was it that such a well-known physician couldn't find a remedy to save himself? Dharmakanta was seized by a deep urge to go and meet Swarna. But he was burdened with a lot of work. He would be able to go to Calcutta only after meeting the peasants of Kamrup and Darrang and seeing their condition. That would take him another month or two.

2

Dharmakanta finally found the third house on the second lane of the old Baithak-Khana Road. At first, as per the address given him by Tora, he had gone to the Scotch Lane house of the Baruas. But he learnt from the neighbours that, after his wife's death, Gunabhiram Barua had shifted to his Baithak-Khana house. Dharmaknata was numbed by the news of successive misfortunes that had befallen the Baruas and was now afraid to face Barua Dangoria. What if he had lost his mental balance? But the eagerness and warmth with which Gunabhiram received him dispelled all these apprehensions and Dharmakanta felt that here was a person who had been tempered as gold is through fire. Misfortunes had not been able to break him. Seeing his calm and composed face with its long white flowing beard, Dharmakanta's esteem for him increased even more. He was quite surprised to find that instead of talking of his misfortunes, Gunabhiram quickly took Dharmakanta to his study and showed him some of the letters he had exchanged with the authorities of Calcutta University for instituting a prize in his wife's name. He told him that the prize would go to the student who secured the highest marks in Assamese in the B. A. examination.

"You know how eager she was about books and learning. Though she herself didn't get much of a chance to study, yet she was always pleased when others excelled. She also wrote a book called *Neeti-Katha*. Do you remember that?" There was a slight tremor in Gunabhiram's voice as he said this. As Dharmakanta listened to Gunabhiram, he remembered how once when he had stepped into their Maniktala Street house, he had found both mother and daughter busy correcting the manuscript of Swarna's book, *Arhi Tiruta*.

After a while, Swarna entered carrying a tray of tea and snacks for the visitor. Dharmakanta did not notice any particular change in her dress, for like other married women, she had on a light-coloured saree and also wore some ornaments. He had been afraid of finding Swarna in the white saree of the typical Bengali widow. But now he was quite relieved and happy to see her appearance and was genuinely thankful to the Brahmo Samaj for making this possible. Swarna tried to greet Dharmakanta with her usual smile and he saw that the successive tragedies of her life had left a deep mark on her face. But her bright personality continued to shine through. She heard all the news from Dharmakanta and then enquired about Lakhi. With a deep sigh, she said, "How many girls are there who can stand on their own feet as Lakhi has done? If only I too had her strength of mind!"

"Why are you saying this, Swarna? You are so much more educated than Lakhi. And, above everything else, you happen to be the child of a rare couple who have never compromised on their convictions, even if that meant going against the accepted social beliefs. So, I just cannot believe that you will accept defeat."

"Bless me, Kakaideo, so that I can be like my parents," Swarna said, her voice almost choked with emotion.

Dharmakanta skilfully tried to change the topic and said: "Why don't you go back to your studies? Ever since the *Asam Bandhu* stopped publication, you too have stopped writing. Now you could write stories and poems for the *Jonaki*. Lakshminath Bezbaroa is related to you all. Just send your writings to him and he will publish it I am sure."

"He has said the same thing to me. But I don't feel like writing anything these days. Now my main job is to take care and educate my three brothers and my little girl. Ai gave me this responsibility as she lay on her death-bed. I don't like thinking about myself anymore."

Dharmakanta did not know what to say. Surely, he couldn't ask Swarna to be selfish. Wasn't he himself quite selfish and leading the life of a gypsy after having thrust all his responsibilities on his wife? But what could he really do? For, it was Lakhi herself who had insisted that he work for his country while she took upon herself all the responsibilities of running the home. Now, looking at Swarna's brothers and her little daughter, Dharmakanta thought that maybe someday they would turn out to be quite famous and successful. But, he asked himself, would they then have the time to remember Swarna's selfless sacrifice? For a moment, Dharmakanta felt rather guilty for the indifference and ingratitude with which society had all along treated womankind.

3

Swarna missed her mother at every step. But she never showed her sorrow in front of her brothers. For them, she was now the one who would fill up their mother's place and it was her constant endeavour to ensure that they never felt neglected. Only after her mother's death did she come to realize the almost endless responsibilities of running the household. She knew now that, no matter the number of servants one had, it was an onerous task to ensure that everything worked smoothly. At her husband's place, Swarna did not have to take on so many responsibilities because Nandakumar and his sisters were always there to help out. But now her father was gradually leaving all the duties to her. On the face of it, Gunabhiram's household did not seem to lack in anything. Compared to many others, Gunabhiram had brought up his children quite comfortably. He would buy the costliest clothes for them from the Calcutta market and when it came to food, Gunabhiram possessed what may be called royal tastes. Though it was the normal practice at home to have Assamese and Bengali dishes, yet he would often order European food for his children from elite restaurants. Moreover, there were always guests to be entertained, for many well known persons from different parts of the country used to regularly visit the Brauahs. Apart from the famous Brahmos of Calcutta, regular guests at Gunabhiram's Calcutta residence included the Raja of

Gauripur, the zamindar of Bogoribari and the Satradhikar of the Jakhalabhanda Satra. Also, there would always be some relative or the other who would come to visit them. Now that her mother was gone, it was Swarna's turn to look after all these people and see to it that they were taken care of properly. She tried to put up a happy face as she went about her many duties but her heart was never in it. She would eagerly look forward to those evenings when Assamese students like Lakshminath Bezbaroa, Hem Goswami, Padmanath Gohain Barua, Radhika Prasad Barua would come to visit her father for advice and guidance. On those occasions, Swarna would discuss with them many a matter ranging from literature to developments within the country and outside. She valued those evenings greatly when there were almost endless discussions regarding *Jonaki* and whether political articles should find a place in the journal. Although one of its editors, Chandrakumar Agarwalla, had written that politics be kept outside the ambit of *Jonaki,* yet there was a group of students who were opposed to this view. Even during Dharmakanta's stay in Calcutta, this issue had generated much heat and Swarna recalled how one day there was an impassioned debate in their house with Dharma insisting that at a time when the nation was passing through a critical phase, no journal could ever steer clear of politics and remain neutral, for it was a historical duty which each new writer was expected to perform. But several of the young men present that day had protested, saying that the place of literature was always outside politics and this had resulted in a discussion on the difference between *rajniti* and *praja-niti*. It was as if a storm over old and new viewpoints had been raging in Gunabhiram's sitting room, bringing with it a certain freshness into Swarna's mind.

Their sitting room was also witness to a lot of political discussion. For, it was in this room of the Old Baitak-Khana Lane house of the Baruas that the final list of representatives to the Allahabad session of the Indian National Congress, from among the Assamese students of Calcutta, had been drawn up. Dharmakanta was present on that day and, despite everyone insisting that he be sent as a representative to the session, he had not agreed. He insisted that he had a lot of work to do in his home state and that, once back in Assam, he would have to organize the peasants because he believed that the future of the nation could be moulded by the village people alone. With Dharmakanta opting out, the meeting had finally approved the names of Radhanath Changkakoti, Lakshminath Bezbaroa and Bholanath Barua.

Swarna would generally keep quiet during these political discussions. But she would listen intently to the arguments and it didn't take long for her to realize that most of these young men were loyal subjects of the British. At Anandamohan Bose's house, she had also met several leading political personalities like Surendranath Banerjee, Umeshchandra Banerjee, Durgamohan Das, and Dwarkanath Ganguly. Listening to their views she felt that they were convinced that there was nothing better for the Indian people than to be ruled by the British Empress. Their only point of grievance seemed to be that the educated Indians had not received their due from their colonial masters and, hence, should try to realize their rights through constitutional means. Though Swarna could not grasp the full meaning of the term "constitutional", yet having heard it quite often, she had grown familiar with that term. But, among all these views, she found Dharmakanta's arguments to be surprisingly different. He saw the British government to be an enemy of the Indian people and believed that the country would prosper only if this government was overthrown and an Indian one installed in its place. But only a small handful of Assamese students seemed to support this view and even they were engaged in working for the Congress. Swarna simply did not understand how this was possible.

Among the political personalities she had met, it was Kadambini Ganguly she liked the most. Kadambini was the first Indian woman to have passed out of the Calcutta Medical College. Right from the days of her childhood, Swarna had known this graceful woman as a family friend whom her father had always held up as a role model to prove that girls were in no sense inferior to boys. But once she got married to Dwarkanath Ganguly, Gunabhiram had stopped meeting them, though he changed his mind later on.

Swarna clearly remembered the day when Kadambini along with her husband Dwarkanath had come to visit them and seek her father's blessings before embarking on their voyage to Chicago to attend an industrial fair there. Gunabhiram had reflected for a moment and then gone inside only to come out with a delicately woven silk riha-mekhala which he gifted to Kadambini and said:

"Will you please wear this dress in Chicago? Just show them the clothes Assamese women wear."

Swarna recognized the riha-mekhala set. Her father had brought it from Nagaon for her mother. But her poor mother had never had a chance to wear it.

Kadambini was all smiles as she asked Swarna: "Please show me how to wear this dress. If I don't wear it properly, then its very worth would be lost."

Swarna took her inside and showed her how to wear it and Kadambini looked splendid in her riha-mekhala. Looking at her, Swarna couldn't help the feeling that if only she had been an Assamese lady how proud her state would have been of her! Would there ever be an Assamese woman physician, she wondered?

4

Swarna's family could not stay in peace even for a year at their Old Baithak Khana Lane house. Just a few months after her mother's death, Karuna too was caught by the same illness. The poor boy had appeared for his Entrance examination that year and everyone had expected that he would come out with flying colours. Of all the children, Karuna, with his quiet disposition, seemed the most interested in studies and in Nagaon, encouraged by his father, he had brought out a school journal called *Lora Bandhu* As for Swarna, she would always boast of her brother in front of her friends. She was convinced that one day her intelligent brother would qualify for the Indian Civil Service. But a few days before his examinations, Karuna suddenly developed high fever. Though the medicines initially helped to bring down the fever, yet his condition continued to worsen. And, when all the medical advice from Indian and foreign physicians proved to be of no avail, Gunabhiram decided to take him out of the city. The doctors had told him that there was a chance of the disease being cured if they moved him to a dry location. Finally, accompanied by two helpers, Gunabhiram and Karuna left for Purulia. Just as they were about to leave, Gunabhiram called Swarna aside and said:

"Maisena, I am leaving Kamala and Jnan with you. You are now both a father and mother to them."

It was with a smiling face that Swarna bid good-bye to her father and brother, for she had believed that her brother would return fully cured from Purulia. Not having much of an idea about the complications that life often threw up, she seemed quite hopeful. But when Karuna's condition did not improve even at Purulia, a helpless Gunabhiram went with his son to Madhupur in Bihar, which some of his friends said was a healthy place. Realising the problems that her father was facing in looking after Karuna all alone in an alien place without friends, Swarna decided to move there along with the children. She requested a relative of theirs, Nabinram Barua, to accompany her to Madhupur. Gunabhiram had quite often helped Nabinram and his brother Jiwanram during their stay in Calcutta and Swarna knew that, after her father, these members of Anandaram Dhekiyal Phukan's family were her nearest relatives.

Accompanied by Nabinram, they proceeded to Madhupur. It seemed the excitement of a first class train journey made them quite forget the real purpose of their journey. But once they reached Madhupur, a blanket of sadness engulfed them. Karuna was bedridden and the medicines weren't having any effect on him. As for Gunabhiram, he was totally absorbed in looking after his sick son. The doctors had suggested that the patient be given chicken soup but the Brahmin cook wouldn't touch that. So, Swarna started making the soup herself on a kerosene stove. And, even though he was so sick, Karuna would appreciate his sister's cooking with a wan smile. On seeing this Swarna's eyes would fill with tears. There seemed to be no way out for her except to keep on praying for her brother's recovery. Then from Calcutta came the news that Karuna had cleared his Entrance examination in the first division. When told about his results, Karuna looked at his sister and said in a tone filled with despair: "Baideu, maybe I will not be able to study at the Presidency College after all." Swarna would lovingly run her fingers through his hair and reassure him: "You will be okay, Karuna. When we go back, you can be admitted to college."

But Karuna would never go back to Calcutta. He left for his heavenly abode from Madhupur leaving everyone grief-stricken. When Gunabhiram came to know that the end was near, he sat by his son's bed and read from the Bhagawad Gita throughout the night. Swarna stonily kept vigil by his side, praying silently. But she did not realize that Karuna's end was drawing so near. And, when his life finally ebbed away, Swarna didn't even notice it. The following morning the Brahmos carried off Karuna's body, once again singing the hymn, "Ei Je Dekha Jai Anandadham". It was the same hymn that was sung when Bishnupriya's body was being carried off for cremation. The sombre notes of the song simply tore at Swarna's heart.

5

On their return to Calcutta after Karuna's death, the Baruas once again decided to change their rented house. Gunabhiram did not wish to stay even for a single night at their Old Baithak Khana Lane residence which was so filled with memories of Karuna. A house was now rented at College Square and once again the family was caught up in all the problems involved in setting up a new home. There was also the additional problem of adjusting to new surroundings. On earlier occasions, it was Gunabhiram who would personally supervise everything and arrange the setting up of the house in a proper manner. But this time he seemed totally disinterested. Seeing Swarna burdened with work, he would ask with a deep sigh: "You are facing a lot of troubles, isn't it Ai? I haven't been able to give you any happiness. I had thought that after my retirement, we would build our own house here in Calcutta. With that in mind, I had also bought a plot of land. But fate ordained otherwise."

As for Swarna, she had never seen her father so helpless. He looked like a dying tree keeping itself erect somehow. This made her quite frantic. All these years, her only refuge had been her father and she dreaded to think of what would happen to her if he broke down in this manner. Trying to plead with him as if he were a child, Swarna would say: "Why are you speaking like this, Deuta? Even now there is enough time to build a house. Once the new house is built, we'll all stay there happily." But Swarna knew only too well that she was forcing herself to say all this.

"No, Maisena. Now I have only one home. That is Anandadham. Your mother is there. Also Karuna. I have no more hope left. Ai, it was with great hopes that I had started the family. At first Brajasundari left me much before her time. After that I set up house so happily with your mother. That too was shattered. I had always thought that without paying any heed to all the ill-will of society, I would be able to stand alone against its prejudices and superstitions. But that was not to be."

Gunabhiram broke into uncontrollable sobs even as he spoke these words. Swarna was dumfounded. She just didn't know how to console her father. Standing by the window and observing the world outside, she felt totally alone. She realized that now it was her sole responsibility to keep her slowly shrinking family together. She prayed to Parameswar to give her the necessary strength of mind.

Gunabhiram could not reconcile himself to Karuna's death and his earlier self was gone for ever. He would try to behave normally when friends visited but as soon as they left, he would at once retreat into his own world. Old friends like Anandamoham Basu, Durgamohan Das, Sibnath Shastri and Gurucharan Mahalanobis would drop in quite often. Then there was Kadambini Ganguly who had just returned from Chicago and who would try to bring some cheer to the Barua household with her witty anecdotes. But nothing seemed to interest Gunabhiram any more. Hemchandra Goswami and Lakhshminath Bezbaroa too tried to revive his literary interests and, unable to turn down their requests, Gunabhiram would occasionally sit down to write his next instalment of *Unwritten History*, only to give it up after just a few lines when his mind would begin to wander. Padmanath Gohain Barua would come to give him the new issues of the *Bijulee* where Gunabhiram's *Asam Yatra* was being published serially. He had given the entire manuscript to Gohain Barua almost a year ago. Otherwise, that too would perhaps have remained incomplete.

Swarna seemed to like their College Square house. The schools and colleges were just a few steps away and this was of great help to Kamala and Jnan. Swarna too would sometimes accompany her brothers to the nearby book-shop from where she bought each one of Bankimchandra's novels. She already possessed a copy of Michael Madhusudhan's *Meghnad Badh* which her father had gifted to her. Though she had heard quite often from her father about Michael's *Birangana Kabya*, she hadn't had a chance to read it. One day she spotted the book at a store and quickly bought it and gave it to her father. That evening, much like earlier days, Gunabhiram was seen passionately reading poetry. Reciting Madhusudhan's verse in a full-throated manner, he explained to his daughter the significance of women's liberation. Swarna was simply enraptured and a surge of self-confidence swept over her.

The very next morning everything turned topsy-turvy. Gunabhiram was down with high fever. Swarna knew this fever quite well. It seemed Gunabhiram too knew that his days were numbered and so, when his fever had subsided somewhat, he called Swarna to his side and said: "Ai, this time I am also about to leave. Now the responsibility is all yours. Take care of Jnan and Kamala. Teach them to stand on their own feet." Clasping Swarna's small, delicate hands in his own feverish ones, he went on: "Though you are a girl, I am certain that you'll be able to do it. I have educated you. Our blood runs through your veins…"

The days passed by as if in a storm. The old, familiar faces appeared again. Dr. Nilratan Sen, Dr. Bipinbehari Sarkar, Dr. Crombey, Dr. Kadambini Ganguly—so many well-known physicians. Yet none of them could conquer that unknown fever. It was as if the intellectual elite of Assam and Bengal had come together at Number Eight, College Square, with visitors crowding the house from morning till late at night. Swarna would take turns between talking to the guests and attending to her father and, whenever there was a little time, she would go to a corner of her room and cry her heart out. But where was the time even to cry? Seeing the plight of Khuki and Choto, she would forget her own grief. It was as if her daughters had been born in the lap of death, with illness, doctors and death having become a part of their lives. But to Swarna's relief, both Jnan and Kamala were growing up and learning to shoulder a lot of responsibility at an early age. They helped Swarna at every step, whether it was fetching doctors or buying fruits and medicines for the patient. There were a hundred other such jobs for them.

Swarna tried hard to apply herself to her duties in as stoical manner as possible. She refused to think about the possible situation when her father would be gone and she would be left alone with her little daughters and her two brothers. She tried to convince herself that, with so many celebrated physicians attending on her father, perhaps a miracle could still be achieved and, till the last moments, she refused to give up hope. But when the inevitable moment approached and once again the strains of the hymn "Ei Je Dekha Jai Anandadham" reverberated in the house, Swarna tried to block her ears and run away from the reality of her father's death. She could now hear the instructions being given for arrangements to be made for the last journey, every detail of which she was quite familiar with. Her father would be taken to the cremation ground in a hired vehicle. The body would be accompanied by Jnan, Kamala and a few Brahmo friends. But suddenly in the midst of all these preparations, Swarna could hear a completely different tune. The Assamese students of Calcutta were singing *sankirtan*. In an instant, the image of the worship-hall of Bilwa Kutir floated before her eyes, and with it came many pleasant memories. She burst out crying.

Just then she heard Lakshminath Bezbaroa saying: "Swarna, we the Assamese students will carry your father's body for cremation. He was like a father to us." Swarna couldn't say anything. But she remembered what her father had once told her, "When I die, there won't be any Assamese to carry my body."

6

Swarna's brother-in-law happened to be a well-placed government official and it was he who took Swarna and the children to his house just a day after Guinabhiram's death. As it was, Kamala and Jnan had been very upset with their father's death, and the idea of having to leave their own house and move into someone else's as guests had completely shattered them. Seeing their plight, Swarna, despite her own helpless situation, decided that whatever the odds, she would live seperately along with her daughters and brothers. So, she explained her position to her brother-in-law and her desire to return to their house at College Square. But meanwhile, without even asking Swarna, Gunabhiram's Brahmo friends, thinking it to be unwise for a young woman to stay alone in a rented house, had already shifted their belongings to a Brahmo Girls' boarding house at Cornwallis Street. Swarna was quite angry with this decision. She didn't understand why people decided that she was weak and helpless. She also failed to see why when Bishnupriya had stayed with them all alone in Calcutta, no one had said anything. Did they think that she wouldn't be able to manage things on her own just because she was a widow? All this made her even more determined to chart her own course. She knew that because of his faith in her, her father had left her brothers in her care. She now felt that it would be insulting to her father's memory if she allowed them to grow up in someone else's house, being dependant on others.

Swarna eventually had to shift to the Brahmo girls' boarding house. But since the authorities did not permit her to keep her brothers with her, Kamala and Jnan were finally lodged in a hostel meant for Brahmo boys. Neither of them were able to adjust to their new surroundings and they disliked the hostel food intensely. Having been accustomed to good food at home, it was now impossible for them to survive on coarse rice and spicy curry. As for Khuki and Choto, they had almost given up eating and, seeing their plight, Durgamohan Das and other Brahmo friends arranged for Swarna to cook her own food. Although this brought some succour to Khuki and her sister, Swarna continued to be filled with remorse whenever she thought of her brothers' plight. She finally requested Anandamohan Basu and her brother-in-law to look for a decent house for them to rent.

In these difficult times, Swarna was helped a great deal by her three friends, Hemaprava, Charuprava and Labanyaprava. These three sisters had always showered her with affection right from the moment of her arrival in Calcutta. And, the day Gunabhiram died, they had spent the entire night with Swarna and her brothers. The sisters now came to visit Swarna at the hostel just a few days after she had moved in. It was with some hesitation that Labanyaprava asked her: "Well, Swarna, weren't you all on good terms with your father's relatives?" Swarna was quite taken aback and answered: "But why? We always saw Deuta showing great affection towards his relatives. He hosted so many of them here so that they could get medical treatment or see the city. And, sometimes when his relatives in Assam were in need, he would also send them money." Listening to Swarna, Labanyaprava and her two sisters nodded their heads sadly. Then, Hemoprava held Swarna's hand and said in the politest of tones: "Only now have we realized how ungrateful and cruel people can be. Yesterday

Ananda Da came to our place and told us that some of your relatives have come from Assam and are claiming to be the real inheritors of Gunabhiram. They said that they would approach the courts to get their share of the property."

Swarna was shocked, "But how can anyone claim Deuta's property when Jnan and Kamala are there?"

"The strangest of things happen in this world, do you understand Swarna? Your relatives are saying that your parents weren't legally married because Brahmo marriages are not recognized by the law. As such, they maintain that all of you cannot be the real inheritors of your father's property".

By then, Swarna was shaking with anger: "These people are wicked! No one came to see us in our time of grief. And yet now they want our property! They think we are weak and therefore think they can cheat us. I will show them that I too can fight! Did my parents educate me at Bethune's for nothing?" Swarna's words were getting choked. But she bit her lips and somehow controlled her tears. Hemoprava and her sisters tried to calm her down and said:

"Don't you worry. You are sure to win if a lawyer like Ananda Dada argues on your behalf. But you will have to do one thing. That is why we have come to you. If you find your parents' marriage registration certificate among your father's papers, then all problems will be solved. Ananda Da says that your father was the first person in Assam to get his marriage registered."

That day, after Hemoprava and the others had left, Swarna wept for a long time. She just kept asking herself if trying to establish the validity of her parents' marriage wouldn't really be an insult to a couple who had freed themselves from the shackles of the world? What was the point in searching for such proof? But the very next moment she realized that she was tied fast by the chains of law, tradition and custom and, even if she wished, she would not be able to free herself. She decided that if not for herself, then at least for the sake of her brothers she would have to endure this. She knew that if she didn't then there would be no one to look after them.

Opening all the boxes where her father's papers had been kept, Swarna searched late into the night for the marriage certificate. The papers were in a mess and Swarna tried to arrange them. But it was impossible to keep them in order in so little space. She had almost given up hope of finding the paper when, inside a neatly tied well-kept file, she finally discovered it. The next day after she handed over the paper to Ananda Mohan Basu, the case was finally decided in their favour. According to Ananada Mohan Basu's advice, Swarna became the legal guardian of her brothers and a trustee of her father's property. The other trustee happened to be Durga Mohan Das's son-in-law, Sir Jagadish Chandra Bose.

7

Well trained nurses were required in order to expand the Nagaon Government Hospital. Pleased with Tora's efficiency, the British doctor of the hospital decided to send her to Calcutta for a six-month training course. At first Tora was quite unwilling to go because she did not want to leave the children entirely to Henry's care. But eventually it was because of Henry's enthusiasm that she decided to go. This was Tora's second visit to the city. She had spent some days there earlier on her way to America with Bronson Sahib. Hence, Calcutta was not entirely unfamiliar to her. But, the first few days of training were so hectic that she did not have any time to think of Swarna even though before leaving for Calcutta, she had sent a letter to her at her Old Baithak Khana Lane address. She had received no reply and had been quite unsure of tracing her in the big city. Then by sheer chance, she came to learn from a Christian girl from Nagaon who was studying at the Calcutta Medical College that one of their teachers, Dr Bepin Behari Sarkar knew the family of Gunabhiram Barua quite well. It was as if the heavens opened up for Tora! She met Dr Sarkar at the medical college and got all the information she needed. She came to know that after her father's death Swarna first stayed with her daughters at the Brahmo Girls' Hostel at Cornwallis Street and then had moved on to a rented house at Brijitola. It was in that house that Kamala was struck by fever and died. After that Swarna had changed house again and was now living at Jeliapara Road in the Bhawanipur area.

The very next day Tora turned up at the rented house in Bhawanipur. Swarna wasn't at home and a maid invited her inside. She was from Nagaon and it was from her that Tora learnt that Kali Baideu and her son, Priyanath, had come from Nagaon to stay with Swarna. She observed that the sitting room, though quite small, had been neatly arranged. There was an almirah full of books in one corner and most of these had belonged to Gunabhiram. She could also see two bound volumes of the *Asam Bandhu*. But it was the four framed and garlanded photographs on the wall which drew her instant attention. One was of Bishnupriya and Gunabhiram together while the other two were of two young innocent faces—Karanabhiram and Kamalabhiram. The fourth photograph was of a young man dressed in European style. Tora tried hard to remember the appearance of Swarna's husband Dr Nandakumar Roy whom she had seen some eight years ago at Bilwa Kutir. She knew that this had to be his photograph. Thinking how lonely Swarna must have been feeling, surrounded as she was with all these sad memories, Tora was filled with grief.

Just then a horse carriage stopped in front of the house. From it alighted Swarna and a young man. Tora recognized the youth. He was Swarna's relative, Kali Baideu's son Priyanath. They used to stay quite often at Bilwa Kutir. On seeing Swarna, Tora was surprised to find that, despite all her misfortunes, she looked as beautiful as before. She was so relieved to see that even without the vermilion bindi on her forehead, Swarnalata looked radiant. Pulling the *oroni* on one side of her head, Swarna was about to enter the house when, much to her astonishment, she saw Tora in front of her. She instantly embraced her and burst into sobs. Recalling that particular evening when all three friends were together at Bilwa Kutir, Swarna said: "All my dreams are shattered, Tora. That I am still alive is quite a miracle." One by one Swarna related all that had happened to her. Husband, father, mother, Karuna, Kamala—it was as if a procession of the dead passed her by. Swarna's tears had dried up by the time she was recounting Kamala's death.

"I tried a lot to save him, Tora. The poor chap depended on me completely. He kept holding my hand till his last moments. When the fever first started, our doctor friends had advised that he be taken to Darjeeling. I made all the arrangements and sent Jnan and him to Darjeeling. But his condition only worsened there. After his return he stayed with me for about a month. The doctors said that they were all suffering from kala-ajar. It seems people from Assam carry this infection. But we left Assam so long ago!"

"Swarna, it is difficult to understand the nature of these illnesses. The symptoms appear long after the person gets infected. I have seen many people suffering from this fever at Nagaon. There it was like an epidemic." Trying to change the subject, Tora asked: "Where's Jnan gone?"

"Acting on everyone's advice, we have sent him to England. After Kamala died, he was a complete wreck both mentally and physically, and I had almost gone mad trying to save him from this killer disease. First, I sent him to Bombay with one of our physician friends so that he could benefit from the sea breeze. When he returned from there, everyone suggested that perhaps in England, he would be safe from this illness. It's almost two months since we sent him there. I have just been to the bank to send him some money. I have heard from one of my school friends, Mrs Gupta, that Jnan is now staying with one Mrs Spear and starting his studies. Shri Durgamohan Das and Dr Jagadish Chandra Bose had arranged everything."

"That means you are staying alone now?" Tora asked.

"Kali Baideu and her son Priyanath are with me now. But

how is it possible for them to stay with me always? I really don't know what I will do once they leave. The Brahmo Girls' School has been asking me to come and teach there. But I don't feel like leaving Khuki and Choto all alone. Khuki is always sick. I am very worried about her as well." She then introduced her two charming daughters to Tora. The elder one was about seven years old and was studying at a nearby English school.

The two friends spent the entire day together. Swarna enquired about all her friends and acquaintances from Nagaon, and Tora told her all she knew. Panchanan Sarma had, along with a few other friends, started a girls' primary school and he had been helping Lakhi ever since Dharmakanta was arrested and sent to jail. And, the moment Tora mentioned Dharmakanta, Swarna became eager to hear about him.

"Please tell me what has happened to Dharma Kakaideu. When he came here last, he had brought with him a memorandum from the poor peasants of Assam. I remember him discussing it with Deuta."

"He had also come to our place around that time and told us about uniting the peasants and forming some organization. Then I didn't understand much of what he said. But now we realize that he has been able to put into practice whatever he was saying."

"Dharma Kakaideu had also said the same things to me; that in foreign countries the poor peasants and factory workers had united and formed organizations which have been instrumental in overthrowing the king and in establishing a 'people's rule'. He had given me a book on the French Revolution. Really strange things seem to be happening in those places."

"Strange events have been taking place even in our Assam," Tora added. "You will be surprised to know of the manner in which the poor peasants united and fought against the British government in Rangia, Patharughat and Kamrup." Saying this,

Tora tried to recount some of the incidents relating to the peasant uprisings that she had heard about from Dharmakanta.

On his return from Calcutta, Dharmakanta had first gone to Dibrugarh. But he could not stay there for long. The peasants of Kamrup, Darrang and Nagaon were agitated over the British administration's decision to raise land revenue rates and were holding people's assemblies or raij mels at several places. They had also decided not to pay the enhanced revenue. Thousands had gathered in these meetings; and at some places the peasants were so worked up that they came out with their spears and staves, ready to fight the administration. Having heard of all this, Dharmakanta, accompanied by some of his comrades, had rushed to Lower Assam. All of them were members of the "ryot sabha". On arriving at Kampur they had realized that the situation was quite serious, with the peasants determined not to pay taxes. They had taught a bitter lesson to the mandal and his officials who had come to collect revenue and had even beaten them up on some occasions. Dharmakanta had learnt while at Guwahati, that the government was contemplating action on the basis of the report submitted by the mauzadars and that, in order to teach the people a lesson, the sepoys were being kept on the ready. So, along with his comrades Dharmakanta went from village to village telling the people that whatever the consequences, they should always stand united, for unity was their real strength. Addressing the people's assemblies, Dharmakanta would tell the peasants a story from Aesop's fables which was about how an old father used a bundle of sticks to give a lesson on unity to his sons. The people not only immediately understood the meaning of the story but also accepted the moral of it. Whenever they got to know that an official had come to seize the belongings of a peasant because he was unable to pay tax, they would resist collectively and throw the *tekela* out of the village. The resistance was fast building up and whenever someone tried to pay the revenue on the sly, the entire village would come together and socially boycott that individual. Moreover, if the people heard about some mauzadar making life difficult for a peasant, they would march in a procession to the Mauzadar's house, squat in front of it and refuse to move unless he knelt before them and begged forgiveness. As for Dharmakanta, he would remind the demonstrating peasants that the power of united action was always more than that of weapons. The government, he argued, would never dare to use force on unarmed people, for it was contrary to British law. But one day the police surprised everyone by entering the village in force and arresting all the elderly people who were promptly sent to the thana at Rangia. Dharmakanta was among those who were arrested. When the prisoners were brought to the thana, it was clear that it would not be able to accommodate so many people. Seeing this, the police officer in charge ordered that a bamboo enclosure be built in front of the thana and the prisoners kept confined there under the open sky. It was Dharmakanta who dared to protest against the irrational order but the elders, fearing that the situation would become worse, just kept silent. The bamboo enclosure was put up within a few hours and a couple of policemen were posted at the entry. It was here that the people, who had been given some plain rice and salt for dinner, spent the long winter night, shivering in the cold.

The next day was the tenth of January 1894. Tora remembered the date well because it was her daughter's birthday. Dharmakanta had learnt from the sentries at the gate that the Deputy Commissioner McCabay Sahib had reached Rangia from Kamrup the previous night and had brought with him several truckloads of policemen. As the commissioner reached the thana, one could hear people raising slogans some distance away. Immediately there was an alert within the thana premises and the Superintendent of Police ordered his men to throw a protective ring around it. Dharmakanta and his comrades peeped through the bamboo fence of their enclosure and saw that the field in front of the thana was brimming with thousands of people who, following requests from their leaders, had begun to squat, all the while raising slogans demanding a cut in the land revenue and the release of the prisoners. The crowd was unarmed and appeared quite peaceful with only a few of them carrying bamboo staves. Seeing them, Dharmakanta was sure that the police would never set upon such a peaceful assembly. He had in fact hoped that the Commissioner would come out of the thana premises to assure the people that their demands would be met. But nothing of that sort happened. McCabay Sahib himself came to the verandah of the police thana and ordered the police to fire upon the crowd in order to disperse them. In an instant there was mayhem, with the sound of guns being fired and the air filled with the anguished cries of people who had been shot. There was no actual count of all those who fell to police bullets on that fateful morning. The field had turned red with the blood of peasants.

As she was relating the incident, Tora was getting more and more agitated, with beads of sweat dotting her forehead.

"What happened after that? What did they do to Dharma Kakaideo? How many of our people were killed?" asked Swarna anxiously.

"So many had died that no one can give the exact figure. It is said that the police dumped all the bodies in a roadside ditch and burnt them. Our people were too simple, Swarna. Most of them didn't have any idea about guns and bullets. At first, they had thrown clods of earth in anger against the bullets. But on seeing their compatriots falling down one after another, the people ran helter skelter. Dharma Kakaideo was sent from there to the Guwahati jail. Several persons from Guwahati approached the government to release Dharmakanta. But it was of no avail. There were many serious charges against him and his articles published in *Digvijay* were being cited as proof of his treason. Actually, the police had discovered the identity of Dharmakanta's father. That's why they implicated him in a false conspiracy charge and got him jailed for a year."

"Poor Lakhi. She must have suffered a lot; isn't it?" Swarna asked after intently listening to Tora all this while.

"We got news of Lakhi after quite some time. Though we had heard something about Dharma Kakaideo, yet we weren't sure. Only when he was transferred to the Nagaon jail did we come to know about him through a letter that he had sent with one of the jail guards. We finally sought permission and went to see him in prison. That was the first time I saw a jail. Naturally, we were a bit scared. But they had kept Dharmakanta quite well. There were no problems about food and he was also allowed books and paper. But he seemed quite disturbed and had requested us to bring him news of Lakhi and the children. It was clear that the Rangia incident had gravely upset him. For, he kept saying repeatedly: 'So many people died in front of my eyes. How can I ever forget it? There must be a solid protest against this. How can one tolerate such brutal action on unarmed people?'" I was really nervous that day, Swarna, because the fire I had seen in Dharma Kakaideo's eyes that day does not go out so easily."

"Did all of you see Lakhi?"

"Oh, yes. When I met Lakhi's father and told him everything, he decided to come with us to Dibrugarh. We went to Diburu by steamer from Silghat. It is a beautiful town and lots of British live there. By the time we reached Lakhi's place, it was almost evening. From the doorstep we could hear her singing a Brahmo devotional song—the one that's sung at your home, "Nath Tariyo".

"That's actually a borgeet. Deuta was very fond of it. Ai too would ask me to sing it when she was bedridden," Swarna said with a distant look on her face.

"Lakhi's father had silently stood at the entrance for a long time and only after the song was over did he announce our arrival by clearing his throat. Finding us in front of her house, Lakhi was completely taken aback. Then she quickly bowed down and touched her father's feet. The meeting of father and daughter after all these years was a touching sight and I just could not control my tears. Gradually, we told Lakhi everything. She had already got news of Dharmakanta's arrest and told us that the police had come and, after having searched through his papers, taken away copies of the newspaper *Digvijay*. From what she said it was apparent that she had taken all this in quite a mature manner. The Brahmo headmaster of her school had been of great help and in order to help her tide over the crisis, he had increased her salary by five rupees. Her mother-in-law now stayed with Lakhi. It was nice to see that her mother-in-law, who had initially disapproved of their marriage, now stayed with her and loved her as her daughter. However, she didn't eat with them and cooked her food separately.

"Her father had wanted to take Lakhi to Nagaon. But she did not agree and told him that this was the greatest test of her life and she would have to pass it all by herself. Respecting his daughter's sentiments, he had left after having blessed her. Lakhi has also decided to take the Entrance examination this time. She is sure to pass," said Tora decisively.

"But has Dharma Kakaideu been released?"

"Yes, of course. He left for Diburu after spending a night at our place. But I have cautioned him again and again to consider everything well before he does something. How long will poor Lakhi struggle alone?"

"Well, it is some people's fate to struggle all alone," Swarna said with a sigh.

Tora kept on looking at Swarna and then said all of a sudden: "Swarna, why don't you get married again?"

Swarna stood silent for some time with her head lowered and Tora could see that her cheeks were flushed. As if about to say something to Tora and then suddenly checking herself, she replied: "I have pushed out all such thoughts from my head. An unfortunate woman like me cannot ever think of spoiling another person's life."

"Pray, tell me Swarna, is any one's life really free from misfortune? Why are you blaming yourself? Please do give up such useless thoughts. I am sure there will be no dearth of good and honest persons to marry a gifted girl like you. Haven't your father's friends said anything about this to you? Why, the Brahmos are all for widow re-marriage aren't they?"

"It's not that they haven't suggested it. Some of them have. But I haven't agreed because of my brothers. What will happen to them if I leave?" Tora sensed that Swarna seemed to have forgotten that one by one everyone had left her already. Affectionately slapping her on the back, she said: "Jnan has already gone to England. I don't understand what really holds you back now?"

Swarna didn't reply. But it seemed that after a long time she suddenly felt somewhat light and free. It could have been because, after all these days, someone had held out some hope for her future. Just then a chanawallah passed by shouting his wares. Swarna went to the window and waved at him to come and giggling like a small girl asked Tora: "Have you ever tasted Kolkata's chatpatti? Once you have had it, you can never forget it for the rest of your life". Choto and Khuki looked at their mother in surprise. For a long time now they had never seen her so cheerful. Instantly, they developed a strong liking for the new mashima from Assam.

8

When Tora went back to Nagaon after having completed her training, she was quite disappointed. Citing a financial crunch, the administration had abandoned its earlier plan to improve the functioning of the government hospital. With that, the very reason for her being sent to Calcutta so as to improve her qualifications no longer seemed to exist. In the end, the doctor of the Nagaon hospital advised her to try for a transfer to the civil hospital at Guwahati. He told her that there at least she would get a chance to put her new skills to use. Meanwhile, she received an offer of a job from the Nagaon Mission as well. The Welsh Mission was planning to set up a new hospital at Shillong and they needed a qualified nurse there. And, even as Tora was weighing her chances, it was Henry who ended up solving everything. There was a vacant post of second master at the Guwahati high school and Henry asked for a transfer to Guwahati and got it earlier than he had expected. Actually, he had been planning to move to Guwahati for quite some time for he had felt that once in Guwahati, the outside world would become more approachable and open up faster. If one travelled by the new mail steamer boats, one could reach Goalanda from Guwahati in just two days. From there it was just a night's journey to Calcutta. The British too were aware of the growing importance of the place and had set up offices and educational institutions there. A new road was also being built from Guwahati to Shillong. Over and above this, the most attractive thing for Henry was that the government was considering setting up a college in Guwahati. Once the college came up, Guwahati, like Calcutta, would become the centre of intellectual activity, many journals like *Jonaki* would be published from there and the number of educated people would increase. It was with such hopes that Henry had persuaded his wife to come with him to Guwahati.

Initially, Tora was quite unhappy about having to leave Nagaon. Having spent the most significant period of her life in this small town, it was naturally full of many memories. It was here that she had received unforgettable love and care from the Baptist Missionaries. The memory of Bronson Sahib being fresh in her mind, she remembered how she had wept uncontrollably on hearing of his death and wondered if she would ever be able to emulate in her own life the lesson of selfless service and sacrifice which she had learnt from Bronson Sahib. She had never thought him a foreigner because for her there was no similiarity in his way of life and behaviour with that of the ruling sahibs. Henry, however, had started viewing things from a slightly different angle. He increasingly felt that the white missionaries were not opposed to the British rulers and even after the brutal killings at Patharughat, Rangia and other places, they had not uttered a word in protest. He failed to see how people committed to working for the good of humanity could decide to keep quiet when there was such repression. One day, Henry had read out to Tora a piece from an old volume of the *Orunodoi* entitled "A Description of the Treacherous People of Nagaon" which, in all probability, had been written by some missionary priest. It was full of hatred for the Assamese people and deep admiration and respect for the British rulers. Even then, Tora could never forget what her mother had said about the missionaries: "It is only because of the missionary men and women that we are able to live like this, Tora. Else, who knows what would have happened to us? Never be ungrateful towards them." It was not that Henry was ungrateful. But he did not want his past to keep him shackled. He wanted to think freely.

In Guwahati, Tora and Henry's days were filled with a lot of activity. Situated on the bank of the Brahmaputra, the atmosphere around the civil hospital was calm and quiet, with the river breeze blowing gently throughout the day. Things were quite comfortable for the couple, with the hospital being just a stone's throw from their living quarters in Panbazar and Henry's school located just a few hundred yards away. Though Tora's working day usually began from ten in the morning and stretched till four in the evening, she quite often had to work extra hours because of the shortage of nurses at the hospital. Apart from the occasional night duty, she also had to assist the surgeon during emergency operations. It was in Tora's nature to always do the extra bit with a smile on her face even though she missed spending time with her children. Her son Naren was in primary school, while her three-year-old daughter stayed at home and was looked after by an old maid of the Guwahati Mission.

The Baptist Mission was situated just near the Civil Hospital and was a complex of several beautiful old bungalows which overlooked an attractive brick-laid church building. Adjacent to it were the newly-built sahib's residences and the club house which were beautiful brick structures. They formed part of the row of huge official bungalows which stood alongside Strand Road as it skirted the mighty Brahmaputra. Nearby was the historic Dighalipukhuri, a centuries-old large rectangular pond surrounded by trees and a major landmark of the town. Tora and Henry would often go for walks along its banks. However, that portion of the road on the northern bank of the Dighalipukhuri which passed the European club was barred for Indians in the evenings, with sentries posted at both ends to prevent tresspassers.

As for the local people, they had never thought it necessary to protest such an arrangement, instead they seemed to view this as a privilege of the ruling race. They would in fact often satisfy their curiosity by standing on the banks of the Dighalipukhuri and straining their necks to catch a fleeting glimpse of the memsahibs going to their club.

It was the thirteenth day of June of the year 1897. The sky had been overcast since the morning and, as she was getting ready to go to the hospital, Tora casually glanced at the southern horizon. It was looming with thick, dark clouds. Knowing that it was about to rain heavily, Tora quickly cooked food for the family and, after finishing her meal, got ready to leave. She wanted to get to the hospital before it started to pour. As she was about to leave, just as on other days, this morning too her little one insisted that her mother lift her up and give her a kiss. Fearing that her nurse's uniform would be soiled, Tora somehow managed to placate her child and left for work after planting two kisses on her cheeks. She glanced back at Henry, gave him a smile and, after promising to be back early, walked briskly towards the hospital.

As Tora approached the front of the hospital, large drops of rain had already begun to fall. And, just as she stepped on the verandah, the rain came down with full force. But once inside her ward, she had no time to think of the weather. After doing the rounds with the surgeon and checking the patients' charts, she got busy in attending to the out patients. There was a bad burn case among them. A young boy, some eight or nine years old, had been admitted the previous day. He had been scalded by boiling water from his abdomen downwards and there seemed to be little chance of his surviving. Though the doctors were trying their best to save the child, yet in such cases a whole lot depended on the nurses. The boy was screaming continuously and Tora kept changing his dressings with the utmost care. Seeing that the boy's mother was crying uncontrollably in the verandah in front of the ward, Tora went over to her and asked her rather brusquely to show some restraint. Though she felt bad for the woman, yet she knew that nothing could be achieved by creating a commotion. She spent the greater part of the day with the boy and by evening he was given medicines and put to sleep. Because of this the atmosphere in the ward had calmed down. The boy's mother too had gone home.

As Tora's duty hours ended, the nurse on night duty arrived. And after briefing her properly for the night, Tora was about to leave. She noticed that it was still drizzling. But, just as she opened her umbrella and stepped outside, it seemed someone gave her a mighty push. She fell on her knees to the ground. At first she thought that her head was reeling for the earth under her feet seemed to be moving in waves. Tora clutched at a patch of grass. It was an earthquake! All around her people were shouting and screaming in fear. The entire hospital staff, doctors as well as patients, had rushed outside. Some were praying to Sri Ram with folded hands while others were looking at the sky and calling upon Christ to save them. The two brick houses in front of them collapsed like a pack of cards and, in the midst of the rumbling, Tora could hear the screams of those who were trapped under the debris. To, add to the panic, two huge peepal trees in the hospital compound were uprooted and fell to the ground with huge thuds. There was a deafening sound all around and it appeared as if cannons were being fired from all directions. Finally, when the tremors ceased a little, Tora stood up and looked around. Suddenly she heard the wails of a child from within the hospital. It struck her that the boy with the burns must have been left inside. By then, a portion of the hospital building had already collapsed, although the front part was still accessible. Without thinking of anything else, Tora instinctively ran inside through the opening. Everyone watched in amazement. Scrambling over the rubble, she managed to reach the ward where the boy was lying on the bed screaming. Within seconds, Tora wrapped him in a bedsheet and carried him towards the door. Just then there was another huge tremor. Those who were standing outside could see the roof of the hospital cave in with a mighty sound. Tora couldn't come out.

That entire night it rained heavily, with intermittent tremors adding to the panic of the people. No one in Guwahati stayed inside their home on that fateful night. The waters from the Brahmputra entered the town and inundated it. Several areas adjoining the river including the hospital compound were filled with water. In many places the wells had been filled up with sand and there were gaping holes in the middle of the streets. While almost all the brick buildings had been completely razed to the ground, the thatch and bamboo houses survived the apocalypse.

The next morning the hospital surgeon himself went to Henry to give him the news of Tora's death. Describing Tora's great sacrifice, he said: "Following the great ideal of our Saviour Jesus Christ, Tora gave her life up for others. Such a death is really noble."

Tora's colleagues too were full of praise for her service to humanity. But at that moment, all these words of consolation were meaningless to Henry. Though the earthquake hadn't been able to damage their small house, yet Henry felt that all he was left with was a shell. Without Tora the very spirit of the house had gone.

The administration took charge of everything, right from recovering Tora's body from the rubble to arranging for her funeral. The Mission too extended its help to each of the families that had been affected by the earthquake and took Henry's children under its care. Though Henry's colleagues and students kept coming to offer their condolences and give him company and several prayer meetings were held where people fondly remembered Tora and paid their homage to her spirit

of devotion and sacrifice, yet all this just could not do away
with the feeling of endless emptiness that seemed to envelop
him. Henry took leave from his school and continued to stay
at home. Most schools and offices were closed following the
earthquake. Houses which had collapsed were being built anew
and damaged buildings repaired. But this time the government
buildings were being constructed not with brick and mortar, but
with bamboo and thatch.

Henry received a long letter from Swarna. She wrote saying
that Tora had now really become the brightest star in the sky and
would continue to guide all of them from a distance. She requested
Henry to come and spend a few days in Calcutta. Reading the
letter over and over again, Henry thought that there was a time
when the very idea of going to Calcutta would have excited him.
But now even that exciting city seemed to have lost all its charm
for him. He carefully placed Swarna's letter under the copy of the
Bible that lay on his table. These days he had begun to regularly
read the Holy Book. His lacerated heart was trying once more
to understand the significance of Christ's message of love. Earlier,
when he was with the Mission, he used to read out passages from
the Holy Bible to console many a soul in grief. Now he chose a
particular saying of the Saviour to console himself: "Blessed are
they that mourn, for they shall be comforted."

A month or two after the earthquake, Dharmakanta came to
visit Henry. He was now fully engaged with his work at the
printing press which had already brought out several Assamese
books. Now that he was also planning to bring out a weekly
newspaper, he had to visit Guwahati quite often. Sitting by
Henry's side that evening, Dharmakanta talked of the days gone
by and the experiences they had shared in Nagaon and Calcutta.
In the end he revealed the real purpose of his visit: "Lakhi has
asked you all to come to Dibrugarh. Visiting a new place would
make you feel better; we too would like it. If you so wish, you

could work at the press with me. Or, you could take a transfer to the government school there."

Henry replied with a wan smile: "I have been thinking of going to see you people. But meanwhile I have taken a decision regarding my future. I have committed myself to go and work at a new school run by the Welsh Mission in Shillong. Once the road re-opens, I will go there."

"That means you have decided to go back to the Mission?" Dharmakanta asked in surprise.

"I had no other option. I am a very lonely man, Barua. Since my childhood the Mission has been my home. Having met Tora, my life had taken a new and unexpected turn. My world had suddenly grown large. But now that inspiration is gone for ever. Now I am just seeking some anchor, at least for some time. The Mission will be able to give me that peace of mind. No one else really can."

Henry was speaking in a slow and measured manner lest Dharmakanta misunderstood him. As for Dharmakanta, he just kept looking at him in wonder. He had never understood Henry's inner thoughts. Slowly, nodding his head he said:

"I never could understand you, Henry. But I still feel that you could have built up a fraternity of friends and well-wishers even by staying outside the Mission."

"Your way of seeing things is very different, Barua. You will never understand me," Henry said, giving up on trying to reason with Dharmakanta. Dharma raised both hands in a gesture of defeat and said smilingly: "Really, this time too I have lost with you. But I have not given up hope. Some day you will return to our midst. If I do not call you to come and join us, the times they will."

And, as he was about to depart, Dharmakanta laid his hands affectionately on Henry's shoulder and said: "Now, will there be any space for people like us in your family?"

Henry replied in a hurt tone: "Don't make me feel bad about

this, Barua. You all—you, Lakhi and Swarna—are so close to me. It is my memories of you that will help me start life afresh. Moreover, how far is Shillong really? If the roads improve then we will keep meeting quite often. You can come and be my guests. I have also written to Swarna. Once her brother returns from England, both of them should come to Shillong."

9

The great earthquake of Assam had also shaken Calcutta, and several old buildings in the city had collapsed. However, this was nothing compared to what Assam went through. Having read the accounts of the earthquake in the newspapers, Swarna was filled with anxiety about the fate of her relatives and friends in Assam. With the roads and postal services badly affected, she hadn't had any news from them in a long time. And, when the news finally started filtering in, Swarna was much relieved to learn that her friends and acquaintances at Nagaon were all safe, though a few houses had collapsed. But she was completely distraught with the news of Tora's death. Though she had dealt with quite a few deaths in her own family, yet she couldn't really accept the fact that Tora was no more. She felt that some part of her own existence had been suddenly darkened by her death. For, all these days Tora had symbolized all that she had herself wanted to be. And, whenever she met Tora, she had always got a new measure of inspiration to keep living. She now remembered how the last time they had met, Tora had asked her to get married. It was her advice that had suddenly rekindled certain longings in her mind which, otherwise, had lain dormant.

According to the newspaper reports the actual devastation caused by the great earthquake was in the Khasi and Jaintia hills. Several villages situated at the foot of the hills had just disappeared under the massive landslides created by the quake. There was no real count of the numbers of people buried alive. All the beautiful government bungalows in Shillong were reduced to rubble and several Englishmen lost their lives. Among those killed by the quake was Deputy Commissioner McCabe who had ordered the police firing at Rangia.

Swarna lowered *The Englishman* which she had been reading and said to the Bengali bhradralok sitting in front of her: "Somehow, people do have to pay for their sins one day or another. McCabe sahib couldn't run away from his sins even by going to Shillong."

The person Swarna was talking to was Khirode Chandra Roychoudhury, the Principal of Hoogly College. Everyone knew him to be a well educated person with a sterling character. A widower with two children, Roychoudhury was about forty, though he looked much younger than his age. After having met Swarna at Jagadish Bose's home, a friendship had sprung up between the two. Gradually this friendship got strengthened and both of them decided to get married. At first there had been a great deal of hesitation in Swarna's mind, for having lived alone all these years, she was somewhat unwilling to go in for such a major change in her life. But the eagerness of her friends and well wishers coupled with the almost endless patience of Khirode Babu had finally helped Swarna to arrive at a decision. And, now encouraged by Khirode Babu, she was once again going back to her studies, although she was not at all willing to take the Entrance Examination as desired by him. What would she do, she asked herself, by passing examinations?

Khirode Babu smiled at Swarna's comment about McCabe and said: "You too seem to believe in poetic justice. But I don't. So many good people have suffered without any reason in this world of ours. And so many crooked people are spending their days in happiness. A lot of innocent people died in this earthquake."

Swarna's face suddenly turned ashen. Her eyes welled up

with tears thinking of the letter she had got from Henry a few days ago. Khirode Babu felt bad about what he had said. He had seen how the news of Tora's death had affected Swarna. Swarna kept quiet for some time and then absentmindedly folding the newspaper, said in a philosophic tone: "Life and death are not in our hands, Khirode Babu. Each one of us can only continue doing our duty as best as we can. One can discover a meaning in death if one engages oneself in good and meaningful action. Evil deeds can make one's end quite terrifying." Swarna continued after a while: "I have seen death from such close quarters that for me the dividing line between life and death is indeed thin."

"You shouldn't be saying such things at your age, Swarna. Your whole life is before you. It is of living that you should think now. We'll talk of death when we both grow old, okay?" The last words were said in a lighter tone, but they were full of affection.

Swarna did not protest Khirode Babu's words. Looking at the calendar hanging on the wall, she changed her topic and said: "Next year Jnan is coming back. I will then be free after handing him his goods and property."

"That means you are thinking of taking *baanprastha?*" Khirode Roy said in jest: "That means I too will have to get prepared to leave for *banabaas* with you within a year. Otherwise, even before we get prepared, the twentieth century will announce its arrival."

"The twentieth century!" Swarna exclaimed like a small girl. "It's so good to think about it. Deuta used to say that in the twentieth century the world will change entirely. Man will do everything with the help of the machine. It will take just two to three days to go from Calcutta to Nagaon. And, our society will be rid of all its superstitions. Will we ever be able to see those days?"

Swarna stood up and, leaning on the railings on the verandah, looked into the distance. It was about to get dark. Slowly, the gas lamps of Calcutta were lit one by one.